For Lydia —

Summer Squall

Happy reading + bridge playing.

Love,

Sarah Jones

Sarah Jones

11/13/19

MILFORD HOUSE

Milford House Press

Mechanicsburg, Pennsylvania

MILFORD HOUSE

an imprint of Sunbury Press, Inc.
Mechanicsburg, PA USA

NOTE: This is a work of fiction. Names, characters, places and incidents are the product of the author's imagination or are used fictitiously, and any resemblance to actual persons, living or dead, business establishments, events or locales is entirely coincidental.

For information about special discounts for bulk purchases, please contact Sunbury Press Orders Dept. at (855) 338-8359 or orders@sunburypress.com.

To request one of our authors for speaking engagements or book signings, please contact Sunbury Press Publicity Dept. at publicity@sunburypress.com.

ISBN: 978-1-62006-313-2 (Trade paperback)

Library of Congress Control Number:

FIRST MILFORD HOUSE PRESS EDITION: July 2019

Product of the United States of America
0 1 1 2 3 5 8 13 21 34 55

Set in Bookman Old Style
Designed by Chris Fenwick
Cover by Chris Fenwick
Edited by Chris Fenwick

Continue the Enlightenment!

For Roz, who knows how to listen,

and the lake ladies, who know how to laugh.

Of this be sure:
You do not find a happy life;
you make it.

-Thomas S. Monson

*H*er light cut through the dark and played across the coral reef, revealing its ridges and valleys. An outcropping, the color of a sunset, caught her attention. She inched a gloved hand forward, expecting it to give like a soft bath sponge. It was rock hard. On the ocean floor below, startled creatures scurried for hiding, their movements raising small clouds of sand from the lunar surface. In the distance, a murky shape swished. *Not a shark*, she told herself. That's what the dive master had said. *Not in these waters.* But still, in a night dive, anything was possible. She shivered despite her dive vest.

Turning away from the reef, she looked for a light, but all she saw was black water. No light beam. No blue fins. At forty feet below the surface, nothing was visible, she realized. Not even herself, in this all-black gear.

She wrapped her arms around herself, fighting off panic, but still it came, closing around her like a coffin. Only a few hours earlier, she had explored these same waters with the dive master. He had pointed out schools of turquoise fish and a seahorse hidden in a bed of orange fans. She had smiled at him, grateful for his presence. But tonight, as she peered through a fogged mask, all she saw was this inky black.

Nausea crawled up her throat, and she bent over, expecting to heave into her mask. "Oh, God," she whimpered, her heart beating rapidly like a triggerfish ready to attack. "Oh, God. Help me."

CHAPTER ONE

*B*eth stomped on the brakes and braced herself. The impact to her rear bumper knocked her forward and then back into her seat. All around her, Atlanta drivers bleated their horns as she eased off the interstate, trailed by the car in her rearview.

"Shit," she muttered as she got out, driver's license and insurance card in hand. In a practiced motion, she pulled her auburn hair into a ponytail and cinched her navy raincoat tighter, ready to face the person who had battered the bumper of her new Acura. The driver, a teenager, was already out of his car, phone to his ear, when Beth approached him. *Calling his dad*, she thought. Either that, or he was already on the phone when he hit her, not paying attention to traffic. In the rain, no less.

When he ended the call, Beth took an aggressive step toward him but then stopped. The kid wasn't the only one driving distracted, she realized. She was too – lost in thoughts about kissing Mark in her kitchen, him lifting her with one arm onto the counter to bring her face closer. Then in bed, dancing to one another's rhythm as if they had always known these steps.

Softening her face, she approached the kid. "It's okay," she said, as he handed over his insurance card. She resisted an urge to pat his arm. *Poor guy*, she thought. He would probably be grounded for a month.

As she waited for the police to arrive, her thoughts returned to Mark. Had it been three weeks since she met him? It seemed like . . . well, she didn't know how long it seemed. All she knew was that she wanted it to keep going. She smiled in memory of the night they met. She and her best friend Lori had been at Johnny's Hideaway, a local dance spot where

Beth's favorite DJ played, when Mark approached her. That wasn't so uncommon, a guy hitting on her. Johnny's had a reputation as an old-school pick-up bar. What was different about Mark was his attentiveness. He asked questions and nodded or smiled at her answers, keeping his eyes fixed on her. After she and Lori left, he had called to make sure she had arrived home safely and asked her for a date for the following night. Now he was taking her sailing on Sunday.

Traffic sounds faded as she visualized him. A strong chin with a cleft that deepened when he grinned. Hands that could span an octave and a half on a piano as easily as split a cord of wood. Shoulders so wide she wondered if he had trouble passing through doorways. The guy most people would want by their side if disaster arose. Had he been on the Titanic, he would have survived and pulled others to safety – his powerful arms pushing rescue boats through the water.

God, she sounded like a fourteen-year-old with a crush on the cute guy in second period. Only this time the cute guy was a high school wrestling coach. So different from the men she had dated with their constant talk of sales commissions or office politics.

A glance at her watch caused her contentment to vanish. Daydreaming was not on her to-do list. First stop, a press check for the convention guide. Her rep had emailed that the cover photo was out of register. That would delay the books arriving at the mailing house, which would mean another stop she had to make. Then there was the mandatory staff meeting. Her boss would be pissed if she were late for that. And if the meeting ran over, which often happened, no way would she make her three o'clock therapy appointment. She wanted to talk to Emmett— Dr. Em, as she called him. Now she might as well call to reschedule.

"Come on," she exclaimed, accidentally tooting her horn in frustration. Her hand traveled into her purse, searching for her Xanax. She lifted the bottle into her lap and cradled it. With only a moment's hesitation, she shook out a capsule and swallowed.

"Gardiners do not suffer from depression," Beth's mother had often told her, especially if some poor soul unburdened herself in Sunday School. "We are made from sturdier stock," she'd whisper, shoving Beth with her Bible toward their regular pew.

"Shut up, Mother," Beth muttered. Dead and gone a year, her mother's strident voice still echoed inside Beth – ordering her, criticizing her, threatening her. Making Beth feel that nothing she accomplished would ever measure up.

With disgust, she threw the bottle into her purse as her mind traveled back to her family home in Tennessee. All those rules that had been force-fed at the dinner table, served right along with fried chicken, mashed potatoes, and green beans – well-seasoned with her mother's maxims, part Ben Franklin, part Southern Baptist, and a healthy dash of Appalachian folk wisdom. Beth had swallowed these nuggets of advice like One-A-Day vitamins.

"And look at me now," she muttered. Seeing a therapist, taking drugs, and still afraid to talk about that night in college. Ten years had passed, but that room, that taste, that smell still haunted her, even as she slept. Just last night, she had dreamed she was underwater, struggling to get her foot loose from a rope wrapped around one ankle. The more she struggled, the more it tightened. She even toppled a glass of water by her bed as she flailed her arms in her sleep. That was the part of the dream that bothered her the most – the reaching for help and finding no one there.

"Shit," she said again. It was fast becoming her favorite word.

***

Thirty minutes later, accident report in hand, Beth eased back into the flow of traffic. The kid was again behind her. What awaited him when he arrived home with a citation, she wondered? Would he get a chance to explain? Would they ask if he were injured? Would they hug him, their hearts pounding with worry? Or would someone stare down at him with disgust and say, "You are an embarrassment to the family"?

As traffic again halted approaching downtown, Beth's eyes settled on the back of a trailered boat a few feet in front of her. *Why Knot?* it proclaimed in blue nautical lettering – a length of rope extending from the last letter with a fishing hook on the end.

She cocked her head to one side. *There's a reason why a rearview mirror is small,* she thought, *and the windshield is expansive. It keeps your eyes focused on the future, not the past.*

"Soiled girls," her mother's voice again, "often find themselves alone for life." She shook her mother from her head and stared at the bumper. "Why not?" she murmured. Why not Mark? Why not happiness for a change?

CHAPTER TWO

" Feel the wind," Mark instructed her. "Where's it coming from?"

Her eyes closed, Beth turned her face first left, then right, and pointed. "There," she said.

"Now look at the wind indicator on the mast. Does it agree?"

She looked up and nodded.

"See?" he said, with a quick squeeze of her shoulder. "A good sailor feels the wind. Now keep the bow pointed into it while I raise the mainsail. Don't let it fall off," he cautioned when the wind took the sail. "The wind can be tricky on a lake. Keep your bow headed up until the sail is unfurled. That's it," he said as he cleated off the halyard. "Good." He patted her back. "Now fall off to port." She moved the tiller. "That's starboard. Port." She corrected.

"Great." He squeezed her shoulders again, bringing a grin to Beth's face. "Now we'll raise the jib. If the wind is coming from starboard, which sheet should you use?"

"Port?" she asked.

"That's right. I'll take the tiller. Use a hand-over-hand hold, little fingers toward the sail. That way if the line slips, your hands are protected."

She raised the sail and cleated it, then reached again for the tiller.

He cut the engine. "That's it," he said. "Lesson one of sailing."

"Raising the sails?" she asked. She was still biting her lower lip in concentration, her eyes fixed on the bow.

"Minding the captain." He adopted a mock pirate voice. "Arr. Come here, me beauty, and give your captain a kiss."

She leaned over and kissed him. "So, you're a pirate now?"

"That I am, me lassie." He stretched his legs and leaned back with his hands behind his head. "It doesn't get much better than this. The wind, the water, the quiet."

She nodded in agreement. "But when there's no wind?"

"Arrr. That's when we break out the rum, me pretty. That's when we break out the rum."

Beth scooted over so Mark could take the tiller. It gave her an opportunity to do her mental happy dance to celebrate how well the day was going. Already she had absorbed the language of sailing and the points of sail, taking notes on index cards.

Her eyes rested on his hands. He was so masculine at the helm. So confident, so in control. So much the opposite of her.

Mark turned her way and gestured for her to draw closer. She cuddled next to him, leaning her head on his shoulder. "Let's sleep on the boat next weekend," he said, kissing the top of her head. "Get out of the city for a change. Gaze at the mountains. Sleep under the stars."

They both shared a connection to mountains. Mark was from western Pennsylvania, close to the North Country Trail near Slippery Rock. His father had been his Scout Master, he had told Beth, often taking him and his two younger brothers on weekend excursions along its path. He came from a family of big men who liked to be outdoors.

At six-foot-two, Mark was the smallest of the Berger boys. His dad, as a young man, had been known in his hometown as "The Crusher" for the way he attacked a fastball. He had been called up from a farm league team to play center field for the Pittsburgh Pirates for one season before a knee injury prevented him from running the bases. Mark kept a framed print in his office of his dad's eight-by-ten glossy, as much for inspiration as intimidation to the high school students he now coached.

"He was my hero," Mark told Beth one night, as they sat on her patio. "Most boys feel that way about their dad, but to me, he was more than just a great guy. He had this huge presence. A big laugh. A strong handshake. Everybody loved him."

Beth took his hand, lacing her fingers with his. "How did he die?" she asked in a low voice.

"Heart attack. He didn't even know he had a blockage. He just dropped dead."

Looking back, Beth knew this was the moment she fell in love. Listening to Mark talk about his dad. Sitting snuggled together with his arm around her shoulders. Her back turned against any past that would dare interfere with any facet of her constructed life. Her friends worried that things were moving too fast. "But so what?" Beth had countered. "If he's the right guy, why wait?"

Like Mark, Beth was rooted in the mountains. Both her parents came from a long line of Appalachian settlers who melded into the mountains – hard working people whose character resembled the terrain. Stubborn. Unyielding. Neither parent wanted to live anywhere but in the southeastern corner of Tennessee where they were born.

The hills of Tennessee were Beth's playground, beyond them the purple mountains of North Carolina. She spent her summers camping by mountain streams where her father and brother caught rainbow trout on lines baited with nightcrawlers. She loved how solid and eternal mountains were, but from a young age, she had dreamed of a life beyond this small corner of Tennessee, maybe in Asheville or Charlottesville, maybe Atlanta. Somewhere with bright lights and entertainment, far away from her mother's domineering presence but close enough to come home for holidays. Her mother had always said, with noticeable hurt in her voice, that Beth's first baby step was toward an open door.

But as much as she loved the mountains, her favorite childhood memories involved the ocean. One week each summer, her family vacationed with cousins on her dad's side in Gulf Shores, Alabama. Beth loved splashing into the water, then screaming as she ran back to shore pretending she was chased by a sea monster. In a photo album, she still had a faded picture of her wrapped in an oversized beach towel, her dad hugging her close. In her mind, the words *beach* and *vacation* were synonymous. You escaped to the beach; you came home to the mountains.

"Mountains or ocean," Mark asked as they left the boat dock. "If you had to choose, which would it be?"

"Can't I have both? One for home and one for play?"

"Mountains or ocean," he repeated.

And she, wanting this moment and this relationship to last more than anything she had ever wished for, took a deep breath and said, "Ocean. I'd choose the ocean," praying she guessed right.

Husband and home. That's what she longed to say. But now was too soon to admit as much to him.

Mark turned to her and smiled as if sealing a deal.

CHAPTER THREE

A smile worked its way across Beth's face as she arrived at Chastain Park. Lori had beaten her there and was stretching her legs. When she saw Beth, she pointed at her watch and wagged a finger.

"I know, I know," Beth called out as she slammed her car door. "I had to stop by the office. Sorry!"

"I thought we agreed. No more working on the weekend for you, missy."

"True, but I had to finish something before Monday." She looked around. "Where are Janet and Anna?"

"They went on ahead. You know Anna. Push, push, push. Go, go, go. I keep telling her it's just a thirteen-mile walk, not a marathon. And Janet needs to pick up her kids. Not sure why her husband can't do it, but . . ."

The four women had met at a fitness club years ago. They nicknamed themselves the Core Four because they always placed their yoga mats side by side in front of the instructor. Anna had convinced them to register for their first Rock & Roll Half-Marathon in Savannah, more a street party than a road race, she had stressed. The friends had already booked their rooms at the Olde Harbour Inn on River Street. Their training now involved walking three laps around the park every Sunday morning.

Beth loved her friends, but Lori was her closest. It was Lori who comforted her after her mother's funeral. Lori who Beth called a few months later when she couldn't get out of bed, dizziness and nausea gripping her in waves, accompanied by chest pains and a numbness that scared her. It was Lori who bustled her into her car, driving through a torrential downpour to a nearby urgent care facility, where a doctor diagnosed a panic attack. Lori was the friend who picked up Beth's

Xanax prescription and researched therapists while Beth slept until evening.

And Lori was the friend whom Beth came closest to telling about something shameful from her past.

"Love you're wearing the shirt," Beth said, pointing to the bright blue long sleeved t-shirt with a silhouette of four women, arms locked, below the block lettering of their team name. She had ordered them from one of her vendors. "We may not win the race," Beth had declared when she gave them the shirts, "but if there's a trophy for best dressed, we'll bring that one home."

An hour later, they staggered onto the patio of a coffee spot near the park. A tanned woman in an Emory sweatshirt waived them over to a table and handed them both lattes. "Tell me again why we're doing this," Lori said, dropping heavily into a chair.

"So I can have a weekend away from my husband and the kids," Janet answered.

"So I can get my butt into size two jeans," offered Beth.

"Stop it, you two," said Anna. "It's so four fabulous women, who never see each other anymore, can spend a wonderful weekend together in a great party town."

"You're the one who travels all the time," Lori said, digging into her backpack for her phone. "Where to now?"

"Geneva," Anna answered. "I'm meeting with a client for the whole week. No play time at all."

Of the four women, Anna was the most accomplished, working as an international consultant in finance and accounting. She was also the oldest of the four, nearing fifty, and took pride in reminding the others of the struggles women had gaining upper management positions. She had coached Beth on how to ask for a raise, and at Beth's last review, she used Anna's tips. "You know I'm worth it," Beth had said to her boss, as he signed off on a seven percent increase to her salary. His secretary gave her a fist bump when she walked out.

"Bring us up to speed about you and Coach," Janet said. She glanced at her watch. "I have exactly thirty-seven minutes before I need to pick up the kids from soccer practice."

"Mark," Beth said with a broad grin. "It's going great. He's working this morning with the Chattahoochee River Keepers." She turned to Anna. "You've done some fundraising for them, right? The people who go along the river and pull out trash?" When Anna nodded, she looked back at Janet. "Anyway, he's supposed to drop by here afterward. We have a cookout at the lake with his sailing buddies, but I wanted him to meet y'all. Finally."

"Excellent," Anna said, and then wagged a finger at her. "But please don't let him take up all your time. Okay? I mean Sunday used to be girlfriend day."

"Give her a break," Lori interjected. "It's time she met a good guy after the losers she's dated." Seeing Beth bristle, she patted her hand. "Tell them how Mark took your car in for service and got it detailed. That's not something what's-his-name would have done." She snorted with laughter. "And re-member that guy who asked you to drive him to a party that turned out to be his girlfriend's birthday? And you thought he was bringing you as his date? Remember?"

Beth jerked away her hand. "Hey, they weren't all bad," she said. For a moment, she pictured the boy from back home. Her first kiss was from him. Her first date. Her first everything. His deep eyes. His kind smile. His warmth. So long ago. But now she had Mark making her feel sexy and alive.

Just then, her tall, dark-haired man approached their ta-ble. He had a white visor pulled low on his forehead and wore khaki shorts and deck shoes. A navy sweatshirt thrown around his shoulders was the only concession to the cool weather. Beth jumped up and gave him a hug. He draped an arm around her neck as he removed his sunglasses.

Anna rose and held out her hand. "Anna Hopson," she said.

"Mark Berger," he responded.

Beth laughed, suddenly nervous. "Sorry," she said as she made the introductions to Lori and Janet.

Mark's eyes traveled to each woman's face. "Good to meet you." He flagged over a waiter and ordered coffee before turning back to the others. "Beth says you're training for a road race. How's it coming?" His arm still around Beth's neck, he pulled her closer. "I wish I could get this one to run the river trails with me."

"I've seen those trails. They're uphill," Beth protested and then nudged Lori. "Besides." She lifted her cup. "I'm just here for the lattés."

Lori held her cup up to Beth's and toasted.

For a moment, no one said anything. Beth pushed her hair behind her ears and then fluffed it back out. She looked up at Mark. "Maybe we should get rolling. We don't want to be late."

Mark's eyes traveled around the table, sizing up his audience. "We've got time." He pulled out a chair for her and then one for himself, folding his long legs under the table and crossing his arms.

"So, this is the Core Four." He chuckled. "All for one, and one for all."

Beth shifted in her seat. "Something like that," she answered.

His smile broadened. "I bet Beth has given you the stats on me."

Janet and Anna exchanged a quick look.

"What?" Beth protested. "I haven't . . ."

"It's okay, Beth," said Mark, giving her a squeeze. "They can ask questions."

Anna squared her shoulders. "Okay. Here's one. Your name's familiar, but I don't think from the River Keepers. I've heard it somewhere but can't place it."

Mark shrugged. "It's a common name," he answered. "I bet the phone book's full of Bergers. Plus, my family's from Pennsylvania, not Georgia."

"Maybe, but I keep thinking I've heard it somewhere." She drummed her fingers on the table. "What about Casino Night at the Atlanta Ski Club? I'm one of the organizers. Every single guy I know has attended that event. Maybe you were a volunteer one year?"

"Don't think so. Gambling's not my thing. But if you need help next year—"

Janet interrupted. "Maybe you've heard of him through sports." She drained her coffee and turned to Mark. "Beth said you're a coach, right? My kids are in soccer. Any tips?"

Mark shook his head. "Sorry. It's wrestling, not soccer. But I also run summer tennis camps for kids." He dug a card from his wallet and handed it to her. "Here. Your kids might enjoy this. I teach footwork that would help on the soccer field."

Janet glanced at the card and laid it aside. "I'll look into it."

Lori spoke up. "Beth says you have a teenager. A daughter. What's she like?"

"Like my ex," he answered. "Mouthy, demanding, and, at the age of nineteen, already thinks the world owes her."

"Wow," Lori said, eyes wide at Beth. "Sounds like a handful."

"I'm meeting her soon," Beth muttered. "She lives with her mom."

"Right," Mark continued. "But wants to move out on her own. I told her when she graduated high school, I would pay for one year of college, and if she flunked out, which she did this past semester, she'd need to pay her own way. So now." He paused to drink his coffee. "She waits tables at O'Charleys."

An awkward silence engulfed the table before Lori spoke. "I waited tables in college," she offered. "It's hard work, trust me." She glanced from Mark to Beth. "Good for her."

Beth nodded in agreement.

"She's still growing up," Anna added. "Not everyone is meant to go straight into college. I once told my son — he attended a tech school before getting accepted to Georgia Tech — 'It's not where you begin your studies but where you end them.'"

"Fair enough," Mark said, stretching his legs beneath the table and leaning his head back into his hands. "With that out of the way, what other questions do you have? I'm an open book."

Beth turned to Mark with a serious face. "They already know enough. You don't have to answer any more questions."

"Relax." He squeezed her shoulders. "I'm enjoying this." He bent his head from side to side releasing a kink. "Let's see. What else I can tell you?" He looked up, pretending to give the matter serious thought. "My favorite color is blue. I'm good at public speaking but hate spiders. The last book I read was *The Firm*. I'd like to sail around the world someday, and if my house caught on fire, I'd save my dad's baseball jacket." He turned to Beth. "He played one season in the majors."

"You like courtroom dramas," Anna said. "Beth's a big reader too. You should read something together."

Beth nodded in agreement.

"Na," Mark replied. "I wouldn't say I'm a reader, although I have an annual subscription to *Sports Illustrated* and read *GQ* at the barbershop."

Beth interrupted. "Enough about parenting and reading lists." She shook her head at her friends in a scolding manner that failed to hide her smile. "We are definitely out of here." She reached for Mark's hand. "We don't want to be late for the cookout."

He stood languidly and pulled Beth from her chair. "Great to meet you, ladies." He extended his hand to each woman. "Hope to see you again, maybe up at the lake."

Beth blew a kiss to her friends and then turned and scampered after Mark like a cheerleader following the winning team off the field. When she caught up with him, she raised a hand for a high five. He was looking at his phone and didn't notice. She glanced over her shoulder. Her friends were huddled together, coffee cups and muffins pushed aside. No one was smiling.

CHAPTER FOUR

*A*s the captain announced that the flight from Chicago was in a holding pattern, Beth groaned. She looked at her watch. Best case scenario, the plane's wheels wouldn't touch down on the Atlanta runway until well after six. That meant that she would be right in the middle of rush hour traffic.

She leaned her head against the seat in front of her. After three long days working a convention that extended from early mornings to past midnight, she was exhausted. Managing registration was especially draining. But it was the only way to become a show manager. The thought brought a chuckle. Maybe that would get her bumped up to first class.

She shifted in her seat and thought about what to say to Mark when she could turn on her phone. They were in that in-between stage of the relationship where both were being cagey about their feelings, neither wanting to be the first to declare themselves. Or maybe that was just Beth. She was, frankly, despite their differences, head over heels about Mark, as she had said to Lori, who then cautioned her to protect her heart. "Let him be the first to say what he feels for you," she had advised. "Remember, you've had a broken heart before."

She nodded as if Lori were seated beside her. No wonder her friends were waving the caution flag. Beth was the first to admit it. She was a magnet for commitment-avoidant men. She had dated them all, it seemed. But if Mark were that type, he wasn't sending out the signals. He used the "we" pronoun often, referring to future events like holidays and bucket list trips. Definitely a good sign.

But something wasn't quite right, especially whenever she traveled for work. Like last night, on the phone. Mark was talking about wrestling practice and then veered into questions about the male/female ratio at the convention and how many guys were hitting on her. She had laughed and answered like it was a joke, but still. Could he be jealous?

She leaned back and considered the question. If he were, it would be new territory. None of the men she had dated before had shown the slightest amount of jealousy. Career-driven, yes. Thoughtless, certainly. Boring, often. But jealous? Nope. At some level, it was flattering. But honestly. What in the world was giving him any reason to worry?

Sure, she hung out with the guys in lobby bars when the trade floor closed and had running jokes with them that overflowed to emails, but this was how she generated ideas for the articles she wrote for trade magazines. Most men had wives and families they went home to, and Beth knew how to handle the others. She had a job she liked and a boyfriend she wanted to keep.

It was her fault, she concluded. Maybe she needed to brag more on Mark, play up how much she admired him, how he was better, faster, stronger than other men.

Testosterone was a tricky substance.

She looked again at her watch as the captain announced they would continue the holding pattern. *Shit*, she thought. She would like to see him tonight, but she didn't want to appear needy. That would make their relationship DOA. Maybe she could convince him to spend the night at her condo, but he was funny about that. It hadn't taken her long to realize how he preferred his man cave, complete with dishes in the sink and laundry piled on the floor. Not a problem, but still, something to work around.

In the three months since they met, she didn't mind the drive to his place when she was in town. By the time she got there, he had his "Licensed to Grill" apron on (she smiled even now remembering how silly he looked), steaks ready for the George Foreman grill, and an open bottle of red wine. They had a routine: stay in on Friday nights, go out on Saturdays, and sail on Sundays. Plus, she often spent the night at his place in the middle of the week, if she wasn't traveling. But lately, her business trips had increased, and so too had Mark's complaints.

"Red flag," Janet had said after yoga the week before, and Anna and Lori had nodded their agreement. But as Beth had countered, she saw only green lights for her and Mark. No relationship was without speed bumps.

As she stared out the window at the cloud coverage below, she thought about how life had changed since moving to Atlanta ten years earlier. Back then, she had felt obscured by a giant cloud that at any moment could be obliterated by a storm front, exposing her past in all its raw ugliness. She looked away from the window, remembering. How could she have been so naïve? So trusting?

Beth shook her head. No need to think about things that were best left buried.

***

Forty minutes later, she boarded the rail transport to the terminal and grabbed a handhold. "You have such a glamorous job," Lori had once commented, counting off the cities Beth visited. Beth tried to explain that her life felt anything but glamorous. All she saw of these cities was the inside of a convention hall. "I stand in high heels on a concrete floor for hours and try to look helpful, and then attend cocktail parties and dinners that last forever," she had moaned one afternoon, after a strenuous week in San Francisco. "Not that I don't like my job," she corrected herself. "But most nights, all I want is to curl up with a book and a cup of hot tea."

As the train came to a stop, she jostled up the escalator around slower moving passengers and headed to the car park. She had learned the ground rules of flying early. Never check your bag, have your boarding pass ready, save the frequent flyer points for an upgrade on long flights, and wear comfortable shoes.

Mark answered his phone on the third ring. "I'm home," she said, trying to put energy into her voice as she exited the parking garage. She missed him, but God, she was tired.

"Great, babe. What time do you think you'll get here?"

She wiped a hand across her forehead, pushing her bangs to one side. "Listen, Mark, I'm whipped. The flight was late leaving. I didn't get bumped up and had to sit in a middle seat in the cattle car."

"Then get on up here, and I'll give you a back rub."

"Sounds wonderful. But could that back rub happen at my place?"

She pictured him turning his head from side to side the way he did when he didn't like something, rather like a bull pawing the ground.

"Aw, Beth," he began, and she knew the rest without even listening. How he was already enjoying a bourbon and cigar on his back deck. How he wanted to get up early for his morning run. How he preferred his king size bed over her queen one.

She merged onto I-85, avoiding an SUV that swerved into her lane. "How about I bring coffee and croissants in the morning?" she said into her cell. "I can be there early. We could have breakfast in bed." Glancing over her left shoulder, she accelerated into the outside lane.

***

By the time she arrived home, Beth felt rather proud of her negotiation skills. She had held her ground, something she was still learning how to do. A bubble bath and a chilled glass of white wine were just what she needed. "Sometimes I think you watched too many reruns of *Donna Reed* instead of *Mary Tyler Moore* as a kid," Anna had joked when Beth mentioned how Mark wasn't willing to spend time at her place. "It's not all about pleasing the man, you know," she had said. "You have needs too." And Beth had agreed. But still, old habits die hard.

She dropped her bags inside the front door, catching a glance of herself in the hall mirror. Her eye makeup was gone; her face was pale from three days of little sleep. She kicked off her heels and stretched to relieve the ache in her lower back. Then she walked into the living room and lit a candle. Soon lavender and jasmine filled the room with a soft fragrance. She loved coming home. Before leaving for every business trip, she cleaned the condo so she could enjoy its freshness as soon as she walked in the door.

Her eyes traveled around the room as she crossed to the stereo and turned on the local smooth jazz station. This place was her pride and joy. Four years ago, she stood in front of the fireplace with her realtor and signed the offer. The two-bedroom unit had been owned by a University of Georgia graduate, a frat boy most likely, who painted the walls the official UGA color – red Pantone 200. The dining room was used for a pool table, complete with mirror tiles glued to the walls. The kitchen had so much grime that she had it gutted and reconfigured with new cabinets and appliances, including a glass tile backsplash. The two bathrooms still had their original 1970s brass fixtures. Those too went. But the result was all Beth – soothing pale peach walls, recessed lighting, deep crown molding, and gleaming hardwood floors.

She had been meticulous about the decor in a way that reminded her of the dollhouse she had as a little girl. It was a gift from her grandmother – a woman whom Beth adored as a child, whose soft voice and gentle touch smoothed the wrinkles from any bad day. Beth would sit for hours with her dollhouse arranging tiny furniture, opening and closing miniature windows, and moving minuscule people from room to room. Time would pass, and Beth would be lost in its peaceful serenity. It was a life under her control – a place just for her and no one else. But then things changed. Her sister was born, and the dollhouse was no longer big enough to escape into.

But look at her now. Safe in her own place.

She picked up a small blue bowl that sat on her bureau. Its weight felt heavy in her hand, as her thoughts traveled to the potter who made it. "Once I'm famous," he had told her, "I'll make you a full set of these." She turned it, rubbing her hands across it, tracing the potter's strokes. Then she sat the bowl back down.

"Time for that drink," she said.

She was not much of a drinker. She had learned that danger in college. But a nice glass of La Crema chardonnay on a Friday night was a well-deserved treat, she reasoned. The only thing missing, she thought as she sank into the bubble bath, was Darcy, her cat. He used to sit on the side of the tub swatting at the water, extending one paw below the surface before pulling it back, shocked by its wetness. God, how she missed that little bundle of fur.

She had adopted him as a kitten from a shelter right after she moved to Atlanta. From that day on, he had served as her morning alarm clock and her nighttime feet warmer. But more than that, he had absorbed every tear she had cried and ever hug she needed. When she found him one day staggering and falling to the side, a call to the vet brought the news she didn't want to hear. He was having a stroke.

She wrapped him in a blanket and held him to her chest as she drove to the vet, feeling his silky fur between her fingers and the soft velvet of his ears. He was still in her arms when the vet told her he was gone. When she arrived back home, she wrapped herself in his blanket and cried.

It was the stillness that got to her. A door closed. A life passed. Eight pounds of comfort gone.

Lizzie, she thought as she ran more hot water into the tub. *That's what I'll name my new cat.*

Later, after a grilled cheese sandwich and roasted tomato soup, she crawled into bed, flicking through channels until pausing on an old episode of *Sex and the City*. Of course, the plot was preposterous, and so were the outfits worn by Sarah Jessica Parker. But she had to admit, the show examined the same questions that plagued her: How do you find a healthy relationship when you've never experienced one? How do you find a safe harbor from the storms of life?

She turned off the television and thought about the column Carrie Bradshaw might write to answer these questions. It would be one Beth would have clipped and stuck on her bathroom mirror.

Like the women in the TV program, her friends were her family. She couldn't imagine life without them close by. They seemed happy about her and Mark. Well, maybe happy wasn't the word, but willing to accept him. They had their concerns. That's what friends did.

She picked up her phone.

"Beth," Mark murmured. "What's up? Did you change your mind about coming up here?"

"I'm already tucked in. Just calling to say good night."

"Then what time will you be here tomorrow? Want to join me for a run?"

Beth stretched in bed. "Think I'll pass on the run. But listen. I'd like to go by Pet Smart to look at kittens."

"Aw, Beth. Get a dog. It can run the trails with us."

"I know, but I'm a cat person. In fact, I've already picked out a name. Lizzie, like Elizabeth Bennet in *Pride and Prejudice*." There was another reason for selecting the name, but no need to tell that to Mark.

He yawned. "You and your books."

A few minutes later, she put down the phone and fluffed her pillows. She felt good about herself. She hadn't caved to someone else's wishes. More than that, it had been months since her last panic attack, and she had weaned herself off Xanax. Mark was what she had needed all along – not drugs, not therapy. She stretched her arms above her head and yawned. She could already feel Lizzie curled against her stomach, and in the morning, Mark's arms would be wrapped around her.

Green lights and checkered flags, she thought as she went to sleep. That's how she saw their future.

CHAPTER FIVE

*B*eth tooted her horn just as Lori emerged from the front door of her townhouse, her recyclable shopping bags tucked under her arm. "Got your list?" Beth asked.

"Got it," Lori replied.

"And your recipes?"

Lori patted her purse. "Plus, I've got my list of plants to buy. It's time to play in the dirt, as they say on the radio. She rummaged in her bag and held up a furry mouse. When she squeezed it, the sound caused Beth to jump. "For Lizzie," she said, putting the toy in Beth's lap.

"You are such a good aunt to her. We play every day with the laser pointer you found. God, I'm glad I have her."

"Has she warmed up to Mark?"

"Not quite. But the few times he's stayed over, she waits until he's snoring before she crawls in beside me."

"Smart kitty."

For years, the two women had a tradition of shopping together every Sunday afternoon at the Decatur Farmer's Market off Clairmont Avenue and afterward going to Beth's condo to cook for the week. Both were amateur chefs and devoted to episodes of celebrity cooking shows. They liked to perfect recipes like Thai cashew chicken (Beth's weakness) or Cajun shrimp (Lori's go-to favorite). They especially enjoyed shopping for unique ingredients to jazz up salads, which they packed into individual containers and took as their lunches each day. Plus, it gave them the opportunity to catch up.

"You've got to admit it's less crowded on Thursday nights," Beth said, as they stopped at the cheese counter to sample double cream brie.

"But I miss our Sundays. It's not the same watching a chick flick without you and a serving of pasta primavera. All those healthy vegetables we added made me forget how much cream and cheese we used."

"I know. Thanks for being flexible, but Mark . . ."

"I know. I got it. You have a boyfriend."

For an awkward moment, Beth felt guilty about having Mark, not just as a boyfriend but perhaps forever. And Lori wasn't seeing anyone. She claimed she preferred her single status, having grown up in a large family. But Beth thought differently and wondered if she talked too much about Mark. Something she needed to watch. No guy was worth losing a friend over.

They paused in front of a display of handmade pasta, their weakness, selecting a tagliatelle that would hold up well with sautéed beef and spring onions.

Beth pursed her lips. "I miss it, too." She turned and looked around the store, surveying the customers before turning back to Lori. "But you know what I *don't* miss? All those families coming here after church and sampling everything and the kids getting sugar highs and laughing and running into everyone's carts. I mean, I feel like a failure looking at those happy families." She dropped the package into the shopping cart. "And Anna and Janet are mad at me for missing our last happy hour."

Lori turned to her. "No, they aren't. You know Anna. What's that Gloria Steinem quote she repeats so often? 'A woman without a man is like a fish without a bicycle.' And Janet is too busy hauling her kids to and from soccer practice to form an opinion about you and Mark. Plus, she and her husband are fighting, so don't expect her to cheer for you and Mark." She waited a moment before adding. "But you are wrapped up with him. Scuba lessons, tennis matches, sailing . . ."

"I'm being a bad friend, aren't I?"

Lori hugged her. "Just a busy friend, plus you're still sad about your mom's death. That may be what's bothering you." She nodded toward a woman pushing a toddler. "It's only natural for you to think about happy mothers and daughters and the what-ifs of life so soon after losing your mom, even if you didn't get along when you were younger." She squeezed her again. "Don't be so hard on yourself. Your friends will always be here for you. And if Mark doesn't treat you right," she struck a mock fighter's pose with her fists raised. "We will come after him."

Beth laughed. "Even Anna?"

"Especially Anna."

Beth turned away to allow the pain in her chest to subside as memories from the previous year pressed downward.

It was back in June, and she had just returned home from work when her phone rang. It was her mother calling to say she had stage four pancreatic cancer. She had announced it as if she were telling Beth what she had bought for dinner. "I got cancer in my pancreas. Stage four," she had said. The next day, Beth took a leave of absence from work and moved back home so she could ferry her mother to her chemo appointments in Chattanooga.

That was when Beth shut down emotionally, watching the slow drip of poison while her mother sat – her eyes closed, her hands folded in her lap.

A month later, Beth had no choice but to honor her mother's request to stop chemo and secure hospice care. "I'm tired," her mother had said. "I don't want to be poked anymore."

Beth sat by the bed when her mom breathed her last. One minute she was there; the next she was gone. It was that quick. It was that final. Beth had always thought death involved a struggle, a fight. It had been that way when her dad died five years earlier. "He fought hard," her mother had said when Beth arrived at the hospital too late to say goodbye. But here death had happened right before her eyes. A simple slipping away.

The hospice nurse had led her out of the bedroom and into the kitchen, pushing a cup of tea into her clasped hands. When the undertaker arrived, Beth stood out of the way as they rolled the body to the hearse. When at last she was alone, she sat for a long time in the silent house before rousing herself and calling her brother and sister. It was time to get busy.

From an early age, Beth had known her place in the family – sandwiched between Paul, an over-achieving brother whose name now topped the letterhead of a prestigious Nashville law firm, and Jessica, or Jess, as she liked to be called, her carefree younger sister who at the age of twenty-four was still finding herself, working as a barista in Chattanooga. Beth was the middle child who took care of everything.

At the funeral, she sat between Paul and Jess and tried to focus on the minister, but the memory of countless Sundays sitting just like this, in birth order, interfered. As kids, they had nudged or pinched one another during the service, trying to get the other in trouble – behavior that at best got them a stern look from their mother or at worse being dragged by one arm down the side aisle and into the vestibule where their legs were slapped.

Beth had turned her head toward Paul and looked at his profile. He had the beginning of a double-chin, she'd noticed with a small bit of satisfaction, but as always wore an impeccable dark suit. Exactly what a top corporate lawyer should wear. She looked next at Jess. Her hair was dyed platinum, a look that didn't go with her skin tone, but then Jess always liked to be different. Which explained the red boots.

What a family, she had thought.

The following weekend, Beth had stood on the porch as Paul filled a U-Haul with furniture and yard tools for his lake house. "Tell me again why someone who never works with his hands needs tools?" she asked but didn't receive an answer.

Meanwhile, Jess packed the china and silverware and stored it in the trunk of her car before returning to the house and picking up their mother's jewelry box. "Mom said she wanted me to have this," Jess stated. Beth only shrugged.

After both cars pulled out of the driveway, she sat on the porch steps and dropped her head into her hands. Her body ached and she felt drained – not just from the two-hour drive from Atlanta, but from the task that still lay ahead. Her mother's will named Paul as the executor but specified that Beth should clear the house.

She leaned her head back and focused on a tree branch that reached over the porch. A robin was busy building a nest close to the trunk. Beth heard somewhere that over a single robin's lifetime, it builds up to thirty nests – a process that involves collecting hundreds of twigs and tufts of grass before coating each nest with mud. "And now I must empty the nest," Beth told the bird.

She walked to her car and removed collapsed boxes. Hours later, as sunset cast shadows across the house, fifty years of linens, Christmas decorations, books, and knickknacks were ready for Goodwill to pick up.

She looked at the one item she had chosen for herself – her grandmother's Singer sewing machine. Beth had learned to sew on it – first clothes for her dolls and later skirts and dresses modeled after outfits in *Seventeen* magazine. Her grandmother had always taken her to the local fabric store and helped her pick out the right cloth for each outfit, teaching her how to rub the cloth between two fingers to gage its quality – a habit Beth still followed when shopping for clothes. The sewing machine would fit well in her entranceway.

With the front door key clutched in her hand, Beth had walked one last time from room to room – staring out a window, pausing in a doorway, running a hand across a kitchen counter, seeing through adult eyes a place that held equal parts of joy and sadness. She climbed onto the kitchen counter to double check the shelf Jess had cleared. In the back of a top shelf, she found four Waterford glasses shoved into a corner. They had been a retirement gift for her father. When she came home for her rare visits, he always made a Four Roses Manhattan for each of them, complete with maraschino cherries. Beth felt again on the shelf and pulled out a dusty bottle of Jack Daniels. "It's football time in Tennessee," she could hear her father saying as he turned on the television to watch his Vols. She poured a shot into a glass, added a splash of water, and raised it as a toast. Then she took the drink outside and sat once again on the steps, listening to the sounds of night falling.

Her parents' relationship had been a mystery to her. They were like two people living in parallel worlds – her father going to work as an accountant, coming home to read the newspaper and watch the news, always willing to listen to Beth if she sought his attention, but never engaging with her. Present, but absent. Content to let his wife run the household.

In contrast, her mother filled every inch of space in their home. In fact, Beth was never allowed to close the door to her bedroom, which was why she learned to retreat inside herself, safe in her own thoughts with her dollhouse and books and records. How the two of them managed fifty years together was something Beth never understood. They never argued in front of the kids, but they never hugged either. He earned the money; she raised the kids. There, but not there, for one another.

Beth slammed her glass down on the steps. "What sort of people were you?" she yelled before feeling foolish, as her words startled a squirrel eating a nut beneath a tree. Acting out was not allowed in the Gardiner house. It was time to go.

As she locked the front door to leave the house for the last time, she had noticed something sticking out from one of the many boxes of books stacked on the porch. She squatted in front of the box and pulled out a photo tucked between two *Reader's Digest* condensed books. It was a faded picture of Beth and her high school boyfriend, still in its cardboard envelope from the local drug store. They were standing on the fifty-yard line of the University of Tennessee's Neyland Stadium in Knoxville, both wearing orange sweatshirts with the university logo on the front and holding their admission letters. They would enroll as freshmen the following year, and their friends had assumed it was only a matter of time before they would marry.

Peas and carrots. That's what people had called them. A good match.

Beth turned away. Her heart raced, and she felt her chest constrict. She didn't want to think about Drew. It served no purpose to let her mind go there. That was a thousand years ago. But dammit, there it was, her heart shattered and Drew calling out from his apartment, "What did I do, Beth? What did I do?"

***

"Earth to Beth," Lori said, nudging her with the shopping cart. "Are you okay?"

Beth flashed a smile. "Absolutely. Let's get ice cream too. It will go great over sour cream pound cake. And maybe take some to Janet for her kids."

That easily, she slammed the door on her past and turned her thoughts toward Mark. *Why not?* she thought. *Why not take a chance for once?*

CHAPTER SIX

S tanding on her toes, Beth leaned out the window. Asheville was her favorite place on earth, especially in early spring. The sun was rising over a far ridge, and the mountains were enveloped in morning mist that changed the forest from hues of deep green to a soft purple.

Pulling her robe close, she listened to the sound of birds in nearby trees. When she and Mark checked in the night before, it was too dark to see the view. Never an early riser, she somehow woke this morning at the first light of dawn.

She glanced over her shoulder, thinking to call Mark to join her, but he was still asleep, lying on his stomach with one arm stretched above his head. She had fantasied about staying at the Grove Park Inn since she read *The Great Gatsby* in high school and learned that F. Scott Fitzgerald lived there while Zelda was hospitalized nearby. His stories had so captivated her that she had persuaded her high school prom committee to use the Roaring Twenties as the theme. She smiled as she remembered the silver fringe gown she had worn to channel her inner Daisy. So tacky, but then, she was only sixteen.

Her eyes returned to Mark. She didn't even know he existed this time three months ago, and now they were a couple – not boyfriend and girlfriend like in college, but a couple – committed except for the words. He had said as much the night before. She returned to bed and stretched her five-foot-two frame on top of his six-two body. She felt his breathing change as he awoke.

"Good morning," she whispered.

"What are you doing awake so early?" he asked in a gruff voice as he flipped onto his side. He ran a hand through his hair and looked across the room at a clock. "Good God, Beth.

It's not even seven." He snuggled his head against her shoulder. "I need to sleep."

She threw a leg across him. "Are you sure that's what you need? You sure you don't need a good morning hug, or a good morning kiss, or a good morning— what's that Anglo-Saxon word you like to use?" She kissed his neck and worked her way down his side. "Are you sure sleep is what you need right now?" Her lips were now at his waist, and she heard him release a soft moan. "You sure you don't want to make love while the sun rises across the Smoky Mountains?"

In one quick motion, he flipped her onto her back. Beth giggled. "Now that's the man I want on a vacation."

"Shut up, woman," he muttered. "And try not to wake the neighbors."

***

Beth turned in a full circle with her arms outstretched like in the opening scene of *The Sound of Music* before flopping down on the grass beside Mark. "I could live here," she declared.

They had just spent three hours exploring the Biltmore, the Chateau style mansion built by George Vanderbilt in the late 1800s. Gazing out palatial windows overlooking the French Broad River. Craning their necks as they climbed the three-story spiral staircase. Roaming all four acres of opulent floor space. Looking at priceless artwork, including especially Beth's favorite – *The Waltz* by Zorn.

"At Biltmore?" Mark asked.

"No. Asheville, silly. I mean, look." She gestured around. "You've got mountains. Art and culture. Hiking. Shopping. Cool people doing cool things. An old boyfriend and I always talked about moving here after college."

"Only one thing missing," Mark commented.

"You're right. The Core Four."

He shook his head. "No, Beth. Water. There's nowhere to sail."

Beth exhaled and lay backward. "But think about it. Wouldn't this be a great place to live?"

He let out a short laugh. "Get real. You're having a rocky mountain high moment. If I were to move anywhere, it would be Florida." He leaned over her. "And you agreed, remember? Mountains or ocean, I asked, and you chose the ocean."

Her face revealed her puzzlement. "But we were just joking around that day."

"I wasn't. I love being on the water. The sound of the wind as it fills the sails. The surge of the boat. The vastness of it all. I get what those early explorers felt when they set sail from Portugal and Spain."

She removed her sunglasses and peered at him. "Are you thinking of moving to Florida? I mean, not just when you retire or something?"

He scoffed. "I'm not waiting until I'm sixty-five to live by the ocean. I'm saying right now it will happen before then. Maybe sooner than you think." He stood up and held out a hand to pull her up. "Let's get going," he said. "I'm hungry. Come on. I'll treat you to some Smoky Mountain barbeque." He leaned toward her ear. "And if you are a messy eater, I'll lick the sauce off your face."

"Mark," she laughed. "Please don't do that." The thought of her face covered with barbeque caused her to forget about asking him more about his Florida plans.

He grinned and turned toward the car.

Beth took one last look at the Biltmore. It was a magnificent structure, and with the sun setting behind it, the house seemed to glow with rays of light. She remembered the time her mother traveled here with her garden club. Beth must have been eight years old then. Her mother brought home a book that included photos not only of the Biltmore but also of Vanderbilt homes in New York and Newport. Beth would sit for hours looking at the opulent rooms, envisioning the fairytale lives the people must have lived.

She remembered sitting cross-legged in the living room one day with the book in her lap when her mother walked in. "Get your head out of the clouds, Elizabeth, and mind your sister." She couldn't remember what had happened to the book after that. It just disappeared from the coffee table. What would her mother have done with it? And why? Did she think daydreaming was dangerous? Again, all Beth had were questions without answers.

"Let's get going," Mark called, snapping her out of her thoughts. He had the top down on the Mustang. She pushed aside her memories as she ran to the car and hopped in. Mark slung gravel as he accelerated, and the Biltmore and her questions disappeared behind a grove of tall trees.

he cool air-conditioned restaurant was a welcome relief from the heat that blanketed Atlanta. Beth shivered as the maître d' led Mark and her to a corner table. It was her birthday. That morning at work, she had received flowers and a card from the Core Four. "You're not 30," the card stated. "You're 17 with 13 years of experience."

"Not funny," she had told Lori, who had arranged the flower delivery.

As they crossed the floor of Dante's Down the Hatch, an Atlanta landmark, Beth waved to a couple seated in a corner booth. "They beat us," she said to Mark, nudging him forward. Her eyes took in the plush surroundings. A jazz combo was in the middle of a set of Frank Sinatra standards. *Perfect*, she thought.

Grant and Alisa were her favorite couple. Beth had spent many weekends with them, even sleeping at their home after a night of dancing so Grant could prepare his famous Mexican frittata for breakfast. When Beth decorated her condo, Alisa was her interior designer, taking her to places on Howell Mill Road and Miami Circle that were open only to design professionals. Beth credited Alisa for suggesting a soft peach hue for the walls – a color that, according to her, flattered every complexion – and working cream and green into the color scheme to coordinate with watercolor prints of the Smoky Mountains.

College sweethearts, they married after Grant completed his MBA at the University of Georgia. On more than one occasion, Beth had admired a framed wedding photo on display in their den. The couple was posed with their ten bridesmaids and groomsmen in front of the Atlanta History Center. "It was the social event of the year," Alisa had said, in her best

Scarlett O'Hara accent, with four hundred guests and full-page coverage in the *Atlanta Journal & Constitution*.

Twenty-five years later, they had a spacious home, three children in college, and still addressed one another with pet names. At the end of an evening, Grant would always turn to his wife and say, "You're still the prettiest girl at the party." To Beth, they were perfect.

Only last week, Beth told Alisa that her therapist warned her not to fall in love too quickly.

"He's right, you know," Alisa had responded, much to Beth's dismay. "Plus, Mark's ten years older than you," she added, "which can become challenging. Lifetime relationships take a long time to grow lasting roots. The easy part is falling in love, and," she added with a finger wag at Beth, "if I know you, you're headed that way fast. But be careful. Don't let the excitement of meeting the right man blind you to what Mark must do to *be* the right man. If there are things you don't like, tell him about them early on. If he cares enough, he'll change."

"Yes, Mom," Beth had replied. That was how she thought of Alisa. The mother whose advice she could trust – so opposite to her own mother whose sharp tongue and iron hand Beth had feared.

When they reached the table, Grant stood and enveloped Beth in a hug. "Happy Birthday, Rocky Top." He and Alisa were fans of UGA football, and with Tennessee a big rival, he never missed an opportunity to rib her about her hillbilly roots. She had joined them the previous year to tailgate in Athens when Tennessee played Georgia and won, she liked to remind him.

"Thanks, Herschel," she replied, using the name of his all-time favorite Georgia running back, Herschel Walker.

An hour later the two couples were lingering over their second bottle of wine when Mark asked, "Have you two ever been on a sailboat? I'm teaching Beth to sail and thinking of taking her to the British Virgin Islands next month. Interested?"

Beth looked from Mark's animated face to Alisa, and her eyes widened with surprise.

"Are you asking us to join you or take lessons?" Grant asked.

"Either," Mark replied. "Both. I can always use help pulling lines."

"Will the boat have a bathroom?" Alisa asked.

Grant hugged her to him. "It's called a head, sweetie, and yes, you'll have a place to plug in your hair dryer."

Mark ignored her question. "There are days at work when I look up at a poster in my office. It has a sailboat anchored off a tropical island with white sand and deep blue water, and man, what I wouldn't give to be there." He looked away as if seeing himself standing behind a wheel. A wistful expression crossed his face. Beth reached for his hand to pull his attention back to the table, lacing her fingers between his.

"It's your hobby," Grant said. "Like me working in my garage on an old Corvette I'm restoring. Once I'm done, Alisa and I are taking it to a car rally in California, aren't we, sugar?"

Beth spoke up when she saw Mark shift in his chair. "I think it's more than that for Mark," she said. "Captain Mark. I think that's who he wants to be when he grows up."

Mark's smile broadened, missing the kidding tone in her voice.

"To Captain Mark and sailing," Grant said, winking at Beth and raising his glass for another toast.

"And to love," chimed in Alisa.

"And birthdays," added Beth.

"To dreams coming true," Mark added, turning to Beth. She leaned her forehead against his and squeezed his hand.

***

It was after eleven when Mark led her down a hotel corridor in midtown Atlanta. "Close your eyes," he said, as he inserted the door key into the slot. He guided her with one arm into the room. "Now keep them shut until I tell you to open them."

She heard him moving about the room. Water began running into a bathtub, and she detected a sound like a match being struck. Some more bumping about, then she heard what sounded like a cork being pulled from a bottle.

"Now, open your eyes," he instructed. Beth looked about the room, taking in the votive candles on every surface of furniture. A vase of red roses stood on a small table between two filled champagne glasses. Leaning against the pillows was a box of Guylian chocolates, her favorite.

"Oh, my God, Mark," she said, as she walked into the bathroom where a bubble bath awaited. She turned back to him and into his arms. "I can't believe you did this. I'm speechless. Turning thirty is so worth the wrinkles."

He gave her a long kiss. "Do you like it?" he murmured.

"Like it? I'm overwhelmed."

"There's just one more thing." He pulled a box out of his jacket pocket and gave it to her. It was wrapped in silver paper with a red velvet bow. She opened the box and gasped as she pulled out a gold chain with a single teardrop sapphire. "I thought it might work with your blue eyes."

She turned toward a mirror and held up the necklace. "Here, let me do that for you," he said, as he connected the clasp. He turned her back toward him and held her in an embrace. "Happy birthday, Beth. I'm in love with you. Hope that's okay."

She reached her arms around him. "I'm already there," she replied. "I'm already there."

He reached again into his pocket and pulled out a small blue box. "In that case...." He dropped to one knee.

Beth gasped. Her hands flew to her open mouth as tears pooled in her eyes. Mark opened the box and lifted out a rose gold ring with a single sapphire surrounded by a halo of seven diamonds.

"It was my mom's," he said, as he reached for her left hand. "Now it can be yours." He pulled her down beside him. "Beth, will you marry me?"

She nodded, sobs preventing her from speaking. He slid the ring onto her finger. It fit. "Is that a yes?" he asked.

She nodded more and then threw herself at him. "Yes," she said between gulps. "Definitely yes."

CHAPTER EIGHT

" Ta-da," Beth exclaimed, as she held out her hand to her girlfriends.

The Core Four sat stunned – their mouths open, their eyes wide.

Lori spoke first. "Oh, my God, Beth!" She pressed one hand against her chest. "You're engaged? That's incredible." She stood and gave her friend a hug. "When did this happen?"

"Last night," Beth answered. "I was caught off guard. Mark had this amazing setup with a hotel room and champagne and flowers and chocolate and, well," she held her hand out again. "A ring."

Lori hugged her. "And you said yes."

"You bet I said yes." Beth looked at her ring and smiled.

"This calls for champagne," Janet proclaimed, as she stood to signal for a waiter.

Beth's eyes traveled to each friend and stopped on Anna. "You don't look happy."

Anna shook her head. "No, no. That's not it." She leaned in. "I'm just surprised. It seems," she paused. "Fast. Four months, right?" Beth nodded. "But sure. Of course, I'm happy for you. Mazel Tov, as my Jewish grandmother would say. May you have a long life and many children."

Beth held up a hand. "Please. No kids. Raising my baby sister was enough, remember? Plus, there's Mark's daughter, Heather, to think about. He was still in college when she was born, which was why he got married," she added. "I get a nineteen-year-old daughter without morning sickness, terrible twos, teenage attitude, or college tuition." Beth shrugged. "Anyway, we're meeting her today to share the news."

Her friends sat back as if blown into their chairs by a strong wind. A waiter appeared and placed a stemmed glass in front of each. They all watched as he uncorked the bottle.

"Congratulations to me," Beth proclaimed when the waiter left. She downed her glass. The other three exchanged a quick glance as they sipped theirs.

"And the date?" Lori asked, just as Janet blurted, "Are you sure?"

Beth sat up straight. "June first," she said. "So, mark your calendars now." Then she turned to Janet. "And yes, I'm sure." She poured another glass before folding her arms. "What is it with you three today? I thought you'd be happy for me."

Anna leaned forward. "I'm sorry, Beth. I shared something with Lori and Janet just before you arrived. It's probably nothing. But you should ask Mark about it."

Beth screwed her face in puzzlement. "What are you talking about?"

Anna glanced at Janet who gave her a quick nod. "I remembered where I had heard Mark's name. I don't know the details, but it seems there was some scandal at the private school where he once taught. Something about man-handling a kid."

"What?" Beth asked, color draining from her face.

Anna reached for her hand and held it. "I don't want to spoil your joy. Honestly. But ask Mark about it. Just to get everything out in the open before the 'I do's'. Okay?"

The three watched as Beth absorbed the news.

"O-kay," she muttered, as an image of his hands came to mind. "I'll do that." She pictured his long fingers, the squared nails, a scar on his left hand from a hockey match. With a decisive shake of her head, she smiled and topped up everyone's glass.

"To marriage," she proclaimed, as she raised her glass aloft. "And to the Core Four!" she added.

"To the Core Four," they echoed.

Beth scanned the table, examining each face – Lori's smile of support, Janet's what-the-heck wink, Anna's drawn brow. For a moment, she felt like she was boarding a ship and waving goodbye. She discarded the feeling and held her glass higher. "And to Mark and me," she said and downed her champagne in one gulp.

***

A few hours later, Beth pulled into Starbucks and watched as a young woman open the door. Something about her carriage made Beth believe the girl was Heather. Blonde, tall, and slender, she wore black boots that climbed above her knees and a gray sweater dress belted at the waist. But her outfit wasn't the giveaway. It was the set of her chin. Confident. Even cocky. Just like Mark when he played tennis.

Deciding to give father and daughter time alone, Beth turned off the engine. In a few moments, she saw Heather join her dad at a window booth. He didn't stand up and hug his daughter, Beth noted. Strange.

She watched as Heather sat, crossed her long legs, and leaned forward, pushing a frothy drink to the side. Whatever she was saying brought a frown to Mark's face. His arms folded across his chest. Then both his hands smacked the table. Beth jumped even as Heather did. What was going on? She reached for the door handle, unsure what to do, then let go. Best not to interrupt.

Meanwhile, Mark was wiping up spilled coffee and glaring across the table. Heather apparently said something else, and Mark pushed himself back from the table, knocking into another customer.

Oh, dear, Beth thought. *Oh, dear*. She got out of the car, her eyes still on the scene. Mark was reaching across the table to Heather, but she shrugged his hand off and stood. After a few steps toward the entrance, she turned back to her dad and yelled something.

She and Beth reached the entrance at the same time. "Hi," Beth stammered. I'm Beth." Their blue eyes connected for a moment, and then Heather was past her. Beth watched as she jerked open the door of her car, cranked the engine, and slammed the car into reverse.

"What's going on?" she asked Mark when she reached his booth. "What's wrong?"

He ignored her, his arms once again crossed, his face glaring out the window.

"What happened?" she asked. "What was she crying about?"

He shook his head in disgust. "She's just like her mom." He grabbed his phone from the table and stood. "I don't want to talk about it. Let's get out of here."

"But Mark," Beth said, trailing him outside. "If something's happened, I need to know. Maybe I can help." She reached for his hand. He shrugged her off. "Talk to me, Mark," she said again.

He didn't speak until he reached his car. "It's nothing. Leave it alone. Heather is just being a little bitch. Like I said, she takes after her mom." He looked across the parking lot and exhaled. "I'll get it sorted out. It's none of your business."

Beth's eyes opened wide. "You're wrong," she answered. "We're getting married, so it is my business."

He slammed the car door and cranked his engine. "Leave it alone, Beth. I'm going for a run. Talk later."

Beth stood in the parking lot and watched him leave. *Like father, like daughter*, she thought, but then chided herself. She walked toward her car, feeling sick to her stomach. But not for Mark, she realized, for Heather. All that tension. All that anger. She knew how that felt, all too well. Only Beth would never have been allowed to say something and escape without a slap across the face.

She weighed her keys in her hand, trying to decide whether to follow him to his house or drive back to hers. *Take Mark's advice and butt out*, she thought, or lobby for more understanding on his part. And what to do about Anna's information? That needed clearing up. She got her phone out and dialed Lori. This called for a girlfriend chat. A long one.

Thirty minutes later, Beth sat in Lori's kitchen with a cup of tea cradled in her hands.

"What are you going to do?" Lori asked.

Beth shook her head in frustration. "Probably call him and try to arrange another meeting with Heather, but...." She shrugged her shoulders in a hopeless manner and looked down at her tea.

Lori reached forward and patted her knee. "Why don't I add a little whiskey to that cup? A little Irish courage to get your strength ready for that phone call?"

Beth smiled and held her cup forward. "Sure. Why not?"

amily, Beth thought as her car approached down-town Nashville. *Can't live with them, can't* . . . well, that said it all. It had taken several days, but at last, she persuaded Mark to contact his daughter. "Fall on your sword if you have to," she had told him. "Be the adult." That last remark earned her a glare, but a week later, Mark said he and Heather had talked. Beth didn't press for details.

She had also asked about the private school incident.

"It was nothing," Mark had said. "Just showing a kid a move and he slipped and hit his head. His parents got all worked up about it. I had already accepted an offer to coach at a school closer to my house, so I quit." He had shrugged. End of conversation.

Meanwhile, Beth had her own family concerns – how to plan a wedding that included her siblings. At her mother's funeral, she had suggested celebrating Easter together as a family. With the engagement, now seemed the perfect opportunity to introduce him to her family. But as she and Mark pulled into her brother's tree-lined driveway, she doubted her judgment.

Throughout the drive from Atlanta, the closer they got to Nashville, the more Beth tapped her fingers on the steering wheel, tension coiling up her spine like kudzu vines ready to choke the life from her. The stress had progressed into a pounding headache and her old familiar chest pains.

"Honestly," she told Mark, "I'd rather be on an egg hunt with thousands of screaming toddlers than spend the day with my brother." But here they were.

She eased her car onto the brick-paved parking pad and turned off the ignition. Paul's house was in the Belle Meade neighborhood of Nashville, on Honeywood Drive. "The most exclusive neighborhood in the city," she said with an eye roll. "Nothing but the best for my big brother."

Mark stepped out of the car and stared for a moment at the Corinthian marble columns flanking the three-story brick home. "Holy shit," he said at last. "Is this where your brother lives? I mean, crap, this place is amazing."

Beth followed him as he crossed the lawn to get a better view of the five-acre estate. "It's called Woodbloom Manor," she said. "You know, for all the trees and gardens. Pretentious, right?"

Mark turned to her. "You told me your brother was a successful lawyer, but I didn't know crime paid this good."

"He's a corporate attorney, and he married old money." She mimicked climbing a ladder. "Now he's climbing his way to senior partner." She rolled her shoulders to release tension and then nudged him forward. "Let's go inside and try not to genuflect when I introduce you."

At that moment, Beth's sister, Jess, ran out the door. Her hair was dark and curly now, but she still wore the red boots, Beth noticed. They looked better with the jeans she had on instead of the lacy black dress she wore to the funeral. Beth hugged her. "You made it," she said.

Beth's heart always ached when she thought about Jess. She was six years old when her father took her to the hospital to meet her new sister. As she stood by the bed, half hidden behind her father, her mother had extended the infant toward her, as if expecting Beth to take the crying baby away. She remembered trying to hold the newborn in her arms like she did her favorite doll, but Jess cried even more until her father reached for the child and returned her to her mother.

From that day on, Beth's life changed in ways she was only now examining. Jess's crib was put in her room, and over time, Beth was expected to help wash, feed, and bathe her sister. For years afterward, her mother seemed to want nothing to do with her youngest. Only later in life did Beth realize that her mother may have suffered from severe postpartum depression.

Yet here they were celebrating the holiday together like a normal, happy family – Beth still feeling somehow both responsible for and irritated by her sister's presence.

"Been here a week," Jess answered. "Paul's put me up in the pool house so I can come and go as I please. I'm thinking of moving here and waiting tables for a while."

"No more Chattanooga and lazy Sundays tubing down the Tennessee River?"

"I'm thinking music is more my scene." Jess looked from Beth to Mark, only now noticing him. "Well hello, handsome," she said in a sultry voice.

"Ignore her," Beth said, seeing Mark's broad grin. "She would flirt with a signpost." She watched with amusement as Mark added swagger to his walk as he caught up to Jess. But when he put an arm around her, Beth's felt a chill until Mark looked over his shoulder and winked.

"Let the holiday begin," she muttered.

Three hours later, Beth rinsed dishes in the kitchen as Ashley, Paul's wife, piped whipped cream onto slices of Lane cake. Beth had made the dessert the day before using her grandmother's recipe. It called for a quarter cup of whiskey, but Beth always added more to keep the cake moist. "A little sad" is how her grandma had described its texture.

Beth had remained quiet throughout dinner. She and Mark were the ones with big news, but it was Paul who dominated the conversation. Time with him always put her back in the family home where for every stage of her life, his accomplishments eclipsed everything. Full-ride university scholarship, check. Top of his graduating class, check. Big league law firm, check. Marriage to the sweetheart of Sigma Chi, check. Weekend lake house, check. Beautiful daughter in private school, check. Today Paul was holding forth on a Supreme Court case he was set to argue. Check.

"How long have you known Mark?" Ashley asked as she placed the dessert plates on a silver tray.

"Actually only a few months," Beth replied.

Ashley raised one well-groomed eyebrow. "Love at first sight?"

Beth thought before she answered. She and Ashley had never been close, probably because their lives were so different. Ashley had a private Pilates instructor who kept her lean frame in top shape. She played tennis twice a week at the Belle Meade Country Club. She had been president of her sorority at Vanderbilt and now served on the board of the Nashville Junior League. Her home had been featured in *Southern Living* and *Home Décor*. Her daughter, Isabelle, had the brains of her father and the looks of her mother. Beth sensed that Ashley viewed Paul's siblings as the poor relatives but was too well mannered to be anything but the perfect hostess. Or maybe that was Beth's own insecurities poking up their ugly head.

"You could say that," Beth said. "My friends think so. But for me, it's the real deal. I've dated enough. So has Mark. Of course, he can be a bear – I think because he grew up in a house full of boys – and I'm sure you know the usual horror stories about me."

Ashley waved away the remark with her hand and then opened a bottle of white Bordeaux. Gesturing to Beth to hold out a glass, she poured both a drink and then sat the bottle down with a heavy clink to the counter. "I envy you, you know," she said.

"Really? Why?"

"You have your own life. A career. Good friends. And now you're engaged to a hunk."

"Well, thanks, but my life's nothing to what you and Paul have."

"Oh, please," Ashley said. She gazed into her glass for a long moment before speaking. "You grew up with him. You know how he is. We never do anything that isn't good for the firm. Do you know where we would be today if you hadn't suggested coming for a visit? At the country club having dinner with some corporate CEO whose business Paul wants to secure. Honestly, the man is consumed by work."

She sat her glass down and picked up the dessert tray. Beth could tell she was beyond tipsy. "Here. Let me carry that for you," she offered.

Ashley handed it to her and walked toward the dining room before turning back to Beth. "If Mark and you are in love, that's great. And if the sex is good too? Well, don't tell me about it because I will be jealous. But don't rush into something. Trust me." She nodded toward the dining room. "Look before you leap."

With a quick flip of her blonde hair over one shoulder, she adjusted her pink silk blouse and opened the door before Beth had a chance to respond. She shook her head to clear it before returning to the dining room. "Where's Mark?" she asked.

"Went to look at the pool," Paul answered, putting down his cell phone. "Mark's a double-A tennis player? Good going, Beth. I told him I didn't remember you being any good when you played in high school, but maybe you've gotten better. Did Ashley tell you about the deep-sea fishing trip I'm taking next week with a client? I'm looking forward to reeling in a Blue Marlin." He made a casting motion.

"And Jess?" Beth added, noticing that Paul was the only one left at the table.

He reached for his phone to check calls before answering. "Not sure. She mentioned going to the Bluebird Café for some music. Tried to persuade Mark to go, but he begged off."

Beth felt the vice tightening around her head as she absorbed his words. She placed the tray on the sideboard and looked from her brother to his wife, whose face was now blank except for a prim smile.

Ashley met her eyes and lifted her glass in a toast. Beth lifted hers in return.

CHAPTER TEN

*W*ith an arm resting on her dance partner's shoulder, Beth glanced at her watch. Where the heck was Mark? His flight to Miami should have landed well over an hour earlier. If he took the hotel shuttle, as she had recommended, he should have arrived in plenty of time to shower, change, and meet her in the ballroom. Surely, he hadn't gone for a run on the beach. After all, she had left a note and an Atlanta Dance Club shirt for him on the bed. He wouldn't wear it, but still, she was doing her best to make him feel part of the group. And they had met dancing.

When the song ended, Beth gave her partner a quick hug and walked off the floor. But when the DJ began "One Drop of Love," a West Coast Swing favorite, another man grabbed her hand and spun her into his arms.

"I love this song," Beth said to him, and for the rest of the number, she forgot about Mark.

She had flown to Miami two days earlier for work and was excited to introduce Mark to the dance world. For several years, she had attended weekend events sponsored by local dance clubs. Dallas, Chicago, Boston, St. Louis – making new friends and renewing friendships with old acquaintances.

She loved the energy of these weekends – the booths that sold everything from CDs to dance shoes and jewelry, the way many dancers wore their club's logo shirt, the hardwood sprung dance floor that made it so easy to move. For an entire weekend, from midday until way past midnight, everyone danced. And when they weren't dancing, they were mingling in the lobby with a drink in one hand and their dance shoes in the other.

"We just dance. That's all," she had told Mark when she suggested he join her in Miami. But he had seemed dubious. And now he was late.

She walked off the dance floor to get a drink of water and heard a voice say, "Thanks for waiting for me in the room."

She stepped back, knocked off balance by Mark's tone. "You made it," she said, giving him a hug.

He pulled away. "My flight was late, and I had to spend ten bucks to get a cab here. Then I had to wait while you danced with John Travolta." He nodded toward the floor. "I wanted us to spend time together this weekend, not just dance."

"I'm so sorry," Beth said, nudging close to him. "We can spend all morning in the room."

He put a possessive arm around her. "I still think you should have waited. You knew this was the first one of these events I've attended."

"Again, I'm sorry. It didn't even occur to me that you'd be bothered. I thought you would read my note, and everyone was already down here so...." She stopped and caught her breath. "I'm sorry. Let's just dance, okay?"

Just then, a man walking by reached for Beth's hand and cocked his head toward the dance floor. Beth automatically smiled at him as she held up one finger to signal for him to wait. It was considered rude to turn down a dance. Mark exhaled.

She looked up. "Are we okay?" she asked. "Let's you and I dance the next one. Okay?"

Mark at first pretended not to hear but then gave her a quick nod. She smiled and followed her new partner to the floor and fell into step with him. But she didn't enjoy herself.

Mark's sport was tennis. She knew that. There he dominated. Since he took up the game, he said he had practiced his serve thousands of times, placing balls down the middle, painting the outside line, putting on topspin to keep his opponents off balance. He knew how to win, and, as Beth had observed at his last match, when he lost, his racket often landed in the branches of trees.

She glanced toward him. He was still standing by the door, gazing over dancers' heads, looking bored and out of place. Beth's heart sank. Perhaps it was time she became a better tennis player, she concluded. So Mark wouldn't feel left out.

CHAPTER ELEVEN

*T*he realtor placed a packet of materials on the coffee table. "If your home is listed by this weekend, there's a good chance for a full price offer by the end of next week. May is the perfect time for listing." She looked around the room. "This place will show well. Excellent job with the finishes."

Beth smiled at the compliment and then looked at Mark. "What do you think? Should I sign now?"

She heard the hesitation in her voice and knew already what his advice would be. They had talked it over several times already, and each time Mark made it clear he didn't like the hustle and bustle of living downtown. "Plus, we're only thirty minutes from the lake," he always emphasized, sounding more like a vacuum cleaner salesman reviewing the features of the machine than Beth cared to admit. "You want to sail with me, right?" he would continue. "Think about the nights we could spend there. The stars. The solitude." And Beth would nod her head in agreement, pushing away any nagging desire to disagree, allowing the solid arms wrapped around her to chase away any doubts.

"You could sleep on it," Mark answered, their eyes still locked together. "But why wait?" He smiled and drew her close, his voice soft and sensual. "Plus, the quicker you sell this place, the sooner you'll be living with me."

Beth nodded. Marriage required compromises, she reasoned. Now, this was one she needed to make. After all, home is where the heart is.

The realtor saw the opportunity and extended a pen toward her. Beth held it for a moment above the document, and then with a flourish, signed her name.

"Excellent," the realtor said and held out her hand. "I'll call you tomorrow about holding an open house on Sunday. Get your packing boxes ready. You'll probably get multiple offers. And congratulations," she added, as she turned toward the door.

Beth collapsed into a chair and looked again at Mark. "I did the right thing, didn't I?" It was a rhetorical question. She didn't expect an answer. But if she felt the need to ask the question, did that not say something about her answer?

Later, after she watched Mark drive away, she returned to her seat. She thought about how hard she had saved for the down payment on the condo, putting bits aside until she had the needed amount to move out of a rental unit. She had forgone vacations, theater tickets, and girlfriend shopping trips for years to build up her savings. Now, with Buckhead condos in high demand, she stood to make a tidy profit.

So why did a part of her feel like she was making a mistake? Why was a nagging voice sounding like Dr. Em saying, *what's the hurry?* He, too, had questioned her on the speed of the relationship, and she had yet to make an appointment to tell him about her engagement. She paused and counted the weeks on her hands since she had last seen him. Too many.

She fixed a cup of tea and went out onto her deck, leaving the door open so Lizzie could join her. The dogwoods and azaleas were past their peak, and the ground below them was carpeted with spent flowers. A sense of sadness settled on her as she thought about her condo. It was perfect, she concluded, and in less than a month, it would belong to someone else. Her new home would be a tract house north of the city with a two-car garage and a chain-link fenced back yard.

Snap out of it, Beth, she told herself as she sipped her tea. *You love Mark. It's just a condo. It will be fun to take on a new decorating project. Your place is with him, and together you can create a home.*

She pulled Lizzie into her lap and leaned back to watch the rustling of the dogwoods. She remembered her mother once explained the Christian symbolism of their flowers, their petals shaped like crosses and their pink tips like small drops of blood. "They remind us of our sins," her mother would say. Beth never liked placing such a heavy meaning on a unique tree. To her, they were a delicate blossom that turned a hopeful face to the sun. Kind of how she felt right now. Fragile, yet hopeful.

But now that she had allowed her mother into her head, her thoughts stayed there like a wasp feeding on fallen fruit. When Beth had moved to Atlanta after college, she didn't even let her parents know her address until after she had a job. In fact, the last time she had been in the same room with her parents was spring of her junior year, when she went home, hoping to find love and comfort and finding neither. "Every family has one black sheep," she had overheard her mother say to her father. That night, Beth had returned to her dorm room and turned herself into a black sheep – cutting her auburn hair and dying it jet black, a look she completed with dark eyeshadow and liner. Out went her pastel dresses. In their place were black turtlenecks and baggy cargo pants.

She kept this look until she checked into an Atlanta motel the night after graduation. The next day, she had booked an appointment in a hair salon. Three hours later, she emerged with a hair color similar to her original. At Rich's department store, she bought one suit, two pairs of slacks, three blouses, and a pair of black pumps. A week later, she was a copywriter for a small ad agency – a position that gave her the skills needed to become an assistant marketing manager with a tradeshow management company. And she didn't look back. Sure, she had returned home for a visit now and then, but mostly, she kept that door shut — that is until her mother passed, and Beth had to open Pandora's box. All those memories from so long ago.

She pushed Lizzie off her lap and walked into her bedroom. Her eyes landed on the blue bowl. She looked away. *Time to get those boxes packed*, she thought.

CHAPTER TWELVE

*M*ark dropped a box onto the floor and stretched his shoulders. "That's the last. Good God, Beth. How many books do you own?"

She glanced at the box. "Those aren't books. That's crystal. See where I wrote *fragile* in big letters? I hope you didn't break anything."

"Right. Sorry." He went to the refrigerator and pulled out a Gatorade. "Guess I better get the truck back to U-Haul. Think you can handle the unpacking? If you're finished when I get back, we could go to the park for a run."

Beth looked up from where she kneeled. "Why don't you run without me? I've got way too much to do here."

After she heard the front door close, she lay back on the floor and stared at the ceiling fan whirling above. Moving from the condo had been harder than she expected. Every book, every lamp, every decorative pillow had a story behind it. Now as they lay scattered around Mark's living room floor, she realized that through his eyes, they were just dust collectors with no meaning or purpose.

"It's just stuff," she said to the ceiling fan, hoping that by repeating Mark's words, she would convince herself. She reached into a box and pulled out an item. It was a mercury glass vase wrapped in three sheets of packing paper. The antiques shop owner on Roswell Road had told her it was made in Bohemia in the mid-eighteen hundreds. She held it up to the light the way the owner had to demonstrate its delicate construction. A reproduction was available for a fraction of the cost at any home goods store, but Beth liked to think about the one artist who had crafted this piece. It sat on her bathroom counter, always with fresh flowers, and made her smile each morning as she applied her makeup. She reached for the packing paper, rewrapped the vase, and then placed it into a box labeled *Personal*. In it were items like this one – things that might not work in Mark's current house but would decorate a future home. Maybe a place overlooking a lake with mountains in the distance. This was her dream, and she allowed her thoughts to wander before getting back to the task at hand, but her mind remained on paint colors and fabrics.

She stood with a renewed burst of energy and turned about the room. Her eyes landed on the fireplace. "I live here too," she muttered, looking at a collection of sports trophies placed in no particular order on the mantel. *It won't be home until I make it home*, she told herself.

Crossing the room, she picked up a trophy. It was for an Atlanta Lawn Tennis Association city final – Men's A-1 Doubles. One by one, she examined them. Some dated back to Mark's college years. A couple were from Peewee baseball, so tarnished she could barely read the inscriptions.

She looked around and focused on a high ledge that separated the kitchen area from the living room. Turning back to the mantel, and before changing her mind, she removed the trophies and carried them into the kitchen, where she cleaned and polished each one.

Next, after finding a stepladder in the garage, she arranged them on a high ledge. Some stood facing toward the entryway, welcoming the warrior home; some looked toward the living room. After a few adjustments and adding a small spotlight she unearthed from her Christmas decorations, she stepped off the ladder.

Hands on her hips, she critiqued her work. With a satisfied nod of her head, she returned to the open box and lifted out the mercury glass vase, placing it on the mantel before going outside to clip greenery to add to it. Again, she unpacked items from her personal box, deciding on a ceramic cat. Alisa had given it to Beth as a housewarming gift for the condo. She placed it beside the vase, giving it a little pat. She then returned to the box and located the blue bowl. It, too, was added to the mantel.

Satisfied with her vignette, she rescued Lizzie from the laundry room. Work could wait. It was time to relax with a cup of tea and her favorite girl.

Two hours later, she heard Mark's car pull into the garage. Jumping up, she took a quick look around the room, still satisfied with what she had done. "Whoa," she heard Mark say as soon as he entered the kitchen. "What are my trophies doing up there?"

Beth rounded the corner and saw him staring upward, a six-pack of beer held in one hand and a bouquet of flowers in the other. He sat both on the counter and grabbed a chair. In one fluid motion, he took down the largest trophy and turned to Beth. "What's this all about?" he asked.

Beth started to speak, but Mark was already striding into the living room, toward the mantel. He looked at her arrangement and turned to her, fixing her with a pointed look.

"I just thought I'd add some personal touches," she said, crossing her arms over her chest.

"Well, next time, check with me, okay?" He picked up the mercury vase and replaced it with his trophy.

As he turned to set the vase on a side table, it slipped from his hand and crashed to the floor. Beth gasped and knelt. Her hands shook as she picked up the base of the vase and examined it, and then looked closer on the floor and found the remaining shards. Tears fill her eyes as she held them up toward Mark.

"Oh crap," he said, kneeling beside her. "I'm sorry. It slipped." He kissed the top of her head. "I've got some super glue in my toolbox."

She barely heard him as she struggled to fit together the pieces. "No," she said. "It's ruined."

Mark stood. "Babe. I'm sorry. But you can find another one, right?" He took a piece from her hands and examined it. "Looks like something from Pier One. Bet they're made in China by the truckload."

Beth didn't answer.

"I said, you can get one just like it at the mall."

"No, I don't think so," Beth said at last, not meeting his eyes. "No big deal. It's just stuff."

CHAPTER THIRTEEN

*T*he group leader threw the rubber ball to Beth. "Your turn," he said.

Beth and Mark stood and faced one another. Since she held the ball, it was her job to speak first. She pressed her lips together and brushed her bangs off her brow, stalling. "I like that you're in great physical shape," she said at last, before handing the ball to Mark.

He looked at her with a slight grin. "You like how I'm in good shape?"

Beth reached for the ball. "This is special because...." She looked at Robert, the group leader, like an actor needing her next line. He nodded. She turned back to Mark. "This is special because I can count on your strength to keep me safe."

Robert stood. "Good," he said. "That's the idea. But make the thing you acknowledge about your partner as specific as possible and mirror what is said back to them. Then build on it. Make your partner see that you appreciate who they are." He took the ball from Beth and tossed it to a young couple across the room. "Now your turn."

Beth sat down, feeling a sense of failure, like missing an easy word at a spelling bee. She should have mentioned something more meaningful to a successful marriage than the size of Mark's pecs. God, she was an idiot sometimes. She looked at him. She could tell from his posture he was still irritated about being here – slumped low in his chair, arms crossed, legs stretched out in front, ball cap still on his head. "I have better things to do on a Saturday," he told her several times the week before. But Beth wanted to attend, so here they were. Their argument about her joining her friends for the Savannah road race had precipitated their attending the Saturday workshop – that plus a strong suggestion from the minister who would perform their wedding ceremony.

The applause from the group interrupted Beth's thoughts as the young couple threw the ball back to the leader and sat down. They high-fived one another as if they had just scored the winning shot in a volleyball match. Beth could picture them on the beach at a trendy resort for their honeymoon – her in a string bikini and him in his Speedo, both wearing mirrored dark glasses that wrapped around their eyes. She glanced again at Mark so they could share a private laugh, but he was staring at the ceiling, counting the tiles.

At lunch break, they drove without speaking to a nearby Subway. Beth waited until they were seated, and Mark had attacked his Italian club before asking, "What do you think? Are you getting something out of this?"

He looked at her, still chewing his sandwich, before shaking his head, like flicking water out of his ears from swimming. He picked up his Coke and took a gulp. "I think it's a waste of time." He sat the glass down and looked away, gathering his thoughts. "I mean, the group leader. Robert. Come on, Beth. Isn't he a little bit…?" He wiggled his hand back and forth. He took another bite of his sandwich and continued. "I told you when you first mentioned it we didn't need counseling. The minister didn't actually require it; he only suggested it."

He finished his sandwich and drained his drink before continuing.

"We're fine, and if we have problems, we'll work them out." He held up a hand again to stop her. "Enough, Beth. I agreed to do this so you could see what a bunch of crap these things are." He released a harsh laugh. "I'll bet you ten dollars that at the end of the day we'll be holding hands and singing *Kum Ba Yah.*" He laughed again.

Beth pushed away her Caesar Salad. Other than feeling like she had flubbed the exercise with the ball, she was enjoying the session. The exercises, hokey as they were, might be an excellent way to talk about issues before the wedding, like Mark's relentless campaign to move to Florida. She had assumed it was just talk when he brought it up in Asheville, but lately, she had come into his home office to find him looking at websites for sailing schools there. Her opinion of the state had been reinforced at an early age. "Tacky," she remembered her mother saying the time Beth had suggested a family vacation there. "Just one giant theme park ready to take your money." Beth snorted with laughter as she remembered how her father had weighed in on the conversation. "Land of the newlywed and the nearly dead," he had muttered. Having spent several spring breaks at Daytona Beach, Beth had to agree. Tacky just about summed it up. She was considering whether to share this memory when Mark stood.

"Tell you what," he said. "Let's ditch the afternoon session and catch a movie. Then we can come home, and I'll listen to all the wedding plans. Promise. Even the boring stuff like what appetizers you're passing around while we have pictures made and whether your bridesmaids are wearing fascinators, or whatever they're called." He reached for her hand. "Please, Beth?" He dropped to one knee, still holding her hand. "I can't take any more of that guy. And after the movie, I'll sing *Kum Ba Yah* just for you."

Beth laughed as she always did at his antics, and as they walked to the car, the elephant in the room was relegated to the back seat, like a dog with muddy paws.

CHAPTER FOURTEEN

*B*eth peered through her champagne glass and giggled. The room looked distorted, yet brighter and
more colorful with sparkling pods of light dancing
around. *No, wait,* she realized with a hiccup. *That must be the champagne bubbles.* She sat the glass back down and waved to a server to refill it.

The day was going perfectly. When she planned the wedding just a month ago, slipping away on her lunch hour to
check out a venue or meet with a florist, she had had moments
of doubt. But in the end, it all came together. She stared
across the room and automatically twisted her ring, wondering what her mother would have thought about the event.
Something on the order of "Beware of any enterprise that requires new clothing." She pictured the price tag of her dress.
"Sorry, Mother," she muttered.

As she slid her feet out of three-inch heels and wiggled her
toes, she moaned with satisfaction. Mark turned and put an
arm across her shoulder. "Are you okay, babe? Can I get you
anything? Like excited?" He grinned.

"I'm great," she answered, her smile widening.

"Only great?"

"Okay, I'm excellent, marvelous, awesome."

He held a hand above her glass. "You hate the word *awesome*. It's time to cut you off."

"No way!" she exclaimed, waving once more for a waiter.
"I'm fine!"

She looked across the room again and out to the patio. Her
eyes stopped on a young woman in a black bandage dress
drawing on a cigarette, an empty champagne glass dangling
from her other hand. Heather. Her smile dissolved. She
nudged Mark.

"Maybe you should go speak with her. Bring her back in to meet people. She looks lonely and, well, sad. I thought she was bringing a date."

Mark looked to where she indicated, and a scowl replaced his smile.

Beth accepted congratulations from a coworker before turning back to Mark. "Go on," she said. "Go talk with her and have her join us." She pointed to the place card for the empty seat beside him. "I had her seated at our table. She must not have looked at the seating arrangement."

As she watched him weave his way through the crowd, she bent forward to massage one foot and thought about the day. Awesome might not be the word, but it was close. From Mark dipping her into a long kiss right in front of the minister, to the limo that would take them away after the reception and to the airport and the mystery honeymoon, everything was, well, that word again, awesome.

There had been some concessions due to the short time she had for planning the event – the Vera Wang dress she had seen in *Brides* magazine wouldn't arrive in time, so she had settled for a cream lace and chiffon A-line from a Bridal Warehouse sample sale that didn't need much altering. The lace bodice and deep V-back accented by a small satin bow turned out to be the perfect dress for her frame. She looked down at the front of the gown where a row of clustered seed pearls created the illusion of flowers. Plus, she saved a ton of money. And the groom's cake shaped like a sailboat? Who would have thought a baker at Publix Grocery was that talented? And, he used her grandmother's recipe for Lane cake as the centerpiece, decorated with edible violets.

She put aside her thoughts when Lori took Mark's vacant chair. "I wondered how long you would last in those," she said, nodding to the discarded high heels.

"Thanks for leaving the ballet flats under the table. I'm thinking I can hold up the dress with one hand while we dance. Mark's more the swaying back and forth type dancer anyway."

Lori laughed. "It's about time for the first dance. I'm ready to hit the floor." She nodded toward the musicians. "The lead singer sounds just like Sade. And having them play a classical number as you walked down the aisle...."

"'Canon in D Major,'" Beth said.

"Right. Well, it was beautiful. The whole service. Even Anna had tears in her eye."

"I don't believe that."

"She did! And who wouldn't? Your vows. The flowers. This place." She gestured around. "Honestly, Beth. If you ever leave your job, you could become a wedding planner."

"No way," she answered. "Too much drama." She looked across the room and saw Mark with Heather. He was in her face, lecturing most likely. "In fact, I might need to intervene in some drama right now."

Lori looked where Beth was focused. "Oh, dear. That doesn't look good."

Beth stood, drawing her shoulders back. "Let me take care of this, and then I want a Core Four photograph. Can you get that organized?"

Lori kissed her on the cheek. "Absolutely. You go manage your new family."

Beth's face showed her surprise. "You're right. I have a family. Not just a husband." She grabbed Lori's hand. "Do you think I'll make a good stepmom?"

"Of course you will. You're a kind, loving person. We all know that. It's just going to take time for Heather to get to know you. Right now she can't get past seeing you as the woman who is taking away her dad."

Lori let go of Beth's hand when she sensed Mark standing behind her. She stood and turned to him. "Take care of our girl," Lori said, and then to soften the tone of her voice, pointed two fingers toward her eyes and then toward him. "I'll be watching."

Beth laughed nervously when she saw Mark's eyes narrow. She turned to Lori. "Make sure you're watching when I toss my bouquet. I'm throwing it straight at you."

Lori rolled her eyes. "Sure. Why not? Nothing else is working for me. But," she nodded toward her date. "Today might be different. Maybe you can sprinkle some fairy dust on me."

"Or a spray of pheromone enhanced perfume," Beth joked. "Like the ones we wore in high school."

"What was all that about?" Mark asked as Lori weaved her way back through the crowd.

"What?"

"That whole," he gestured with his fingers, "I'll be watching bit."

"Oh, sweetie, relax. She was just kidding with you."

"Maybe but still...."

"Drop it, Mark." She pulled on his hand toward the dance floor. "Let's make this wedding official."

"You mean have sex right here?"

"No! I mean the first dance. Everybody is waiting for us so they can get out on the floor." She kicked her heels under the table and picked up the train of her dress. "I've got a special song selected just for us."

She caught the eye of the guitarist and the ensemble switched to the opening bars to "Here and Now" as the lead singer announced, "Please join me in congratulating once again Mr. and Mrs. Mark Berger."

Mark leaned into Beth. "Awesome song," he whispered.

She put an arm around his neck. "It was either that or 'I've Got You, Babe.' But to my way of thinking, you can't go wrong with Luther Vandross."

"Indeed," Mark said, drawing her closer.

"I'm happy," Beth whispered. "Utterly and completely happy. How about we skip the cake cutting and get on out of here?"

"And miss that classic photo where I shove a piece of cake into your face?"

Beth laughed. "Don't you dare!"

"Relax. I've got Heather sorted out. I introduced her to a wrestler I coached who now goes to Georgia Tech. Time to enjoy the party."

Beth dropped the trail of her dress so she could put both arms around his neck. "You're right. Let's stay here until the last guest leaves. We have the rest of our lives to be together and only one day with sailboat cake."

CHAPTER FIFTEEN

*W*hen the wheels cleared the runway, Beth turned to Mark. "Okay, husband. You've kept me in suspense long enough. Where are we honeymooning?"

He grinned, took a folded brochure out of his jacket pocket, and handed it to her. She grabbed it.

Twenty dives in the Bahama Outer Islands for an all-inclusive price – food, drinks, air-conditioned cabins, wall dives, wrecks, even sharks. Camaraderie you'll never forget, and memories you'll wish to relive over and over again!

Her mouth opened wide. "We're on a boat for our honeymoon? Not a cruise ship but a dive boat? With sharks?"

A passenger across the aisle turned his head.

Beth lowered her voice. "You know I'm an amateur diver. I mean, when I got my training, I was in a heated pool, and my checkout dive was in a river with manatees. This," she waved the brochure at him, "is the ocean! I have no interest in taking a big leap off a boat into shark-infested water." Crossing her arms, she shifted in her seat so she could face him.

If he noticed her agitated manner, he chose to ignore it. "Sharks aren't interested in divers," he answered. "That's a joke. There's a better chance of being attacked at the water's edge than fifty feet under."

"If you're trying to reassure me, it isn't working."

Mark stretched an arm across her shoulders and drew her toward him. "It will be a fun cruise. Look at the pictures in the brochure. Read the comments. This is a trip of a lifetime, baby. Don't worry about the diving. I'll watch out for you. It's called the buddy system, remember?"

He moved to kiss her, but Beth turned away, drawing the Delta Airlines thin red blanket around her. Mark regarded her for a moment before returning to his sailing magazine. When the seatbelt light went off, a flight attendant pushed the drink cart down the aisle. When she reached their seats, Beth ordered a double vodka. All the euphoria of the wedding had drained from her. With a slight shake to her hand, she poured the alcohol over ice cubes and stared out the window at the land below, as the plane banked through the clouds and set its course south.

***

The horizon glowed red with streaks of purple clouds as the Pirate's Lady crossed from Miami to Nassau. When they had arrived at the docks from the airport a few hours earlier, Beth had thrust the brochure at Mark and pointed to the sleek sailing vessel on its cover. The Pirate's Lady was nothing like the advertisement. It looked more like a large tugboat with a mast stuck on it for appearances only.

With trepidation, she had followed Mark aboard in search of their assigned berth and had gasped at what they found. Instead of a private room, they would sleep not only in a bunkbed, but a bunkbed with another couple housed four feet above them in a similar cramped space, separated only by a thin curtain. In the passageway was a single head that would serve eight people.

"What?" she had hissed. "We're sleeping with another couple? On our honeymoon?"

He had pulled her to the side. "Listen," he began. "I knew it would be close quarters, but trust me. I didn't expect this." He drew her closer. "Try to make the best of it, okay? We'll have fun. Promise."

Now as Beth gazed at the lights of Miami fading on the horizon, the boat moved further from land and further from her comfort zone. Scattered across the stern were passengers who were feeling the effect of too much rum punch. She turned back around. Her stomach lurched, not from rum but from foreboding. She wished she hadn't thrown away her Xanax several months back. If there was ever a time when a panic attack might occur, it was on this trip.

As she felt the ocean chop increase, she reminded herself to keep her eyes fixed on the darkening horizon and her feet planted. That's what Mark had told her to do to avoid sea-sickness. Beneath the sound of the engine, she could hear him talking knot speeds and weather with the first mate. A harsh laugh escaped her. What was she thinking a month ago when she had blithely said to him, "Whatever you plan will be wonderful"? What sort of a woman turns over honeymoon details to a jock, regardless of how much she loves him?

***

Sometime late that night, the Pirate Lady dropped anchor at their first dive site, and by nine the next morning, divers were suited up for their first plunge.

Beth stood on the stern watching the water rise and fall with the pitching of the sea – her stomach moving in sync with the water, the weight of her gear forcing her to bend forward to maintain balance. She was next in line to jump. With fearful eyes, she looked from Mark to the dive master and then back to Mark, hearing the rapid sound of her breathing and feeling the tightness of her dive vest. At last, she jumped and hit the water. With a rush of relief, she bobbed to the surface. She was in. Turning toward the boat, she executed the okay tap to the top of her head. Mark jumped and surfaced to her side. She lunged for him. He grinned and gave her a thumbs up.

For a moment, she treaded water and looked down on the coral pinnacles of the Towers. Their massive pillars reached skyward like bony fingers stretching to grab her. Meanwhile, Mark adjusted his air and signaled for her to do the same.

As they descended, she sensed she was dropping quicker than she should. Her breath caught and her heart quickened. She glanced up for reassurance that the boat was still above. Mark grabbed her arm and pointed to the anchor line to indicate they should get their bearings from it. She exhaled and nodded. With his encouragement, she made a slow turn to look around, forcing herself to slow her breath.

The deeper they dropped, the more Beth willed herself to enjoy the experience. She wrapped her arms tighter around her torso to keep warm and allowed herself to enjoy the sensation of falling.

The visibility was perfect, she noticed, as her panic lessened. Diving was like being dropped into a giant aquarium decorated by a Hollywood set designer. The soft colors, the shapes distorted by her mask, the beauty of it all. This is easy, she concluded and congratulated herself. She reached for Mark and made the shape of a heart with her hands. He grinned and gave her another thumbs up.

Soon she was no longer looking at the boat above but at the ocean floor below. When they touched down some thirty feet below, Mark demonstrated how to adjust her buoyancy, and she swam after him toward the coral. When she saw divers swimming through openings in the coral wall, she grabbed for Mark's arm. No, she signaled. He nodded in agreement. As they finned through the water, sea fans swayed with the current. Beth recognized some of the fish – the blue angelfish with its aqua throat, the four-eye butterflyfish with its distinctive black spot, and the playful blue tangs that darted about. She thought she saw a sea horse and reached for Mark to show him, but then realized it was only plankton.

A rare feeling of peace came over her. From childhood on, she craved quietness. Her home had been a barrage of noise – her brother's trumpet, her sister's screaming, her mother's warnings. Elizabeth, make your bed. Elizabeth, that math grade needs to improve, or you drop cheerleading. Elizabeth, you're getting a whipping for that. Elizabeth Ann, take care of your sister. She knew she was in deep trouble when her mother added her middle name. Now, thirty feet below the water's surface, she heard only the quiet, steady sound of her breath and the slow beat of her heart.

Maybe diving was for her. Maybe Mark hadn't screwed up.

***

Lost Blue Hole, Sugar Wreck, Jeep Reef – as the week progressed, one dive blended in with the next. Plus, they were challenging. Each day Beth struggled more. Her gear weighed fifty pounds – half her weight. But the hardest part, she learned early in the week, was getting back on the boat. She dreaded it after each dive because it called for timing, strength, and nerve – qualities she had in short supply.

"I can't do it again, Mark," she said the fifth morning of the trip. "I'm too exhausted." Yet fifteen minutes later, there she was suiting up. Down on one knee and holding her hand, Mark had applied the Old Berger Charm, as she was coming to call it. It worked. Down they went, Beth right beside Mark as they examined a wreck at eighty feet.

But as they ascended, Beth realized she was in trouble. Either she was coming down with something, she reasoned, or the underwater pressure was getting to her. She tried to get Mark's attention, but his eyes were focused upward. Kicking hard to stay close to him, she watched him grab the tow line, which floated some twenty feet behind the stern. He deftly removed his fins while holding the line under his arm and fastened each fin around a wrist. Pulling himself hand over hand, he approached the steps and expertly placed his feet on the bottom rung before transferring his hands to the ladder. The last she saw of him was the bottom of his dive shoes.

As he disappeared, other divers reached the line before her and pulled themselves to the boat, leaving Beth at the end of the line. She struggled to remove her fins and keep the line tucked under an arm. But just as it was her turn to place her feet and hands on the ladder, a crashing wave hit the boat. The ladder pitched upward, striking her in the face and throwing her backward. One quick view of the sky, and then she began to sink – her face throbbing, her mind reeling. Instinctively, she kicked her feet, struggling to stay shallow, but without her fins, she made no progress. Panic mounted as she saw the bottom of the boat and the last rung of the ladder some fifteen feet above her – the line still floating tauntingly on the surface of the water. Her breath shortened, and panic constricted her chest. She kicked more violently but kept descending. Suddenly she remembered a safety instruction. With trembling fingers, she dropped the weight belt around her waist. Her body stopped dropping, and with a surge of adrenaline, she scissor-kicked again and again, gaining on the boat. With a final kicked thrust, she lunged for the line and grasped its knotted end, riding the pitching sea. With pure survival determination, she pulled herself hand over hand to the boat. As she got closer, she could see a pair of legs on the ladder and a hand reaching for her. She waited for another swell to pass and then let go of the line and lunged for the ladder.

A crew member pulled her up by her dive vest and guided her to a seat. "Are you okay?" he asked, taking off her tank. "Where's your dive partner? He should have been behind you. Let me see your face."

He removed her mask and examined her mouth. "No teeth broken," he said at last. "Your regulator saved you from smashing your face." He handed her a bottle of water. "But your lips are swelling fast. I'll get you some ice."

Mark walked over and sat beside her. "What happened? Someone said you got hit."

Beth looked at him and then down at the bottle. With only a moment's hesitation, she threw it at him. He ducked. "Where were you?" she screamed.

He looked away and then back. "Calm down, Beth. There's no need to yell. You're fine. You just had a little mishap. Don't make such a big deal of it."

She stood up and walked away, leaving her dive gear on the deck for him to wash and stow. Then she grabbed another water bottle and went down to her bunk. The cold felt good on her bruised face but didn't cool her rage. When Mark joined her in their cramped quarters later that night, she kept her back turned to him, elbowing away the hand that attempted to massage her neck. "I'm sorry," he kept saying, but Beth didn't reply.

By the next morning, a diver had posted new nametags for everyone. When Beth saw hers, she gasped. Ladder Lips, it proclaimed.

Mark came up behind her. "You look fine," he said. "Very kissable. The swelling will be gone in no time." Beth ignored him. Her eyes scanned the board until she saw Mark's name. Six Pack. Mark must have seen it at the same moment. "All right," he said with a chuckle, before giving her shoulders a squeeze and turning away.

***

By that afternoon, Beth's bags were packed. For the next two days, she intended to sleep, eat, and fly in the same clothes. Her diving days were over. What had possessed her, she kept asking herself, to agree to scuba lessons in the first place? She hated cold water. Hated being weighed down by gear. Hated her appearance. All the photos of women diving in bikinis were misleading. For the past week, she had basically lived in a full wetsuit and black cap, looking like a penguin and feeling about as agile as one.

As divers readied for the afternoon dive, she sat alone with a copy of *Jane Eyre* open on her lap. She had packed her book club's monthly selection only as a backup. What she had intended to read was the *Shopaholic* series, while lying on the beach with Mark and a Mai Tai. But now as she read about poor Jane, she shook her head in exasperation. She wanted to tell her to turn down the marriage proposal. Lost in her thoughts, Beth didn't notice when Mark sat down beside her. He handed her a hot chocolate and began rubbing her shoulders.

"Are you still mad at me?" he asked, now stroking her hair.

She shrugged off his hand, but he continued. "Please dive with me, Beth," he said. "Please? I'm sorry you got hurt. Can I kiss your face and make it better?"

She laid aside her book and turned to him. "Mark, it isn't just my bruised face that's bothering me. It's you. I mean, I'm your dive partner. I'm your wife! You should watch out for me and you didn't."

"But I will," he answered. "Come on this last dive, and I'll show you. You can't come all this way and not shark dive. Think of the story you can tell your girlfriends. Please, Beth," he whispered in her ear. "I won't ask anything else of you. Do this just for me."

She felt her heart shift, and Mark must have sensed the change. He stood and began readying her tank.

As she listened to the pre-dive briefing, cautioning divers not to touch the coral and to make as few movements as possible underwater, her eyes traveled to the gear at her feet. Wet suit, buoyancy vest, weights, regulator, computer, tank, fins, gloves, cap, mask. It was a whole lot of effort just to see big fish, she thought. She looked again at Mark, and he now gave her a look that said, are you with me or not with me?

She knew that look. Seen it all her life. Elizabeth, do what I'm telling you to do, right now, it said, or else. She bent over and pulled on her wet suit.

As they sank, Beth watched the sharks, swirling under the boat. Swallowing her fear like a dose of castor oil, she followed Mark down, moving her fins only to propel herself forward. Around her were the sharks swimming in all directions. "It's their eyes that are frightful," the dive master had said during the pre-dive briefing. "Try not to look at them." Now, as she swam among them, she felt those glossy, expressionless black orbs on her, their intent only to attack their prey. With an extra kick to her fins, she focused on Mark, following him deeper into the ocean.

Touching bottom, she joined the other divers, who were forming a semi-circle in front of a coral wall, and settled on her knees beside Mark, their hips touching.

As the dive master lowered a baited spear from the boat, sharks surged from all directions. Dozens of them, all sizes, attacking the bait as it descended. Knocking into one another. Chasing after bits of fish. Swishing their bodies through the clear water, as small pilot fish followed their every move, snapping up leftovers. By the time the spear reached the ocean floor thirty feet below, it was stripped clean. It was over in a matter of moments, which made the spectacle more frightening, as the sharks continued to search for food around the coral.

Mark turned toward her. Even with a regulator clinched in his mouth, she could see his broad grin – his teeth as gleaming as the swarming sharks. He stood and applauded, and then signaled for her to follow him as he began his ascent.

Beth placed her gloved hands over her mask. No, she wanted to scream. No, no, no. In the time it had taken for the sharks to eat their lunch, the ocean had changed from a placid aquarium to a dark place of danger, where attacks came from all sides. She knew she couldn't stay kneeling on the ocean floor, but she couldn't swim back to the boat. It wasn't possible to move.

Mark tugged at her arm and again nodded his head upward, impatience rising like bubbles. She could see other divers swimming among the sharks on their way back to the boat. She and Mark were the last ones on the ocean floor. At last, she took the hand he offered and allowed him to pull her up. Her body was shaking as she swam after him, her arms hugging her middle, her eyes avoiding the dark shapes that still swam around her, feeling more like a pilot fish than a partner.

"That was fantastic," Mark said as soon as they were back on board. "Wouldn't have missed it for anything. I want to find out what variety they were. I think most were reef sharks, but there could have been some tigers and blacktips."

He left her and joined the crew in the cockpit. Their laughter echoed against the hull. She sat on her locker, still shaking. Pulling her wetsuit down to her waist, she wrapped herself in a towel, wishing it were a warm pair of arms. She bent over and rested her forearms on her knees. The ache in her chest now extended into her back.

"Are you okay?" another diver asked. She nodded yes without looking up, but the shaking didn't stop. She clasped her hands and twisted her wedding ring. Her fingers must have shrunken because the ring slipped easily over her knuckle – much looser than when Mark put it on her finger.

She looked out across the steel gray water and thought of Dr. Em's advice. "Take it slow," he had cautioned her. The total impact of his words hit her. She had not just ignored his caution; she had taken a giant scuba stride into Mark's life.

How could she have been so eager and naive? And now look at her – shaking, scared, and alone.

***

Airport passengers mingled around them. Mark reached for Beth's hand. "Are you still angry?"

"I told you already," she answered, her tone sharp. "I wasn't angry. I was hurt. Scared. Embarrassed even."

"Embarrassed? Why?"

She turned toward him and pointed to her mouth. "Not the look I wanted for my honeymoon. And the sharks." She shuddered.

He chuckled. "Come on, Beth. Hollywood stars pay big bucks to have their lips look as pouty as yours, and the dive master would have shot a spear gun at any shark that threatened someone."

She cut her eyes at him. "You don't get it, do you? I could have been hurt, and you weren't there for me."

He put an arm around her shoulders and hugged her to his chest. "But you weren't hurt. You're fine." His voice took on a pleading tone as he looked around the airport terminal. "Come on, Ladder Lips. Don't stay mad. How about I buy you a drink? I bet there's a Delta Crown Room here. You're a member, right? Let me buy you a glass of champagne and we'll toast." He pulled her to her feet and picked up his carry-on.

"They're free," Beth said, as she trailed after him.

"What?"

"In the Delta Crown Room. The drinks are free. It's included with the membership."

"Well, that's even better," he said. "Come on. This honeymoon's not over yet." He stopped in his tracks and turned to her. "Here's an idea. I'll book us into the Ritz Carlton for the night. We'll go straight from the airport after we land. We can order room service. You can get a massage. I might get one myself. You can wear that fancy underwear your girlfriends gave you." He pulled her closer. "I love you, Beth. I'm sorry. Let me make it up to you." He raised her face toward his. "Does that sound good? Give me just one smile, and I'll book it right now."

A smile worked its way to Beth's eyes. "Okay," she said. "But it better be a grand room and a good bottle of champagne." She paused. "And next time I say no, please remember to honor my request."

He dropped to one knee in front of her. "Your wish is my command."

"Stop it," she giggled, as passengers bumped around them.

"As you wish," he added.

"And stop quoting from *The Princess Bride*," she said, as she pulled him to his feet and into a hug, looking every bit the newlywed.

CHAPTER SIXTEEN

*B*eth dropped frozen strawberries into the blender and added a cup of rum. As soon as she heard a car arrive, she would add lime juice, sugar water, and ginger. Four glasses garnished with whole fresh strawberries and rimmed with ginger sugar stood ready on the counter, plus a platter of mini croissants stuffed with chicken salad and grapes. Cheese straws and crab-stuffed cherry tomatoes were ready in the refrigerator, along with homemade lemon squares.

Lizzie jumped on the counter, and Beth gave her an affectionate hug before placing her on the floor. When she and Mark had returned from their honeymoon and picked her up from the vet, Lizzie cried out and clung to her during the ride home, refusing to sit anywhere but in Beth's lap. Two weeks later, she rarely left her side, fearful of being deserted once again.

Satisfied with the food preparations, Beth carried a vase of dwarf blue irises to a table on the deck, the cat at her heels. She wanted to begin the celebration outdoors, like the Core Four always did at Beth's condo, complete with daiquiris. It was the first time the friends would see her new home. She had spent the past two weekends painting the walls soft yellow and adding colorful pillows to every chair, ignoring Mark when he cried, "No more pillows!" Aqua bathrooms now boasted fluffy white towels, scented soaps, and creamy lotions, many of them wedding gifts from co-workers. That reminded Beth. She still had some thank you cards to write. With a grab of her notepad, she added that to her To Do list.

Leaning against the deck railing, she nodded in satisfaction at the back yard. At least Mark had mowed the lawn before leaving for his sailing weekend in Florida. He had complained about the task, but she had coaxed him into it with promises of backrubs after completion.

"If you want to make this place look like one of your design magazines," he had told her, "you're on your own." But on reflection, other than having to cajole him to help with everyday household chores, things were going relatively well, she decided. The night at the Ritz returned the romance to the honeymoon, and the further away she was from the dive boat experience, the better she could laugh about it. They even jokingly called one another Ladder Lips and Six Pack now and then, testing the water of one another's mood.

She returned to the kitchen and popped a strawberry in her mouth. Life was excellent, she concluded. Smooth sailing for the newlyweds. She winced at the pun and ate another strawberry. When the doorbell rang, she turned on the blender and ran to open the door.

"Welcome to the burbs," she joked, as Janet, Lori, and Anna arrived. "It's not the end of the world, but you can see it from here."

Anna gave her a close hug. "You're right." She drew back and looked at Beth. "But how long is your commute?"

Beth knew the point Anna wanted to make and fought the urge to call her out for being so blunt. Chances were, they had discussed the topic on the drive. "If I don't hit the road before six every morning, I'm doomed to sit in my car for over an hour," she answered, deciding to let the remark pass.

"And Mark?"

"Oh, he's just around the corner. He can walk out the door at eight and still make his first class."

She popped another strawberry into her mouth and smiled. As happy as her friends seemed for her, she already knew their concern: how Beth was giving away a huge part of her life to gain a small slice of his. *But it's not that way*, she wanted to say. *I'm not lonely and alone. Or fighting off some guy in a bar. Or browsing through online profiles as if finding a man was as easy as buying shoes from Zappos. I'm able to build a lasting future with someone I love.*

"Listen," she said, as she pulled the friends into a group hug. "I know you only want what's best for me. And yes, Mark can be a bull in a china shop, no doubt. But I love him, okay? For better or worse, I'm in this marriage." She guided them toward the deck. "Let's celebrate."

"I agree," said Lori. "Let's drink up, look at wedding pictures, and hear all the juicy details of the honeymoon. A Caribbean cruise, right? I'm so envious."

Beth made a face. "Well, it was on a boat, and the sunsets were beautiful, and by week's end, we had a wonderful time. But let's just say I'm more of a snorkeler than a scuba diver. In fact," she picked up a crab-stuffed tomato, "I prefer my fish on a plate."

"I'm with you on that," added Janet. "If I never hear the words 'Joy bath' again, my life will be complete."

"Was it that bad living on a boat for a week?" Lori asked. "I thought the four of you had a great time."

Beth and Janet exchanged a look and then burst out laughing. "Lori, you're even more naive than this one," Janet said, pointing to Beth. "Sailing is nothing more than camping on water."

"Go on," Anna urged her. "Tell us your version of the sailing lifestyle. Beth tends to omit the juicy details."

Janet looked at Beth, who shrugged her shoulders and turned back to the trays of food.

"Okay," Janet began. "First off, it's crowded, primitive, and regimented. I mean, Mark had ways he wanted something done, so we did it."

"Like what?" Anna asked.

Again, Janet glanced at Beth, asking for permission. "Like baths. Mark called them 'Joy baths.' You know, like the dish soap? He instructed us to lather ourselves up with Joy and jump in the water to scrub. Then we were permitted about five seconds of fresh water at the rear of the boat to rinse ourselves. Am I right, Beth? Or how he never wanted to miss hooking the mooring ball he wanted. I mean, the cove might have four available balls, but if this one," she pointed to Beth, "missed the one he wanted and he had to make a second pass, well, she caught hell for it."

"Not true!" interrupted Beth, but Janet was on a roll. Lori put a comforting arm around Beth.

"She even dove in for one she missed. There she was, bobbing in the water, holding a mooring line like a golden retriever, just to make Mark happy."

Lori snorted, trying to stifle her laughter even as she hugged Beth. "Oh, my God. That's funny."

"Enough," said Beth, smiling despite herself. She held a daiquiri out toward Janet. "Drink this and no more talk about my husband." She paused a moment. "Unless I want to talk about him," she added.

"Here's a thought," Anna remarked. "The Core Four should book a river cruise. There's a great one that goes down the Danube River. It would be a four-star experience."

Lori and Janet raised their glasses high to Anna's. "I'm in," Janet said. They looked at Beth.

"Sound's great, but...."

Anna lowered her glass. "We get it. You need to check with Mark." She started to add more but caught herself.

"Let me show you what I plan for the flower beds out back," Beth said, changing the subject. It was a trick she had learned as a child. Never let someone see what life was like behind the curtain. But Anna was on to her tricks.

"You're not getting off that easy, missy. We want to hear more about your honeymoon."

Instead, Beth gave them a sanitized version of the week, using her storytelling abilities to make the wreck dive sound like a Disneyland ride and the shark feeding no more frightening than visiting a trout farm.

"Mark said they were mainly nurse sharks that have no interest in humans," she finished, avoiding any mention of how angry she became at him for failing to watch her back underwater. Like her mother always cautioned, *don't tell the world your business.*

When she went back to the kitchen to refill drinks, Janet followed her. "Fess up, Beth," she said. "Are you happy? Really and truly happy?"

Beth sat the pitcher down. "Why are you questioning me? I'm happy. Okay?" She exhaled. "Sure. There are kinks to work on and," she gestured around the room, "it's not the perfect place to live, I agree, but I love him, and I believe we can make this marriage work. He's a good guy. Self-centered, maybe, but a good guy." She looked closer at Janet. "Maybe I should ask you. Are you happy?"

Janet looked over her shoulder before answering. "Jack and I filed for divorce yesterday."

"No," Beth said and pulled her into a hug. "I'm so sorry."

Janet nodded and wiped away a stray tear. "It's better this way. We've gone through loads of counseling to where neither of us wants to say another word to the other. And the kids." She shook her head. "The kids will be much better off without living in constant tension."

"Do the others know?"

"I've told Anna but not Lori. She's like you – a Pollyanna about life."

Beth opened her mouth to protest.

"Sorry," Janet said. "But you are. You're like the wife in *Mad About You*. Remember that TV show? She was always so," she raised her hands into the air, searching for the right word. "I don't know, peppy. Always putting lip gloss on every situation to make it look better."

Beth laughed weakly and threw a strawberry at her.

Janet caught it and popped it into her mouth. "Anyway, that's why Anna and I were questioning you about the drive. We want you to be happy." She squeezed Beth's shoulders. "You're happy, and we're happy for you."

Janet turned to rejoin the others, but Beth remained still. In the distance was the drone of a lawnmower – a constant background noise to suburban life. She picked up her drink and then sat it back down. Celebrating her marriage seemed the last thing she should be doing. *Poor Janet*, she thought. No wonder she was so stressed if Jack never helped with the kids. *I should babysit*, she thought. But then she remembered. She no longer lived around the corner from her friend. She was stuck in the burbs. A lonely feeling coursed through her. She missed the Core Fore more than she was admitting.

She picked up the daiquiri pitcher and turned toward the deck when she heard the grind of the garage door opener. She looked at her watch. Mark wasn't due back until late that night. His flight from Ft. Myers didn't touch down until seven.

Before she could the pitcher down, he grabbed her from behind in a hug that lifted her off her feet, causing her to spill the drink on her blouse. "Baby, I have missed you so much," he murmured into her hair. "This trip was awesome, and do I have great news." He sat her back down, took the pitcher from her, and drank. She reached up and wiped a strawberry mustache from his upper lip before kissing him.

"Can your news wait?" She turned and cleaned her top and then gestured to the deck. "The girls are here."

Mark rubbed his hands together and spoke in a crackling voice. "When shall we three meet again? In thunder, lightning, or in rain?"

Beth shoved him. "Stop it," she said. "They're my friends. I want them to like you. And whatever this news is, can't it wait?" She reached for the pitcher and wiped the rim, attempting to put a smile back on her face. "We're only on our second batch."

She turned and walked to the porch. Lori and Anna were seated beside Janet, who had a wadded tissue in her hand. They looked up, and Janet attempted to smile, but then Mark's dark shape came into her view. Janet's eyes clouded, and she sat back in her chair.

"Well, well, ladies," Mark boomed. "Mind if I crash your party?" He popped a chicken salad sandwich into his mouth and wiped it with the back of his hand. Beth laughed, her nerves evident.

Fifteen minutes later, she waved her goodbyes, watching Anna's car until it disappeared. She shuffled from one foot to the other, conflicted over where to turn her attention. Janet needed her friends around her. That was clear. Anna gave solid advice, Lori was good with laughter, but Beth was the one who could listen. And Janet needed to talk. But Mark had news to share.

She walked back into the house and found him in his recliner watching soccer. When Beth entered the room, he muted the sound. She pasted a smile on her face and took a chair opposite him, propping her feet on the coffee table. She never would have done this in her condo, but Mark had so abused the table's surface that Beth didn't even reach for a coaster when she placed her drink beside her feet.

"What's the news?" she asked, her mind still on her friends.

Mark sat up and grinned so wide his back molars showed. "I got a job." He shook his head, still surprised by the news. "A guy in the sailing class works for the local school system in Porto Verde, just north of Ft. Myers. He told me they're looking for a wrestling coach at the high school and wanted to know if I was interested. That was yesterday, so this morning," he glanced at his watch, "only ten hours ago, to be exact, he arranged for the principal to drive down and meet me. Next thing I know, I'm offered the job. That's why I flew back early."

"But you have a job."

"And now I have a new job."

"So, you took it?"

"Well, I told them I needed to check with you, but yeah, I took it. I said yes. And the best part is that the sailing school needs instructors who will work weekends. It's the perfect setup."

Beth stared at him, her mouth slightly open. She looked away and then back before standing and pacing the room. Her brain was on high alert, sending warning signals like a tornado siren. With hands on her hips, she turned to him.

"We can't up and move to wherever the heck Porto Verde is. We live here. We have jobs here, and friends, and activities. And family, like your daughter, Heather. And," she pointed to the front door, "I have a friend who is getting a divorce. She needs me. There's no way we can move to Florida now." She shook her head. "No, Mark. This won't work. I'm sorry. I am. But you'll have to call them back and explain. Who knows?

Maybe in a few years, we can look into it. But not now. Our life is here."

Mark stood and pulled her onto the sofa. He took both her hands into his. "Think about it, Beth," he said, looking into her eyes. "Isn't there something you've wanted all your life? What would you do if you got the chance to have it? You'd go for it, wouldn't you? You'd grab onto it and wouldn't let go." He gripped her hands harder. "I've got that opportunity now to get what I've always wanted. And I want my wife by my side when I do it."

He released her hands, leaned back against the cushions, and cradled his head. "The ocean, baby. I told you that's what I want, and in a few short weeks, that's where we'll be."

Beth shook her head. "This isn't a good idea, Mark. This is too much change too soon."

His eyes narrowed. "This opportunity may never present itself again." He looked away, and his face hardened. "This is the break I've been waiting for." He looked at her. "Don't stand in my way. Please, Beth. One day your break will come. But for now, this is mine, and I want to take it. Say yes."

It was close to eleven that night when Beth walked outside and called Lori. "This is terrible," her friend said. "Janet's marriage on the rocks. You moving. No. You can't do this. You can't uproot yourself now. Don't let Mark push you into doing something you don't want to do."

"But I'm his wife."

"I know you are, sweetie. But think about it. Don't let some man force you to do something you don't want to do, even if he is your husband. That is something Janet might accept from Jack, just to keep their marriage together, but not you. Think about it. What's in it for you?"

Beth lay awake that night trying to formulate an answer to Lori's question, but none came to mind. She looked at Mark and reached a hand toward him but drew it back. He was deep asleep as he always was after sex. It had felt wonderful to have his arms wrapped around her again. Safe. Secure. Satisfied. That was what she had wanted all her life, and now she had it. But were safety, security, and good sex all she wanted? Did she not have dreams of her own? Was she willing to give up all she had built for herself in the past decade to start over?

And what about Mark? What did he want from life? Adventure, she had realized after the honeymoon. Admiration for his achievements. Another mountain to climb. Another tiger to slay. But picking up and moving on a moment's notice? That seemed like something else was eating at him. He had implied that his ex made him feel inferior, like she was always comparing him to her father, a three-star general. Did he simply want to show Beth that he was lord and master of the house?

She flipped onto her side, throwing off the covers. Great questions, but no answers.

***

Beth's boss tapped his pen on his desk and regarded her. "Let me ask you something. How many years have you worked here?"

"Just over eight," she answered. He nodded in agreement. "And you started as a marketing assistant and now you're our marketing director."

"Right."

He flipped a page in a file folder. "And you handle our show guides, our convention advertising, our news releases, articles for trade publications, plus you attend the shows we manage here and in Chicago." As he spoke, he ticked off each duty on a finger. He looked up. "And just about every Monday, you bring in scones." He laughed. "Now I'm not being sexist in saying that but," he patted his stomach, "I do like your cooking."

"Then, you'll consider my proposal?"

He shook his head. "I can't, Beth. As much as I'd like to keep you on staff and help you out, we don't operate that way. You know as well as anyone how hands-on show management is." He leaned forward on his desk. "Think about the last year. How many weekends did you spend coming into the office or going for a press check or working our booth at the convention hall?" Again, he looked down at the folder. "If you were moving to Chicago or even DC, I would consider it, but you're moving where? Porto Verde, Florida?" He looked up and closed the file folder. "No offense, but I don't even know where that is."

Beth stood. "Thanks for listening."

He stood and offered his hand. "Hell, Beth. It will be hard to replace you." He chuckled. "Why the hell did you go and get married? Here I thought you were married to your job."

Beth closed his office door. "Sorry," his secretary mouthed, as Beth walked past her desk to the elevator.

***

Grant already had a glass of wine ordered for her when she joined him and Alisa for lunch. "He didn't go for it," Grant said, as Beth collapsed into her seat.

She shook her head.

"I didn't expect him to, but it was worth asking." He looked at his wife then back to Beth. "Maybe if we sit down with you and Mark and talk things out, perhaps he will see that moving is not in your best interest. At least, not now it isn't."

"Thanks," she responded. "But don't bother. He's made up his mind." She sat, twirling her wine glass in thought. "Who knows?" she said with forced enthusiasm. "I may love it down there. It might be for the best. We can start a new life in a new place."

She looked from one face to the other, longing to read agreement on their faces.

Alisa reached for her hand. "You're right. You may be worrying for nothing. But I've said it before. Marriages take a long time to grow intertwined roots." She squeezed Beth's hands. "But if this move isn't what's good for you, then stand your ground. Lay down your terms."

Beth nodded as if confirming the wisdom of the advice, but the knot in her stomach told a different story. She was on a sinking ship.

CHAPTER SEVENTEEN

*B*eth eased her car down a side street off Peachtree Road. Having lived in this area until recently, she knew how to get Mark close to the starting line at Lenox Mall. This would be his tenth year running the Peachtree Road Race – a Fourth of July event that attracted thousands of amateur and elite runners to downtown Atlanta. For years, Beth had joined her friends along the route to cheer on the runners. Lori would bring Bloody Marys, and Beth would bake blueberry muffins. Anna provided chairs, and Janet brought flags.

But this year was different. She had Mark to think about. As she parked on the narrow street, she reflected on the past month. He had been in serious training mode, running close to forty miles each week, rain or shine. Most of his running was on the forest trails along the Chattahoochee River, but he practiced his sprint running in their neighborhood twice a week. The closer it got to race day, the more fanatic he became about getting his mileage in, as well as the condition of his shoes. He had a favorite brand and would write the date on the sole of each new pair so he knew to replace them once he hit the five-month mark. He had once shown her how the cost of shoes was part of his monthly budget, like cable or electricity. "Kind of like how I budget for my hair and nails," she had answered, putting on a mock serious face.

"It's important I beat my time from last year of forty-seven minutes," he had told her, and Beth had nodded in total agreement as if that were the most important objective in her life too. He had suggested she run with him, but now, as she walked up Lenox Road beside him, she was glad she had opted to be his pit crew. If she were running, he would feel obliged to pace himself with her, and there would go his best-time goal, plus her naturally sunny disposition, as Lori liked to call it.

As she picked up her pace to match his, she realized her sunny side was behind a storm cloud lately. She needed to get that in check, she realized. "No one likes a sour puss," she imagined her mother saying.

"You've got your phone on you, right?" Mark asked as he broke into a jog.

"Got it," she replied, quickening her pace.

"And you'll be watching for me at the three-mile mark?"

"Check."

"Because I may need a Gatorade if the humidity doesn't lift." He slowed to wipe his face with the bottom of his T-shirt. "Christ, it's hot already."

"They'll have water stations along the course, won't they?" Beth asked. "You can get something to drink from them, can't you? And energy bars?"

He ignored her question. "And you'll find me at the finish line."

She gave him a playful salute. "I'll be there."

"Try to park as close as possible to the finish line so we can beat the crowds getting out."

"I'll do my best."

They reached the check-in area, and Mark turned to her. "Well, wish me luck."

She gave him a quick hug. "Good luck," she said. "Break a leg," she added, but he was already striding away from her, his white shirt and blue shorts disappearing into the crowd.

She walked back to her car and cranked the engine so the air would run full blast. The bank sign across the street read eighty-five degrees, and race sponsors had already issued a red alert because of the humidity. By the time the last stragglers would finish the race around eleven, the forecast was for near ninety degrees. Beth had never understood why anyone would want to run in such conditions. Every year, the local media warned runners to pace themselves, to drink plenty of water, to monitor their pulse; and every year they would report how many were treated for heat stroke and other weather-related ailments. She had even given Mark a copy of an article from *Runner's World* about the dangers, but he scoffed at it and tossed it into the garbage.

Beth looked at her watch. It was just now seven. The elite runners would start at seven-thirty. Mark's time group would be a half hour behind them. She put the car in gear. She might find parking behind Peachtree Battle Shopping Center if she was lucky. It was near the three-mile mark, and she had made a big sign to hold. *Go, Mark, Go!* Maybe the girls would join her after all, rather than standing at their usual spot near the entrance to Piedmont Park.

They had pleaded with her to make her muffins and meet up with them. "We never see you anymore," Janet had lamented. But Beth begged off, explaining that Mark needed her along the route. "To hold his hand? To wipe sweat off his brow?" she had asked. Beth knew she was kidding and was allowing her dissatisfaction with her own husband to color her attitude toward Mark. But honestly, she did feel like his Sherpa of late. All the cross-training was taking its toll, as she stumbled along after him, carrying water and towels and fresh shirts. She even canceled walking the Rock & Roll Half Marathon in Savannah with the Core Four so she could travel with him to a half-marathon in Chattanooga. Maybe that's why Janet and Lori were lukewarm about planning their day around her.

When she saw a parking space close to a water hydrant, she braked and eased her car into the space. She glanced again at her watch. "Shit," she said aloud. It was already close to the starting time. If Mark ran eight-mile splits, she wouldn't have time to grab a coffee before elbowing her way through the masses of people already lining the streets. She got out of the car, pulling her shirt away from her neck and tightening her ponytail.

"Shit," she muttered again, as she turned a corner. She had forgotten her sign. She jogged back to the car and grabbed it out of the trunk. Stuffing another Gatorade into her bag, she paused to think how wonderful a Bloody Mary would taste right now, not to mention a good time with her friends. It felt like forever since she had seen them. Maybe she would join them at their usual spot. She tucked the sign under her arm and contemplated her choices: Stand conspicuously near the three-mile water station where Mark had instructed or continue south toward Piedmont Park. She jostled the sign back and forth in thought. *Eeny, meeny, miny, moe,* she said to herself, like a child trying to decide on an ice cream flavor. *Decide,* she ordered herself, as people bumped into her on the sidewalk.

She had her answer. She would think like Mark. He was always spouting how situations should be a win-win. If she joined her friends, that would make them happy and they could help her find Mark near the packed finish line. She grinned at her cleverness and jogged back to her car, hoping that Janet had remembered to bring celery and olives for the drinks.

Lori saw her first. "Thatagirl," she said, giving Beth a high five before handing her a drink.

"I'm proud of you," Janet said, as her kids reached for the muffins Beth held out to them.

"Let's make sure we don't miss Mark," Beth responded.

"Good going," Anna said.

She nodded and looked at her Bloody Mary, thinking about the implications of her actions and hoping she had made the right choice. She pictured Mark's trophy sitting on the mantel in place of her vase and decided she had.

CHAPTER EIGHTEEN

*B*eth pulled into her usual parking space at the Marietta Counseling Center, where Dr. Em worked. Nothing much had changed in the past months, she noticed, except wilted geraniums now grew in place of pansies in the flowerbeds. She jerked open the door and, with a loud exhale, collapsed on the sofa.

"What a dump," she muttered, quoting her favorite Bette Davis line. Only it wasn't Dr. Em's interior she was evaluating so much as her own state of mind. She didn't want to be here, didn't want to be prodded with questions. But what were her options? The day before, Mark told his buddies at the lake that they were Florida bound – an announcement that was met with great cheer. All the guys slapped him on the back and toasted his no-looking-back approach as the ultimate act of manhood. Even the wives and girlfriends were caught up in the celebration, pelting Beth with comments like, "What fun!" and "Woo Hoo!" or "Beach party, here we come!"

But as Beth stood with a half-full cup of warm beer in her hand, something she had learned in high school came to mind. When the conqueror Cortez arrived in Central America, he ordered his ships burned so that none of his men could return to Spain. In some ways, it was the right decision to make, unless, her teacher had said, you were the Aztecs who were mutilated or the poor soldier who simply wanted to see his family again.

She nodded her head as she looked at the celebration on the deck, with Mark in the middle like Peter Pan and his merry band of boys. Die fighting or just die like the Spaniards, she concluded. That was what Florida seemed to her. No exit.

By the time she sat across from Dr. Em, she had all but pulled raw skin from her cuticles. She stuck her hands in her jacket pockets and smiled weakly.

"Great to see you," he greeted. "I didn't realize at first who you were. You made your appointment under a different name. You're married now. Congratulations."

She readjusted her seat and transferred her hands to her lap, one hand lingering on her wedding ring. "Thanks," she answered.

"How long has it been?"

"You mean since I last saw you or since I got married?"

Dr. Em laughed. "Either. Both."

"Two months since the wedding. Six months since I last saw you."

He nodded and flipped a page of his notebook. "Mark, right?"

"Yes. Mark."

"How's married life?"

It was an open-ended question, the kind asked in job interviews. *Tell us about yourself. How did you hear about us? What are your long-term goals?* Beth knew how to handle those. She once carried in her purse a three-by-five reference card with written responses when she was job hunting so she could maintain eye contact and give her twenty-second answer to such pat questions. But today, she knew Dr. Em's underlying inquiry: Why is a happily married woman taking time off from work to return to her therapist?

She looked away and then back to him. "We're having a disagreement, a rather large one." She paused, hoping he would pick up the conversation. She twisted her ring again and then placed her hands under her thighs. "I guess I need to talk about it with someone neutral."

In what felt like minutes but was much longer, she gave him the play-by-play of the past two months – the move to Mark's house, the wedding, Mark's job offer, the pending move to Florida, even Janet's divorce. When she finished, she looked out the window to compose herself. She remembered this view of a parking lot. It reminded her of a similar view from her mother's hospital room. Bleak. Cold. Clinical. Impersonal. A place where sick people come to get well. Or to die.

"How does this make you feel?" he asked.

She glanced again toward the window and then back to him. "Angry," she said at last. "I mean, we had all these guided conversations before we were married about what we wanted in life. The minister required it before the wedding so that we were," she made air quotes, "aligned."

She closed her lips the way she used to zip them shut as a child. She didn't want to come apart in front of him. Part of her was waiting for him to say *I told you so*. She was confident it would happen before the hour was out. But she was willing to risk it just to get some direction. Her self-confidence, if she'd had any to begin with, had taken a nose dive.

What she wasn't prepared to discuss was what she had learned from Anna. If her neighborhood gossip chain was correct, Anna had told her, the full story was that Mark had pinned a student against a wall – an action that brought the kid's parents to the headmaster's office with a demand. Either they would bring a lawsuit against Mark, or the headmaster could fire him. It was a private school, and the parents were big donors. To avoid scandal, the headmaster had given Mark the option of resigning.

When she had again broached the subject with Mark, he had laughed and hugged her. "You know me," he had said. "I'm a big teddy bear. No way would I hurt someone."

"It's understandable that you feel anger," Dr. Em said, drawing Beth's attention back into the room. "That's a lot of change to process for someone who needs stability. Why don't you bring him in for your next appointment?"

Before the sentence was out of his mouth, Beth was shaking her head.

"No?" He leaned forward. "Why not?"

She hesitated and then said, "He thinks it's a waste of time."

"An educator who thinks counseling is a waste of time?"

She nodded but then shrugged. *Go figure*, the movement implied.

Dr. Em tapped his pen against his pad. "What about this. One of the other counselors here holds a couple's group. He's good at leading guided discussions so that participants like Mark don't feel like they're in," now it was his turn to use air quotes, "therapy."

"We tried that before we married."

"And?" he prodded.

"We dropped out."

"That's unfortunate." He regarded her for a long moment. "But you're here now, so that's a step in the right direction. And surely Mark knows that nothing works in marriage if the other partner is forced into compliance." He leaned forward again. "Beth, you've got just as much right to say what does and doesn't work for you as Mark does. Don't let your married identity overwhelm your personal identity."

He flipped back through his notes from previous sessions, like a doctor checking the results from blood tests. Then he looked at her over the top of his glasses. "I know you said your mother was a drill sergeant." He waited for Beth to nod in agreement. "And I know you're accustomed to working under a demanding boss." Again, she nodded. He lay his notes aside. "You're drawn to strong people, Beth. We've talked about this before. And it's good to have them by your side in life. But I can't help but wonder whether there's something more to that. Like you seek a challenge to prove yourself."

Beth started to protest, but he cut her off.

"I'm not saying you didn't marry for love. That's evident. But sometimes other factors influence decisions without us even being aware of them." When Beth didn't respond, he pushed his glasses to the top of his head. "Remember that movie years ago where the news anchor put his head out a window and yelled, 'I'm mad as hell and I'm not going to take it anymore.' Have you ever done that?"

Beth's face drained of color as her mind traveled back.

"Have you ever stood your ground and just said no? Sometimes strong people need reminding that they're not the only ones with power." He paused. "I get it. You couldn't do that as a child. But you're not a child anymore. You have a voice. Now use it."

Beth's hands knotted into fists. She saw a face. Smelled the sweat. Felt the hands. She shook her head to clear the image and rearranged her face into a calm Kabuki mask, hiding all. She looked at him. "I used my voice. It didn't work. Saying 'no' never works."

"Do you believe that?" Dr. Em asked.

"Maybe moving isn't as bad as it seems," she continued, fixing him with level eyes. "Maybe I'm scared of change and need to open myself to new possibilities." She nodded in agreement with her logic. "That's what Mark says. He says I'm change avoidant and that we'll work better as a new couple in a new place."

"And do you agree with Mark? Do you think the only thing you're afraid of is change? Is that why you avoid saying no? Or what about him? What is in his life that makes him need this move? Is there something more at stake for him?"

When Beth didn't answer him, he leaned back in his chair. "I'm your therapist, Beth, but I can only help you if you're willing to do the hard work. There's something bothering you. Maybe something from your past that this move to Florida is triggering." He glanced at his watch. "We've got time to dig into it and," he opened his appointment book, "I've got this Thursday at noon available. We can continue on then."

She smiled weakly and reached for her purse. "I need to think about it. As my mother would say, don't go poking a hornet's nest."

Dr. Em stared at her for a long time. "That's not a good image, but I get it. You're not ready to talk about it. But trust my experience with how the mind works. Things we bury have a way of coming back and biting us in the butt."

She nodded. "I understand. But for now, I've got too much else on my mind. Too much here and now to dig up some old bone, another of my mother's expressions. Right now, my mind is on making this Florida move work."

Dr. Em stood. "Is that what you want?"

Beth answered with a shrug.

"That's not an answer. That's not the Beth Gardiner I know."

"It's Beth Berger, remember?" She stepped toward the door and then turned back. "I'll be back. I'm not sure how soon, but these sessions help." She tightened her ponytail. "I know you think I'm avoiding something, but really, I'm trying to find my way through a maze without a string to follow." She nodded in thought and then smiled. "Fake it till you make it. That's my motto."

She walked out the door and closed it behind her.

CHAPTER NINETEEN

*G*et up. Go to work. Come home. Argue. It became their routine. Like fighters in a ring, they circled one another, jabbing, sparing, and then retreating into their respective corners to fight another round the next day. Beth trying to use every bit of coaching that Dr. Em was giving her; Mark flicking off her jabs like pesky flies. August ended. Beth resigned. Lizzie went to stay with Lori. Mark packed the car.

They debated the move one last time on a clear night, sitting opposite one another on the living room sofa, until both fell asleep from exhaustion. Sometime around two in the morning, they woke. Mark found his keys and then stood by the front door, fixing Beth with a look that clearly said, *coming?* She went to the bathroom, located her purse, and followed him out the now open door, closing it behind her with a solid click.

As Mark put the key into the ignition, Beth turned to him, tear tracks still visible on her face. "Mark, I...."

He held up his hand. "Enough, Beth. Discussion over." He put the car into reverse and backed out of the driveway. Beth punched her sweatshirt into something resembling a pillow and curled catlike into a tight ball.

The plan, according to Mark, was to drive straight through the night, stopping only for gas at the Florida line and again south of Tampa, before arriving in Porto Verde by sunrise. He had pressed this itinerary as if moving were no more complicated than going to sleep in one state and waking in another, like rolling across a bed and getting up on the other side. No worries about friends left behind, or a house to sell, or a cat to board, or a job to find, or a new life to build from scratch.

Eight hours later, the absence of motion of the car caused Beth to wake, shift her body to a more comfortable position and sit up, shaking her head in amazement that she had slept through the drive. Mark was leaning forward with his wrists on the steering wheel, peering through the bug-splattered windshield. When he heard her stir, he nudged her and nodded toward the scene outside.

She opened the door and crawled out, bending to touch her toes, then stretching side to side. Retrieving her shoes from the car, she walked across the parking lot and up a rise, following the sound of the surf.

The gulf was at high tide. Crashing waves competed with the seagulls and sandpipers for space on the beach. The sun glinted on the water, flashing light back toward the sky. A few early morning walkers were already striding along, some holding shoes and wading in the water, others choosing higher ground where the sand was soft and deep. Beth shaded her eyes, walked straight to the water, took off her shoes, and dipped in a toe.

"Nice morning," Mark said. His voice startled her as much by the soft tone as his brevity.

She turned to him. "Is this Porto Verde?"

"Venice Beach, about thirty miles north. I thought we could spend the day here." He nodded in a direction down the beach. "Let's get some coffee. There's a snack bar down there."

Morning coffee in hand, they walked again to the shore and sat just back from the high-water mark. Beth began drawing a pattern in the sand with one finger, circles that spiraled outward like a conch shell. It was a habit she had picked up on a trip to Canyon Ranch near Tucson. She had noticed people walking a winding path laid out with cobblestones and low shrubbery. Their meditative state intrigued her. The next day, she'd returned and followed their lead, walking and thinking. Since then, when in a contemplative mood, she would draw similar shapes, around and around, weighing options.

"There's a house listed online that I think would work," Mark said.

"Really? That would make this easier ...."

"Don't start."

"I'm not. Too tired anyway."

By noon, they found a motel close to the Interstate that allowed early check-in – a place that catered to truckers. While they unpacked their bags, the air-conditioning struggled to cool the room, creating a rhythmic gurgle that muffled the traffic. Finally, with blinds drawn tight, they crawled into bed, each rolling toward the middle, stuffing flat pillows into uncomfortable lumps and settling into a restless sleep.

As they drove south the next morning, Beth stared out the car window at the white line that edged the highway, allowing a blur of gas stations, mom and pop shops, fast food establishments, and trailer park entrances to pass her by. She was resigned. That's all there was to it. Resigned and depressed – not a happy combination for beginning a new chapter of her life, she realized. But what were her options? Mark needed this change. He was searching for something. That was clear. But what about her? When she met him, she thought she had found what she needed. But this? Not even close.

She looked down at the literature she had picked up in the motel lobby. According to the pamphlet in her lap, the road from Venice to Porto Verde had several names: Highway 41. State Road 90. Tamiami Trail. Stretching north as far as Michigan, the highway earned the nickname Bedspread Alley back in the 1950s for all the places where local seamstresses displayed their handiwork for sale to passing travelers. But since I-75 became the north-south corridor of choice for traffic, few drove the two-lane route except locals. All it would take, thought Beth, was for Mark to turn the car around, and this asphalt strip would lead them all the way back to downtown Atlanta. She considered saying something like this to him but decided not to. Instead, she devised other names for the road. Highway to Hell came to mind.

"Did you make an appointment with the realtor?" she asked, forcing herself to speak in a light tone.

He nodded. "All set."

"Maybe we could catch a movie afterward. Get out of this heat."

"There isn't a theatre."

She turned toward him. "Walk through a mall?"

"There's not one."

"Get a Starbucks and sit on the beach?"

He tightened his grip on the steering wheel. "I've told you, Beth. This isn't a resort town. It's a sailing and fishing community. We're on a big bay called Charlotte Harbour. It's an estuary. Rivers from across Florida flow in here before joining the Gulf. The water's brackish – half fresh, half saltwater. More brown than blue. But the sailing is excellent."

"Thank you, Captain." She needed to work on her sarcastic tone, she realized. "But what does that have to do with there not being a movie theatre or a mall or a Starbucks? Or a beach? It's Florida, isn't it?"

He didn't answer. Beth stared at him for a while before closing the pamphlet. Then with a flick of her wrist, she threw it onto the backseat and continued watching the white line outside her window, twisting the ring on her left hand. What was it her father once said about Florida? *Land of the newlywed and the nearly dead.* She was both.

CHAPTER TWENTY

*B*eth put down the phone. It was time for her to stop complaining to Lori. *Stop your whi---,* her mother's voice began, and she cut it off. Dr. Em had counseled to cut the feedback loop to her childhood, and only by stopping it did she realize how powerful that voice had been. Calling Lori wasn't the answer either. She was married. Time to find her own solutions.

Looking out the window, she watched an alligator crawl across, leaving a brushed trail in the grass before easing back into a drainage canal. A month of living in Porto Verde and still the landscape startled her. The sun didn't slowly rise over mountains or set softly behind them; it shot up like a blast from a furnace, from which there was no escape until at last, it dropped just as quickly as it had arrived. Trees didn't turn colors with the change of seasons but remained a constant deep green. Even the texture of the grass was different. She had grown up running barefoot on a soft lawn. Here the grass had knife-like blades.

"It's just weather," she muttered, returning to her laptop, trying to block from her mind what North Georgia looked like when all the trees sported their fall colors, like a rack of cozy sweaters. *September,* she mused, and instead of picking apples in Ellijay, here she sat staring at the same dead-end jobs that her search had found the day before, and the day before that. A hardware store needed an outside sales person who could drive a forklift. The Dollar General wanted a cashier for the night shift. Someone with a passion for hunting, shooting, and fishing – in that order – could become the next marketing assistant at a sporting goods store.

"Yee-haw," she said, shutting the computer in disgust. With a restless flick of her hand, she turned on the radio, which Mark kept tuned to the local weather station. A tropical thunderstorm in the Gulf was expected to bring intense late afternoon showers with lightning and hail. Just as it had the day before, and the day before that. She opened the refrigerator and stared at a bottle of wine. *Tempting*, she thought. Instead, she made a cup of tea and pulled a worn *Cosmo* magazine from her travel bag to thumb through. *What drivel*, she concluded.

"I was worried," she said hours later, as Mark opened the door and shook the rain from his parka. A pile of cleaned shrimp was stacked beside her, their tails in a neat pile. Had Lizzie been there, Beth would have dropped one on the floor for her.

"About me? Na, baby. I'm half fish." He reached for her and pulled her close.

She returned his kiss and considered taking his hand and leading him to the bedroom, but he was already reaching over her for a glass from the cabinet, dropping in ice cubes followed by a shot of Jack Daniels and water. He went into the living room and flipped on the television to golf. She turned off the radio. Their rhythm was off. "Dinner," she called out later, and like a well-trained pet, he took his place at the table and began shoveling in food.

"How was your day?" she asked with forced enthusiasm. He mumbled an answer – something about wrestling tryouts and slackers – and she nodded and smiled as if he had explained the symbolism in a Faulkner novel. God, she needed a project – something to channel her nervous energy. Designing a sales flyer for shotguns was not it. She looked around the scantily furnished room and considered her options. They would drive back the following weekend to pack up the house and pick up Lizzie. Hopefully, when she got some of her things down here, it would feel more like home. Martha Stewart or not, she missed her belongings.

She lay down her fork and leaned back in thought. It was hard for her to convey to Mark how much she loved interior design – prowling through antique markets to find the perfect object to set the tone of a room, bringing home samples of fabric to assess against paint swatches. When she moved into her Buckhead condo, she had made curtains, covered pillows, and framed prints by Claude Monet and Mary Cassatt to complement the look and feel she wanted for her home. Even Mark had commented on her good taste on their first date. "Nice place," he had said. But somehow, he didn't get how much she felt adrift without the anchor of her belongings.

"Tell me again why you like this town so much," she said. She couldn't help herself. The question worked on her like a worm in her brain.

He looked up from his plate. "Drop it, Beth. We're here now. This is our home."

He stood, stretched, and then walked back to the sofa and the television. Chances were, he would fall asleep in front of it, lulled to sleep by bourbon and the raspy sound of rain in the palmetto trees. Beth watched him for a moment, then picked up their dishes and rinsed them before stacking them in the dishwasher. She took her laptop and climbed into bed, reaching for the most recent *Southern Living* magazine while she waited for the computer to reboot. She launched a search, and when a result popped up, she smiled.

Porto Verde custom frame shop needs part-time or full-time person to handle counter sales. Must have an eye for design and a willingness to learn the craft of custom framing. Apply in person.

"Mark," she called. "I may have found a job." She listened for his answer but only heard the low rumble of his snores. Sex would have to wait.

CHAPTER TWENTY-ONE

*F*resh air filled the car as Beth rolled down the window. With each mile north of the Florida-Georgia border, her spirit returned as the humidity level dropped. Leaves were showing fall colors – a hint of orange here, a burst of red there. Football weather, everyone called it. Time to break out bulky sweaters and cowboy boots. But not for her, she remembered. Only one short weekend to pack the house, pick up Lizzie, and then back on the road to Florida.

"What about giving the living room set to Heather?" Mark said, interrupting her thoughts as he maneuvered through downtown Atlanta. "Her mother is paying for her to move into an apartment. I said I'd chip in on furnishings."

Beth pulled her eyes from the scenery. "What will we do for furniture?" she asked. "I'm not ready to dispose of everything, especially pieces from my grandparents. And I definitely don't want to live in a house full of white rattan knockoffs."

"But does it all need to go to Florida? I thought we agreed to downsize."

Beth exhaled and rolled up the window. It had been a grueling ten-hour drive. Her body felt every minute of it. She had leaned forward for most of it, her seatbelt pulling across her chest as if by sheer will she could get to Atlanta sooner.

"We're downsizing because the only place we can afford in Florida is a third of the size of our current house," she said at last. It was pointless to continue arguing over something that had, in Mark's mind, already been decided. "Can't we just store things and decide later?"

"If we get rid of things now, we won't need to rent a storage unit or a big moving truck." When Beth didn't respond, he added, "It's just furniture, for Christ's sake."

Point taken, she thought. But how much longer could she accept the credo *It's just* . . . fill in the blank?

The next morning, while he took a run, Beth sat outside in an antique Adirondack chair. Its green-flecked paint and sloped seat brought back memories of sitting with her grandad on his East Tennessee front porch, while her grandmother made fried apple pies, the smell of cinnamon and sugar scenting the air. He was her Papaw and she his Lizbit. He would pass her pieces of Juicy Fruit chewing gum, which she stuffed into her mouth while she read, feet up in the chair, a pillow tucked behind her back. One summer she consumed every book about a group of kids who solved mysteries in Chattanooga. She had been to those places featured in the books – Lookout Mountain, Ruby Falls, Rock City, the Plum Nelly Art Show. She so wanted to be one of those kids, with a whole city as their backyard, instead of living in a small town that didn't have a movie theater, much less an amusement park. But then, she wouldn't have had Papaw, who took her side in family quarrels.

Looking at mountain ranges had always been a kind of therapy for her. "Look at that," her Papaw would say, as they watched birds circling high above the trees. "They're headed to their nest up on that ridge." While in college, she had hiked to places like Clingman's Dome, high above Gatlinburg in the Smoky Mountains, just to see the view. *Last of the Mohicans* was her favorite movie because of its North Carolina setting. *Mountains are comforting*, she often thought. Like a deep sofa inviting you to stop and snuggle.

She heard the screen door open and Mark's steps. He held a half-empty bottle of Gatorade and stood in front of her, blocking her view. "Everything packed and ready to go?"

She looked at him. "Not quite," she said as she stood. "I'll call Heather and see if she wants the furniture. But I think she's like most young people starting out and would rather get all new stuff from Rooms to Go."

"I'm not spending money on new things for her," he replied.

"Okay. But think about it. When you were twenty and moving into your first place, didn't you want to furnish it your way?" She reached for his hand and swung their arms for a moment. "Be her dad. You already agreed to help her." She squeezed his fingers. "Think of it like this. You're not buying her affection; you're supporting her efforts to become an adult. Kind of like me supporting your desire to sail."

He looked down at her. "If I do that, we won't have the money to sail again in the BVIs."

Beth smiled. "Oh, I think I can live with that."

CHAPTER TWENTY-TWO

*B*eth unlocked the shop door and flipped on the *Open* sign. She pulled in a delivery of moldings from Larson-Juhl and then turned on the electric mat cutter so it would be ready when Deborah, her boss, arrived. She put frame samples back on the wall before organizing the mat corners. *Ten minutes until chaos,* she thought as she glanced at the clock. Grabbing a broom, she swept under the wood chopper.

It had only been two months since she began working there, and she was enjoying it. She appreciated the way mats and molding drew the eye into the picture, took pleasure in helping customers and seeing their delight, looked forward to new art arriving and displaying it around the shop. Much like planning a marketing campaign or putting a magazine to press, she had a knack for envisioning how pieces fitted together. What she didn't like was Deborah's disorganized, frenetic work style. One minute Beth would be fitting a print into the frame and the next Deborah would hurry her out the door to buy wire or masking tape or supplies that could have been ordered in advance. Or she would be helping a customer, and Deborah would bump her away from the counter with her hip, saying, "I'll take it from here."

Deborah reminded Beth of her sister Jess, she realized, as she continued sweeping in front of the shop. Jess, the one whose conception was so unexpected. The one whom Beth was expected to care for, chase after, share with, clean up after, seemingly for the rest of their lives. Jess, who sucked all the attention out of a room, leaving little space for Beth.

Like working for Jess in another body, she thought – her shrillness, her flightiness, her nanosecond attention span. But Deborah had a good eye for framing, and Beth hoped to decorate their home with tropical prints framed on discount. Home décor had always been a passion, but now, she realized, it was a necessity. Her old job provided a channel for her energies and a boost to her self-esteem. But now? She looked at split nails on callused hands holding a broom like Chief in *One Flew Over the Cuckoo's Nest*. No challenge. No incentive. No self-esteem.

She dropped debris into the trash bin and visualized the home she wanted to create. Soothing colors, comfortable seating, low lighting. A loving place. It had all seemed so possible when Mark put the ring on her finger six months ago. But lately, it felt like neither of them understood the other, much less shared the same dreams. She counted on her fingers. When was the last time he did something romantic? Held her hand? Told her he loved her? When was the last time she had felt a rush of joy by his presence? And when had sex shifted from an expression of pure affection into a purely physical act? She couldn't remember, and hearing Deborah's key in the door, she didn't have time to think about it. As she hauled the trash to the dumpster, she tried to discard her worries along with the rubbish. Maybe she could plan something romantic for Thanksgiving that didn't involve watching pro football. *Fat chance*, she reminded herself. Mark would never spend turkey day without the games.

By the time she left the shop nine hours later, Beth was, as her Papaw used to say, bone-tired. She stretched her back and glanced at her watch. The gym's group fitness class had already begun. Plus, she was too exhausted. A soak in the tub and a glass of wine. Maybe some fresh flowers for her blue bowl. That might work. Unlike Darcy, Lizzie was too afraid of water to sit on the edge and play with the bubbles. Beth smiled in remembrance. At least Lizzie liked to snuggle. Beth needed lots of that.

When she pulled into the garage, she saw Mark's red Mustang already parked, its trunk open with tennis gear inside. As she walked into the house, Lizzie ran toward her with her tail straight up in the air. "Has she been fed?" she called but didn't get an answer. She went into the kitchen and got out a tin of Fancy Feast. The sound of the can opener set Lizzie to meowing. "Okay, Okay," Beth said, as she filled the bowl and set it on the floor. "Mama's here." She stroked the cat's back as she gobbled the food.

In the living room, a trail of shoes and socks lead to the lanai. Mark sat with his legs extended on a lounge chair, talking on his cell. "Yeah, three sets," he was saying, his voice revealing his excitement. "We took the first 6-4, then lost the second on Terry's serve 5-7. But we came back and won 6-2." He paused, listening to whoever was on the call and then laughed. "I know, right? They're ranked number ten in the state, so this match will move us up." He paused again to listen. "On Saturday," he answered. "We'll find out our opponents after the match tomorrow." Again, he listened. "Thanks, man. You, too. Later."

He put down his phone and picked up a drink from the table beside him.

"So, you won," Beth said, as she crossed the room toward him. "Congratulations. Sounds like a close match."

He looked over his shoulder at her. "Hey, you're back. About time."

She stopped. "What do you mean, about time? You just got home yourself. And you're playing again Saturday?"

"Is that a problem?"

"Well, kind of, yes," she answered. "We agreed to a picnic on the beach."

He groaned. "Can't we do that Sunday?"

"I have to work Sunday afternoon. Remember?" She picked up a calendar lying on the coffee table. "I even wrote it down." She regarded him for a moment. "Do you ever listen?"

He got up from the lounge chair and walked toward her. "Frankly babe, sometimes I don't. The way I look at it, if I miss hearing something one day, I'll hear it the next." He poured more bourbon into his glass and added ice cubes.

She stepped back. "That's a hateful remark," she said at last.

"Yeah, well, sorry. But," he shook his head and forced a laugh. "You get on a topic, like this picnic, and you don't let it go." He took a long drink. "Anyway, the match is set." He fixed her with a look. "If you want to get out of town, let's go look at boats. That's why we're here."

Beth tried to speak but he continued.

"It's like this, Beth, and try to get it for once and for all. I'm trying to get established here in sailing, and Porto Verde is a boating community. As an instructor, I need my own boat, not one owned by the school."

Beth shook her head, confused about how a conversation about a picnic was now an argument about a boat. She put her fingers to her temples. "No, Mark. You're the one who doesn't get it. We can't afford a boat, at least not right now. And a picnic costs nothing. Plus, you never had this big need for your own boat when we lived in Atlanta. You were happy sailing those owned by the sailing school." She opened a drawer and then closed it hard. "This is what I was afraid would happen. This is why I tried to convince you to wait a few years before we moved here. We could have lived in your house. Saved money. Worked the kinks out of our marriage. But no, you wanted to resign, wanted to move. Just had to get to the ocean."

The glass crashed onto the tile floor, ice cubes and bourbon shooting everywhere.

Beth stood still, her mouth open, her eyes wide. She was a child again, and her mother had smashed Beth's favorite gift from her Papaw. It was a statue of a little girl in a blue dress with a white sash. Her mother was angry that Beth had asked for money to go skating with a friend.

"You just broke my dad's Waterford glass," she said at last. "I can't believe you...." She stopped speaking as Mark shoved her aside and got another glass out of the cabinet. He came back toward her, stared at her for a moment, and smashed it onto the floor.

"Leave me the fuck alone," he said, his eyes boring into hers. He grabbed his car keys and headed out the door. Lizzie scuttled past him and under the sofa as the garage door slammed.

Dive. Dive. Dive! Beth's brain screamed like the commander of a submarine under attack. *Grab Lizzie and don't stop driving until you're in Georgia.* She snatched her purse and pulled out her keys, her every instinct on high alert. *Get going,* she instructed herself. *Get away while you can.* She went into the bathroom. But what did a woman take when she was making a run for it? Toothbrush? Jewelry? Cash? Clothes? Pills? Her cat? She caught a glance of her face in the mirror and stopped, toothbrush in hand. *What was she doing?* her chalk-white face asked, her blue eyes illuminated by tears. Why should she leave? If anyone needed to get out of the house, it would be Mark.

Look before you leap, her mother's voice cautioned her. "Shut up, Mother," Beth said to her reflection.

She placed the toothbrush back into its holder and returned to the living room. Staring at the broken glass, she took deep breaths until her heart rate slowed. With effort, she retrieved a roll of paper towels from the kitchen and, dropping to her knees, sopped up bourbon – struggling to block out its sweet smell. She took her time, making sure no shards were on the floor. Then she towel-wiped the surface and ran the vacuum. Using cat treats for enticement, she persuaded Lizzie to come out from her hiding place and sat on the sofa with the cat in her lap and her phone by her side. She scrolled through her list of contact numbers before snapping the phone shut. This was her problem to solve. Not Lori's, or Alisa's and Grant's. Hers.

"What family doesn't have its ups and downs?" she said at last to Lizzie, a line her mother often quoted from *The Lion in Winter,* her favorite movie. Beth cringed at the thought of what else her mother might have said. She had tried once before to turn to her mother for advice. *That didn't work out at all,* she remembered.

Carrying Lizzie under her arm, she walked to the kitchen and grabbed another handful of treats. With only a moment's hesitation, she took a pint of ice cream from the refrigerator and returned to the sofa. But still, she reasoned, a chat with Lori would calm her. She looked again at her phone and then dialed. Back in college, she had been alone and scared. She hadn't had a close friend to turn to. Now she did.

"We've had our first big fight," she said.

"Are you okay?" Lori asked. "You don't sound okay."

Beth chose her words with care. "This is harder than I thought it would be. Marriage. The move. This place." She paused. "I'm so sorry I keep calling you."

"It's no problem, but I was talking with Anna and . . ."

"Let me guess. She said I was an idiot to marry Mark."

"No, nothing like that. She just said maybe you should talk with someone professional." She paused, perhaps sensing the flush that rose to Beth's face. "You've got a lot on you," Lori continued. "Maybe a local therapist could help you sort things out. But that doesn't mean don't call me," she rushed to add. "I'm here for you. We all are. Remember, we're the Core Four."

Beth was in bed, still thinking about Lori's words, when she heard the garage door open. She looked at the clock. Midnight. Mark's measured steps echoed down the hall. She lay still as he undressed and crawled under the covers. He reached a hand toward her to see if she was sleeping. A few moments later, she heard the deep breaths of his sleep. Willing her body to relax, she pulled the covers tighter under her chin.

Maybe Lori was right. It was time to talk to someone.

***

Flowers and a card greeted Beth on the kitchen counter the next morning. She picked them up and walked outside, finding Mark polishing the hubcaps of her car.

"I'm sorry," he said as he stood.

She nodded.

"I had a bad day at work. That new woman principal is a real ball buster. Gave me a dressing down after school about some parent complaint. I took it out on you. Want me to buy you some new glassware?"

Beth looked across the yard considering. "Let's just forget it," she said. "It's over."

"I lost my temper. It happens sometimes." He shrugged and returned to polishing the wheels.

Beth stared at his back. *But why?* she wanted to ask him. *Why do you lose your temper?* But that might cause another argument. She returned to the house and, before losing her nerve, opened her computer to search for a local therapist. When Mark later came inside, she allowed herself to be hugged, and that night they made love. But as the days passed, she could still hear glass breaking and the vitriol in his voice.

***

The sun had just risen on the horizon when Beth flipped on the kitchen lights. She wanted to have the picnic hamper packed by eight and to be on the road by nine. The night before, Mark had loaded the car with their bikes, an umbrella, lounge chairs, and plenty of towels – grumbling the whole time. Beth had ignored him as she made crab rolls, fruit salad, gazpacho soup, and parmesan breadsticks, whisking about the kitchen.

Now, as she carried the hamper to the car, she realized she had enough food for four people. *The Core Fore would love it,* she thought. But would a day at the beach do the trick for her and Mark? Two weeks had passed since the "glass incident," as she had labeled it. Not one to hold grudges, she had worked on moving forward – accepting Mark's apology, taking time each evening to listen to the minutia of his day, trying not to miss Janet's wit, Anna's insights, and Lori's ready laugh. But despite her effort, she knew the ground beneath them had shifted – a tectonic shutter that might reoccur anytime due to an invisible fault line.

She pushed these thoughts down during the hour drive south to Bonita Bay Beach. *This will be a great day*, she kept thinking, her enthusiasm growing with each mile. That changed as soon as she opened the car door and coughed. "What's that smell?" she asked, covering her mouth with her shirt.

Looking around, she noticed that their car was the only one in the parking lot. Still coughing, she followed Mark toward the shore and up a path through the sea oats, stopping at the top of the stairs that led down to the beach. As far as Beth could see, dead fish covered the beach. Hundreds of them, maybe thousands, counting the ones floating in the water. It looked like the ocean had vomited its creatures onto the shore. The smell was putrefying.

"Oh, my God, this is awful," she said. "I've got to get back in the car. My eyes are burning." Kicking up sand, she hurried to the parking lot.

Mark seemed unaware she had left. With his arms crossed, he surveyed the scene. Some five minutes later, he joined her in the car.

"It's red tide," he said, shutting the door. She had the engine running and the air conditioning on full blast.

"What?" she asked between coughs.

"Red tide. It happens in the gulf a lot. It's an algae bloom that causes fish to die."

"You've heard of this?"

He nodded.

"And it happens a lot?"

He nodded again.

"You knew about it before we drove here?"

He turned to her. "Look, Beth. What can I say? I know you're bummed."

Her face tightened into a scowl. "Bummed is too small of a word. I wanted us to have a special day. I'm sick with disappointment. That's what it is." She took a drink of water from a bottle wedged at her feet and then threw it back onto the floorboard. "Let's go home," she said at last. She was acting like a spoiled kid. She knew it. But at the moment, she didn't care.

He eased the car into reverse and pulled out of the parking lot. "We should have gone boat shopping," he muttered, as he glanced at the beach in the rearview mirror. Beth opened her mouth, shocked by his *I-told-you-so* comment. She started to call him on it but thought better. Best to wait until she wasn't so angry.

They drove in silence, and as she stared at the road ahead, she wasn't sure if that day would ever come.

CHAPTER TWENTY-THREE

" When your husband broke the glass, did he threaten you?"

Beth twisted in her chair. She hated this aspect of seeing a new therapist, even if she had kind eyes.

"Not so much threatened, like he would hit me or something. But I was scared. I've seen Mark lose his temper, but never directed at me."

Helen pushed a long dark braid over her shoulder and leaned forward, her purple glasses dangling from a silver chain. "What about hurtful words?" she asked. "Has he called you names? Spoken to you in derogatory terms? That's abuse too."

Beth thought before answering. A laugh caught in her throat. A picnic, for God's sake. What kind of couple argues about something as simple as that? And her dad's Waterford glasses. It didn't make sense. None of it. Mark had everything he wanted, didn't he?

"He says things sometimes that make me feel punched."

She ticked off people on her fingers who spoke to her that way. The boss at her first job, who yelled with one finger nearly touching Beth's nose. Her brother's demeaning remarks. Of course, her mother's constant barrage of criticism. All those paling to the one person in college who had hurt her deepest. Hurtful words and deeds – all implying Beth was worthless. She had worked hard to prove them wrong. Paying her way through college. Starting a new life in Atlanta. Working overtime. Swimming with sharks. Uprooting herself.

"Do you think he's willing to participate in counseling?" Helen asked, drawing Beth's attention back to the room.

Lost in her thoughts, Beth gave Helen a puzzled look.

"Counseling," Helen repeated. "Do you think Mark will participate?"

Beth scoffed. "My other therapist suggested it too. I didn't even bother telling Mark." A pause. "To his credit, he apologized the next morning and gave me flowers." She snorted. "Two weekends in a row, I got flowers." She visualized the broken glass in one hand and the bouquet in the other. "It's not enough, is it?"

"Then you need a plan."

"You mean like a plan for leaving him?" Beth crossed her arms. "No, I don't want that. I want our marriage to work."

"I was thinking more like a plan for you. A way to rebuild your self-esteem, to fall in love with yourself, so to speak. It sounds like you've lost a big part of yourself with this move. Your marriage will take care of itself once you take steps to care for yourself. You can't fix Mark. You can only work on you."

"But I do take care of myself," Beth reasoned. "I exercise. Eat right. Don't drink too much."

"Excellent. But are you caring for your emotional needs?" Helen pushed her bangle bracelets up her arm and leaned forward again. "Look, Beth. You've taken the first step by identifying a problem and seeking help. You impress me as a take-charge person. I'm suggesting that you take charge of your happiness."

Beth looked away and brushed at tears that welled in her eyes. Outside the sun was at its zenith. Across the parking lot, cars reflected sunrays like exploding flashbulbs. "It feels like I'm going behind Mark's back," she said.

"Then tell him, if you need to. But the key question you must ask yourself is: Do I deserve better than my current circumstances?"

Beth held her gaze. "Sometimes I think I do, and sometimes I think I'm getting what I deserve."

"Then we have work to do. Someone along the way has done serious damage to your self-esteem." Helen reached toward her office calendar. "Tell me, when would you like to see me again?"

Beth thought for a moment. "Is Friday at six open?"

Helen held out her hand for Beth to shake. "Friday it is. See you then."

As she walked to her car, she remembered that Mark wanted to attend the St. Petersburg boat show that weekend and had insisted they leave Friday after work. Beth kicked at the gravel. Her resolve to work on herself would have to wait.

CHAPTER TWENTY-FOUR

*B*eth gazed across Charlotte Harbour and reflected on the past month. *Highs and lows,* she concluded, just like the tide. Days when she and Mark acted like newlyweds, and other days when they behaved as strangers. A high point had been Christmas Eve a month earlier. Neither of them had been in the mood for the Florida version of the holiday – complete with water-skiing Santas and fake snow on palm trees – so at his suggestion, they had packed their bikes and driven to the postcard-perfect town of Boca Grande on Gasparilla Island. All morning they peddled the six-mile ribbon of paths that meandered the island, photographing the lighthouse, peeping in windows of upscale shops, stopping for drinks on the patio at the famed Gasparilla Inn that, as Beth had commented, oozed power and old money from its pale blue ceilings to its dark hardwood floors. Even Mark had enjoyed himself, inventing a drinking game based on the number of preppy pink shirts they spied. That evening, in a burst of holiday spirit, Beth had decorated a small indoor plant with white twinkle lights, gold ornaments, and red garland, and then they attended a midnight service at a nearby church. They had agreed: no gifts – a rule they both broke, with Mark giving Beth her favorite perfume, Chanel No. 5, and Mark receiving the Tommy Bahama shirt he now wore.

And so, the old year ended and a new one began – back to their separate corners, arguing about the merits of sailboats, including the one they now stood on.

"The bilge is clean," Beth heard Mark say from behind her. She glanced back as his head emerged from the companionway, his black hair encircled by an ever-present white visor. "The engine looks good too."

He unfolded through the opening and removed the visor to wipe sweat from his forehead with the back of his hand. Beth turned back toward the water.

"Did you hear me?" Mark asked. "I said the bilge is clean."

When she didn't respond, he ducked under the mast and climbed out of the cockpit on the starboard side.

She kept her place beside the genoa rigging, with her back to him. "Great," she answered, her eyes focused on a spot some thirty feet away from the pier. Mark followed her gaze and saw a dolphin fin disappear. "Sorry," she added. "I was somewhere else for a moment."

"It's an '84, but from what I can see, she's in good shape." He swung himself around the shrouds and joined her on the bow. "What do you think?" he asked when he stood beside her. "Should we buy it?"

She glanced at him. "You know what I think." The mirrored coating of her dark glasses reflected sunlight glinting off the water. "But if you're determined to buy, God knows I don't want to look at any more bilges or take any more notes for you." She waved a small notebook at him before returning her attention to the water and the faint circles left by the dolphin.

"The owner says the sails won't need replacing for at least three years, and all the electronics seem to be working."

"Sounds like you've made up your mind."

They stayed that way for some time – each lost in thoughts that neither wanted to share. It was the third week of what Beth had named the Greater Florida Cheap Boat Search. It had begun in St. Petersburg at 'The Largest Boat Show on the Gulf Coast,' or so the sign proclaimed. Beth had trailed after Mark most of that day, as he examined power boats, cabin cruisers, catamarans, deep sea fishing boats, cigar boats, and sailboats of all sizes. All were decked out in flags from the tops of masts to the sterns. "Happy New Year," she had muttered.

"What I want is an Island Packet," he had said, as she jogged down yet another gangplank behind him, pulling her shirt away from her damp back. "They're built in Florida, so we can tour the plant. Then we'll look at the Morgans for comparison. It's good to know what goes into the hulls. It comes down to this. Seaworthiness. Performance. Construction."

"Check," she had replied, giving him a jaunty salute to inject humor into the day. But by mid-afternoon, after examining Beneteaus, Jenneaus, Hunters, Catalinas and Bavarias ranging from twenty-eight to fifty-two feet, Beth demanded a break. "You look at engine lockers as long as you like," she said. "I need retail therapy."

She was trying on a pair of Docksiders when she noticed an office with a Show Management placard. She put aside the shoes and walked over.

"I worked conventions in Atlanta," she told a young woman at the booth. "Doing the marketing, interfacing with exhibitors, publishing the show guide, writing articles, that sort of thing. Do you know who manages this show?" She left fifteen minutes later with a packet of promotional materials in her backpack and a distinct smile on her face. There was a lot to learn about boating, but show management was a language she spoke.

"Here's what I'm thinking," Mark had said, as they pulled out of the parking lot adjusting the air vents, so they blew at him. "The prices on these boats are ridiculous. Way more than we can afford. It's like buying a new car. You lose value as soon as you drive it off the lot. I'm thinking we need to get at least a ten-year-old boat. Or older, if it's been well maintained."

After that, the sales flyers appeared almost daily on Beth's bedside table.

1998 30' Lance sloop, shoal draft 4'6". New paint 2 years ago. Engine overhauled and runs like new. Genoa sail with new rolling furling. Bimini top. Asking $25,000.

1990 29.5 Jeanneau. She has been one of the great joys of our life. Solid deck. No squishy spots. Yanmar engine in good working order. Well maintained by a good mechanic. New heavy-duty house battery. Asking $12,000.

1994 Irwin. 31' Centerboard Sailboat. 30-gallon diesel fuel tank; 20-gallon water tank. All approved USDG equipment.

BBQ grill. Perfect live-aboard and weekend cruiser. Bottom cleaned monthly. Dinghy included. Asking $29,500.

The last flyer had led them to the boat they now stood on. Mark leaned against the mast as Beth watched another dolphin surface and blow air. "What do you think? Should we make an offer?" he asked.

She stretched her back, releasing tension. "You know what I think."

"You like the Jeanneau better? I thought you said the cabin was too cramped, and it didn't come with a dingy. We'd have to buy one."

She shook her head, still not turning to face him. "No, I'm not in favor of the Jeanneau either."

"Well, what?" He slapped the mast with his visor. "I'm eager to get a boat out on the water, and I think this one is the best. Let's do it."

Before she could respond, the sound of a cart being pulled down the ramp drew her attention. The couple looked to be in their seventies, their faces stranded by the load. She watched as they offloaded water and canned goods into their 42' Catalina. Soon they disappeared below deck.

Beth pointed at the boat. "That's not the life I want," she said. "You're the sailor, not me."

"Have you even looked below?" he asked. "For a 31' Irwin, there's lots of space – even enough room for your cat, if you want to bring it along." He gestured to the open water. "We could sail, baby. Take our clothes off, get full-body tans, ease into a cove when the sun begins to drop, and lift anchor the next morning for another destination. Who wouldn't want that life? We can have that. Right here. Right now."

She removed her sunglasses and pressed her fingers against her eyes. "You should be a DC lobbyist for the boating industry."

"Naw," he responded with a shrug, missing her sarcasm. "That's not me."

Beth turned toward him, her mouth partly open in amazement. She shook her head. "They're mauve," she said at last.

"What?" he asked.

"The cushions. Didn't you notice that putrid color? I'd go nuts." She put her sunglasses back on and shook her head.

Mark stepped from the cockpit onto the deck. He leaned his head back and peered up at the mast. The wind indicator was pointing north. He turned and looked out past the channel markers toward Boca Grande pass.

Beth disappeared through the companionway and returned with a bottle of water. She took a swallow. Mark stepped back on board. "Can I have some of that?"

She handed it to him, and he took a long drink, draining the bottle.

"Okay," he said. "What if I get the guy down to twenty-six thousand? That way there'll be some money for improvements. Would that make you happy? If the cushions weren't mauve, would that make you happy?"

"Honestly, Mark. I was joking, okay?" She shook her head in frustration. "It's not about cushions. Cushions are the least of my concern. Feng Shui has its limits."

"Feng what?" he asked.

She stared at him and then crushed the bottle in her hand.

"It's nothing, Mark," she said, handing him the bottle. "Just do what you want."

CHAPTER TWENTY-FIVE

*T*he February wind propelled the boat further from land. Seated on the transom and dangling her feet in the water, Beth pondered her last session with Helen. They had a good rapport, she concluded. Even better than she had with Dr. Em back in Atlanta. At least that was one decision that had worked. The others she'd made? Only time would tell. *But the clock is running*, she thought. Toward what, she wasn't yet sure. Had it only been a year since she met Mark? It seemed like much longer ago. Their Christmas harmony lasted about as long as the poinsettia plant sitting on the lanai – its stalks all but bare of leaves.

Their argument over the financing of the boat had gone on for days, but two weeks later, Mark used his car as collateral and bought the Blue Raven. Beth didn't even ask about the interest rate. She didn't think it made any difference. He had his boat.

She had talked with Helen about how she had no problem on her job back in Atlanta negotiating with strong-minded people and getting terms acceptable to all parties. But Mark was different. A pro at getting his way. In a category by himself. Like this weekend trip – the maiden voyage of the Blue Raven that Beth had reluctantly agreed to take. She had a different event in mind for Valentine's Day. After a while, it became easier to say yes to Mark's plan. *Plus, who knows?* she reminded herself. It might be as good as those weekends they spent on Lake Lanier – dropping anchor in a cove, making love in the water, watching a glistening sunset.

Or not.

She looked over her shoulder and regarded Mark. He looked in his element, she had to admit. Eyes fixed on the horizon. Hands lightly holding the wheel, allowing the craft to move in accord with the wind and the water. Kind of how Odysseus must have stood as he sailed toward Troy, confident he was doing it for honor, king, country, whatever. But then that journey didn't turn out so well if Beth remembered the story right.

Gazing across the water, she watched Porto Verde disappear behind her, feeling more like Penelope than she wished.

The course Mark had charted would take them across Charlotte Harbour to Pine Island, where they would drop anchor in a gunkhole for the night, securing the boat close to the mangroves on the leeward side of the island. From there, they would sail north, stopping at Pelican Bay, and then east through Boca Grande Pass to Cayo Costa State Park and the Gulf.

Beth had recognized at the time the classic marketing ploy Mark used to convince her to spend three days on this maiden journey. Describe the sizzle; sell the steak.

"We can shell, snorkel, walk the beach, watch the dolphins, drink bourbon from the back of the boat as the sun sets," he promised.

In the end, she threw up her hands and bought it. As she now stared across the water, she prayed that the weekend would bring some sizzle back into their marriage.

When they cast off that morning from their dockage, it had taken close to an hour to meander through the canals before reaching Ponce De Leon Park and the entrance to Charlotte Harbour. The delay aggravated Mark, and, as Beth regarded him, faint signs of this were still evident in his stance behind the wheel, a noticeable tightness between his shoulder blades, a jut of his chin. She had used the time motoring through the canals to store supplies and tidy the cabin, placing colorful throws over the mauve cushions and opening diffusers to help the musty smell. But soon she realized that Mark's sailing accessories would take up most available space. She had stood in the middle of the cabin and regarded it all: charts, foul weather gear, flashlights, safety kits, cases of water, extra line, charcoal, a spare anchor. Plus his diving gear. Plus, they had clothes, food, and coolers. After about thirty minutes of stuffing things into every nook and cranny, she had climbed out, exhausted and irritated.

Now, two hours later, she relaxed sitting on the transom, feeling a gentle wind move the boat along. A pair of dolphins followed their wake, breaking the surface in graceful arcs. The breeze lifted her hair. *Maybe the weekend can be like old times*, she thought.

She closed her eyes, nodding off, and thought she had misheard Mark when he called, "Get up here and get on your rain gear."

"What?"

"Look at those clouds," he said, as she crawled into the cockpit and looked where he pointed off the starboard side. "See how high they are and flat at the bottom? See the rain underneath? It's a squall, and we're headed right into it."

"Couldn't we just turn around and go back?" she asked but knew the answer. Warriors don't run from battle.

"Here. Hold the wheel, and I'll get the gear. Just keep it on its current heading."

She took the wheel and felt the surge of the water.

"Keep it steady," Mark yelled.

A moment later, he was back in the cockpit with his hood up and a safety harness in his hands.

"Put your gear on and this life vest," he ordered. "You need to stay on the wheel while I furl the headsail and put a reef in the main."

He reached for the jib sheet and pulled the line. By now, the sky was dark and ominous, and the wind had increased. Beth shivered, realizing the temperature had dropped considerably. As she fought the wheel against the rising waves, her stomach lurched with each jolt to the boat.

"Ease off. Ease off," Mark ordered. "Something has jammed." He cleated the sheet and went forward, holding the safety lines. He looked back at her. "Pull the sheet while I guide the sail," he instructed.

"I can't and hold the wheel too," she wailed.

"Come on, Beth. Just do it. Figure out a way."

She gripped the wheel with her right hand, leaned forward, and used her left to release the sheet from its cleat. The wind blew her hood off, and the line jerked her arm as she struggled to hold the wheel steady.

"Get it under control," Mark yelled.

"I'm trying," she screamed, silently cursing the weather, the boat, and Mark.

She planted her feet to each side of the cockpit. "Pull!" he instructed again. She did, feeling her body spread apart as if on a medieval rack. Despite her efforts, the jib barely moved, leaving at least seven feet of sail exposed.

Mark returned to the cockpit and cleated the line, his safety harness trailing after him. "Damn furling drum. It's jammed." He slapped the steering wheel in frustration, causing Beth to momentarily lose her grip. "I'm starting the engine. This storm is blowing like a mother."

Beth faintly heard him and kept her eyes pinned to the bow, trying to power up the whitecaps and ease down as they passed underneath. She remembered Mark instructing her back on the lake to steer a boat on a steady heading, which had seemed easy then but nearly impossible with the shifting wind. She heard water hissing as it rushed under the transom. Glancing back, she saw it form a wake like a tail straight up to the angry skies. Her throat tightened as she willed herself to take deep breaths.

"Fuck," Mark said, as he climbed from the cabin back to the mast. "The motor won't crank. I've got to get this mainsail reefed or we're in trouble. Head up so I can lower it. But not straight into the waves." Beth felt frozen, mesmerized by the storm's force. "Do you hear me?" he said. "Head up."

She tightened her hold and tried to keep the boat from pitching as Mark struggled with the sail. He had it lowered close to the first reef point when she again heard, "Fuck, fuck, fuck."

"What?"

"The sail ripped in two places. Dammit." He tied off the line and came back to the cockpit. "Give me the wheel. We've got to sail through it. Stay on the high side if you go below. We need the ballast."

Beth looked off starboard and saw a column of swirling water rising from the ocean toward the clouds. "Oh, my God!" she cried and grabbed Mark's arm.

He shook her loose. "It's a waterspout. Get below now."

She yanked the door open and lowered herself down the steps, dodging the provisions that were now scattered across the floor. She crawled onto the starboard lounge seat and grabbed a handhold.

The boat slammed the waves over and over. When it pitched violently, she fell to the floor and hit her leg against a spare anchor. "Mark!" she cried but knew he couldn't hear her. Out the port windows, she watched the boat keel, the safety lines almost touching the waves. "Mark!" she screamed again but knew there was nothing he could do.

She stayed on the floor and braced her feet to soften the blows. She tried shutting her eyes, but it made the seasickness worse, so she kept them focused out the port windows, hoping to see sky and not water. Vomit rose in her throat, but she fought it back down. Over and over, the boat pitched and shuddered. Each time, Beth cried out, wishing she were any place but here.

She lost track of time, but gradually she felt the storm ease and saw light returning to the skies. Fresh air. That's what she needed. She pulled off her rain gear and opened the hatch cover.

Mark looked down at her. He had pushed back his rain hood, and his dark glasses were back in place. Behind him were blue skies. "Some ride, wasn't it?" he said with a broad grin. "The boat did fine, but I'm pissed about the motor and those sails. Once they dry out, I'll need your help patching the rips." He motioned for her to join him. "Here. Take the wheel while I raise the main. Point into the wind. Now keep it there." He stared upward as the sail filled. "Alright, fall off. I'll ease out the jib, and we're back in business." He laughed. "That's my first time sailing through a squall, but now I know what to do. That's the advantage of a wide beam. No chance of the

Blue Raven being knocked over. We lost time there and got blown off course, but we'll get to Pine Island well before dark and have enough time to find a sweet anchor spot. What are you thinking for dinner? We could grill those steaks and maybe fry some potatoes."

He looked at Beth. Her white knuckles squeezed the wheel while her eyes focused on the water ahead as if it were a tight rope she needed to walk across, one step at a time.

"Did you hear me?" he asked. "Steak and potatoes sound good to you? And maybe some Jack Daniels on the rocks?"

When she didn't respond, he hopped into the cockpit and took the wheel from her. She dropped onto a lounge and pulled her knees to her chest. Her mind formed questions she wanted to yell out but didn't. *Are you nuts?* she wanted to ask. *Are you thinking I will ever consider traveling anywhere again on this boat after going through that, much less have the stomach for grilling steaks?* She opened her mouth to speak, but something about his broad grin and proud chest stopped her. Now was not the time. Instead, she watched the wake of the boat as it moved outward behind them, like a trailing feather leading back to shore. Wishing she could follow it back home.

***

The morning mist was still on the water as Beth sat on the bow of the boat swatting mosquitos. A copy of *Rebecca* lay open in her lap. Her Atlanta book club was reading it, and she hoped to call in for their next meeting. But so far, she couldn't keep her attention on the plot. *Run away as fast as you can,* she wanted to yell at the narrator, who had just arrived at Manderley. Sure, life had turned out okay for her— that is, if you call a house burning down okay. She tossed the book aside in disgust. It slid across the bow and into the water with a gentle plop.

"Shit," she heard Mark say to the motor. *My thoughts exactly,* she nearly said but pulled herself back. Perhaps now was not the time to state her mind. Even Helen would agree with the adage about choosing one's battles, a tactic Beth had employed again and again with her mother.

Neither of them had slept well the night before. It was dark before they set anchor, so Beth had made ham and cheese sandwiches, which they ate while sitting on the bow so Mark could monitor the anchor line. With the cabin a mess and no breeze stirring below, they each made themselves a bed in the cockpit out of flotation cushions, using beach towels as sheets and their rain gear as pillows.

"Give the engine a crank," Mark now ordered. Beth returned to the cockpit and pressed the starter. It sputtered. "Again," he said. This time it sputtered and then caught.

"Ah ha," he cried, as he joined her in the cockpit. "A lead must have worked loose, but she's firing now. Back in business. Let's let her run a while and then re-start after we get the sail mended. Go grab the tape from below. It's in the port side locker."

Beth found the tape and joined him at the mast, determined to be helpful. After all, sailing was the only way to get to land. A snort of laughter escaped at the thought of her and Mark swimming across the bay. Him with his powerful freestyle, and her trailing behind with a pathetic breaststroke.

"Here," Mark said, handing her a sponge and a bucket of water. "Wash both sides of the sail to get all the dirt and salt off. Then I need you to hold it taut while I apply the tape."

She shaded her eyes and looked up at the sail. "I can't reach that high."

"Well, figure it out, Beth. Put one foot here and step there." He pointed at two spars on the mast. "Find a way to hold on."

It took repeated climbs up and down until Mark said, "That's good enough. I'll climb up there and you tear me strips of tape."

An hour later, the patch was complete. With a jubilant shout, Mark cranked the engine, pulled the anchor, and motored out of the cove. He waited until they were in the intercostal waterway before he raised the mainsail and cut the engine. A strong wind blew from starboard, and he eased the sail to port before raising the jib. "Hold the wheel," he told Beth, but just as he pulled the jib sheet, she pointed to the main.

"Look. It's ripping again."

"Dammit," he yelled and tied off the line. "Dammit, dammit, dammit." He landed a fist against the console. "The tape isn't holding. Get the engine back on."

Beth pushed the starter, but nothing happened. She tried again. "It's not starting." Her voice now sounded fearful.

"What?" He pushed her aside. "Let me do it." He pressed the starter button. Not even a shudder. He hit the console again. "Of all the fucking things to go wrong." He removed his visor and wiped sweat from his forehead with the back of his hand.

"What are we going to do?" Beth's voice was tentative. She looked around her. "Maybe we can flag over a boat for help."

He turned. "Those are speed boats, Beth" he snarled. "They're not stopping for us or offering any help, for that matter."

"I thought you had the motor checked when you bought the boat."

"Of course, I did. Do you think I'm stupid? It was running fine, and the owner said he had it serviced just a few months ago." He kicked the cabin door.

"Okay, well..." She caught herself. Mark was not interested in any more questions. She knew that look. Had been raised on it. She went below and brought up water bottles.

He stared at the sky as if reading invisible stars. "We'll have to limp along on just the jib and hope this wind holds," he said. Disappointment and something else in his voice. Beth couldn't tell.

"Are we still headed to Pelican Bay or Cayo Costa?"

Mark seemed not to hear her. Still cursing under his breath, he lowered the mainsail and tied it off, then returned to the cockpit and raised the jib. He let it play out until it caught the wind and turned the boat east.

"Where are we headed?" she asked, but again he didn't answer. Hours later, as the sun set in the west, they dropped anchor near Ponce De Leon Park and rowed their dingy to shore. Beth trailed after Mark as they walked the two miles to their house. When they got there, they dropped their gear in the hallway. Beth headed to the bedroom and crawled into bed with her clothes still on. Before long, Lizzie joined her.

When she awoke the next morning, she wasn't sure if Mark had even come to bed. She called his name but got no answer. Two cups of coffee later, she knew what she wanted to say to him. She waited until he came in through the garage.

"I've been down at the harbor to get someone to look at the motor," he said, as he poured himself a cup.

"Okay," she responded, waiting for her opening.

"And I'm getting someone to help me patch the sail. That tape must have been old. That sail's still good." He nodded, agreeing with himself.

Beth tucked her feet underneath herself to allow Lizzie to join her in the chair. She stroked her for a moment. "We need to talk about all this," she said at last.

He crossed his arms. "I just told you. I'm having the motor fixed and the sail patched."

"That's not what I mean. We need to talk about lots of things." She pushed Lizzie onto the floor. "Not just the boat."

"O-kay," he said, as he took a seat on a bar stool and turned to face her. "What do you think we need to talk about?"

Her eyes searched the room as if looking for a teleprompter. Earlier, the words came easily. Now with Mark's eyes on her, she was losing her nerve.

"Things aren't right between us," she said at last, her voice soft but steady. "I feel like I'm not your partner, the person you love, the one you're devoted to. I feel more like the galley hand than your wife. I'm sorry about your boat but—"

"Oh, really?" he interrupted. "I find that hard to believe. You were dead set against buying it. As we walked home last night, I concluded you were glad the trip was a bust."

She leaned forward on the edge of the chair. "Why would you think that? I mean, sure, I was against buying a boat, but," she shook her head, clearing her thoughts. "I never wanted anything to go wrong, certainly not out in the middle of the ocean."

"It's a bay, Beth."

"Okay." She slammed a palm against the edge of the chair. "In the middle of the bay. Same thing. But Mark, it's not just that things went wrong with the boat. It's how you speak. Like I'm your minion. Someone to order around. And I didn't feel safe out there either."

He sat his cup down hard and started to speak again, but Beth held up a hand to stop him. "I know, I know. You're the captain, and I'm not to say anything negative about the boat while we're under sail. I get that. But yesterday was tough on me. I know you were stressed, but—"

"You're damn right I was stressed," he interjected. "But I had it all under control."

"Maybe you did, I mean, I'm sure you did, but did you take any notice of my reaction? Did you have any awareness of how I felt?"

"Why don't you tell me, Beth?" His voice took on a mocking tone. "Tell me all about your feelings."

She ignored the dig. "I was scared, Mark. And I didn't feel you cared one bit. And that's not all. I've been scared or out of my comfort zone or unhappy, or whatever you want to call it, a lot since we moved down here."

He waved a dismissive hand. "You've said all this before. I don't want to hear it again." He returned to the kitchen for more coffee.

"I know you don't, Mark, but I've got to say *something*. I came here for you because I love you. I left a job I liked, friends, activities, my home, my safety net to be with you. I left what worked for me to build together what would work for us. But it feels like from the day we crossed the state line, I've had to play second mate to what *you* want. It doesn't feel like *us* anymore. It feels like it's all about you."

Her words seemed to echo against the stucco walls. She held her arms out with palms upward. *I'm finished,* the gesture said.

"What do you want me to say?" he asked at last. "You're unhappy. I get it. You miss your job, your friends. What else, Beth? What else are you unhappy about that you need to say right now?" His shoulders dropped, and he dropped onto the sofa beside her.

She looked at him, feeling both drawn and repelled. Part of her wanted to put an arm around him and apologize. But part of her wanted to push her point home.

"I guess that's it," she said at last. "I guess that covers it. But here's a suggestion. Why don't you move onto the boat?"

He turned and looked at her, his face registering surprise.

"I'm not saying forever, but just for a while. Let's have a cooling off period. You know, like in sports? Isn't that why there's halftime? For the players to catch their breaths and regroup? If you stay on the boat, you'll have time to make all the repairs and improvements. After all, if you intend to sail down through the islands, you need to spend more than a weekend on it." She crossed her arms. "I need some time to think, and you do too." She nodded once and then stood and walked to the bedroom. A few moments later, she heard him walking down the hallway and out the door.

Beth lay on the bed and watched the slow spin of the ceiling fan, trying to ease the aching of her heart, wondering whether she had weathered a squall but unleashed a storm.

CHAPTER TWENTY-SIX

*W*ith a proud smile, Beth handed the wrapped picture across the counter to the customer. It was the first time her boss had allowed her to complete a job from start to finish. She had talked with the client about the color scheme of her home and where the art would hang before suggesting several prints. After much discussion, the customer selected Beth's favorite print by Chas Rowe. It featured deep turquoise water flowing along banks of lush yellow-green foliage, their feathered shapes reflected in the stream. The colors were rich, but what made the print special in Beth's mind was the single egret in the foreground, reaching its orange beak toward something below the water's surface. Beth convinced the customer to let the print speak for itself and not overwhelm it with multiple mats. Her boss had disagreed. Mats drove up the price and the profits. But Beth stood firm on using a single white mat, and now the customer's smile told her everything she needed to know. She had nailed it.

When the customer left, she pulled out her phone, wanting to share the moment with Mark. But then she stopped. How many days had it been? She ticked them off on her fingers. Ten. She knew it had to be uncomfortable for him living in this heat on the boat. She felt bad about it. Probably she should break the ice and tell him to come back to the house. Maybe make a meal and watch *Key Largo,* his favorite movie. For a moment, she blamed herself for their argument. She needed to do a better job adapting. But then she caught herself. Why should she always be the one? Why should she twist herself into a human pretzel to please him?

Maybe she would invite Alisa and Grant for a visit. It was time to surround herself with friends. And who knows? Mark might like showing them around the area. Taking them out on the boat, that sort of thing.

She locked the shop door behind her just as her phone rang. A broad grin stretched across her face.

"Hi," she said, her voice soft.

"Guess who?" Mark asked and then chuckled.

She waited.

"Any chance you might be free tonight? I mean, I know you have a busy social schedule and might not accept a last-minute date, but I thought I'd take a chance."

"Is this when I'm supposed to say your place or mine?"

"Let's make it yours. Mine's crowded and, well, the bed is lumpy."

"Lumpy beds are so last year."

"How about takeout food? Is that last year too?"

"Takeout is always welcome, especially if served by a handsome man."

"Then, baby, your delivery is on its way."

Beth clicked off and held the phone to her chest. There was something charming about Mark, no doubt. She had forgotten that. She would probe him tomorrow whether he had learned anything about her deeper needs in their time apart.

But for now, makeup sex was in order.

CHAPTER TWENTY-SEVEN

" Here's the rules," Alisa said." She unscrolled a sheet of paper as if it were the US Constitution. "Rule number one: When boats are on opposite tacks, a port-tack shall keep clear of a starboard-tack boat. Rule number two: When boats are on the same tack and overlapped, a windward boat shall keep clear of a leeward boat." She laid the paper down. "Shall I go on?"

Beth glanced at Mark before replying, trying to read the set of his shoulders. "Sure," she answered. "Go ahead. We're just bobbing in the water anyway, without wind."

She laid her head back and closed her eyes. She had made a vow: no confrontations for the weekend. No matter what Mark did or said, she would not react. After a good three weeks of harmony, they were back in a strained place. When he moved back home from the boat a month earlier, he had seemed eager to reassure her of his love. Their first weekend together, they attended a dock party hosted by the sailing school. Throughout the evening, Mark kept an arm around Beth's shoulder in a protective, even possessive, manner – not committing to join any of the summer trips down through the islands that other sailors were planning. "It's up to Beth," he said at one point, and she gave him a tight smile and took a long draw on her beer. *Just like old times on the lake,* she'd thought – the guys downing beers and their wives or girlfriends clustered together around the food. Out on the dock, she spied the only person she knew – a masseuse at the club named Wendi, who crewed often for other captains. A few years older than Beth, she seemed to know everyone. Beth waved at her and watched as Wendi leaned her head against a bearded guy's shoulder. He kissed the top of her head.

Love is in the April air, she concluded, as Mark smiled down at her, which had made it the perfect time to invite Alisa and Grant, her favorite lovebirds, for a visit. She wanted them to see how well she and Mark were getting along. Mark agreed when she asked him that night after the dock party, but something happened as the date drew near. A subtle shift, but still noticeable. Mark came home later and later from work, and as the weeks passed, he often fell asleep on the couch. "Stop trying to control me," he had snapped one night when Beth asked what was wrong.

So once again, here she sat – trying to read Mark's mood while seated between her two favorite people. Having them by her side felt like being swathed in a warm blanket. In fact, when they arrived the night before, the three of them had pulled together in a tight hug until Beth realized how awkward it must have felt for Mark. She reached for him, but he turned his back. From that moment on, the tension between them was as heavy as the humidity.

Alisa picked the paper back up and cleared her throat. "Rule number three: When boats are on the same tack and not overlapped, a boat clear astern shall keep clear of a boat clear ahead." She looked up. "What the heck does that mean?" When no one answered, she continued. "Rule number four: After a boat passes head to wind, she shall keep clear of other boats until she is on a close-hauled course. During that time, rules ten, eleven, and twelve do not apply."

She laid the paper aside with a flourish, and Grant hugged her to him. "That's good, honey, but I think Mark knows the rules. We're just here to help pull lines. Isn't that right, Mark? We're your crew."

Mark didn't answer.

"He didn't hear you," Beth said at last. "He's looking for wind."

Grant looked at her, and then at Mark, and narrowed his eyes. "This is racing. Right? This is what you do on Sundays?"

Beth again waited for Mark to answer. "I don't so much," she said, cutting her eyes toward him. "But Mark does. He gets other people to crew. I just find it...." She glanced at Mark, unsure whether to say anything more. They were still tiptoeing around one another.

Grant nodded his head, completing her thought. "And how long does a race take?"

Beth again glanced at Mark. "Several hours. Right, Mark? Sometimes five, if the wind is nonexistent like today." She pointed below. "That's why I packed sandwiches and beer." She smiled. "We may be here awhile."

"That must be nice for you," Alisa said. "I mean, you can read and get a tan if you come along, or shop or go have your nails done when you don't race."

Beth released a short laugh. "Right, well, getting my nails done or shopping requires a trip to Ft. Myers, so...."

Mark turned toward them. "What am I hearing here? You're not enjoying yourselves? Do you want me to drop out of the race?"

All eyes turned to him.

"No one's saying that," Beth answered, after an awkward silence.

She drew a deep breath, something she had done a lot of since their company had arrived. "What's wrong?" she had hissed at him the night before, as they crawled into bed. But he didn't answer.

She looked again at her friends and then back to Mark. "But it's not the greatest day for sailing, and since Grant and Alisa are only here for the weekend...."

Mark made an exasperated sound and pressed the ignition button. The engine sputtered and then caught. Grant and Alisa exchanged a look.

"Fine," he said, as he turned the boat and lowered the mainsail.

"Maybe we could motor out to Cabbage Key and get a cheeseburger," Beth suggested. She turned to Grant and Alisa. "It's a restaurant on Pine Island, and supposedly Jimmy Buffett wrote 'Cheeseburger in Paradise' after eating there. We've been meaning to go, but...."

Grant clapped his hands together. "Then let's get four cheeseburgers and enjoy this beautiful weather in paradise.

How's that sound, Rocky Top?" He reached for Beth and hugged her to him. "I miss your smile," he said, and Alisa nodded in agreement. "Let's get that smile back on your face."

Thirty minutes later, Mark motored into the wharf and threw the harbormaster a line to secure the boat, before nodding to the others that they could step off. He trailed behind them as they approached the restaurant.

"I love it," said Alisa, as they crossed the patio and climbed the wooden stairs to the tin-roof front porch.

Beth watched as her eyes traveled the grounds. "Those are royal palm trees and cabbage palms over there," Beth said, pointing to the undergrowth. "They hold the ground in place during harsh weather."

"It's perfect," Alisa said. "Totally natural. But it could use some red pillows on those chairs over there to pull the color from these potted plants."

"Now don't start redesigning paradise, honey," Grant said, in a joking voice. "This is authentic old Florida." He turned around. "Right, Mark?"

When Mark didn't respond, Beth tensed.

"And over there," Alisa continued. "Aren't those little wooden cottages just darling? Blue shutters would be perfect."

Oh, dear, Beth thought, as she watched Grant follow Mark into the bar. *Please don't be rude,* she wanted to say.

"Talk to me," Alisa said, once she and Beth returned to the porch with their rum runners. "Grant and I are worried. You don't seem happy."

Beth gave her a tight-lipped smile. "Guess I'm not doing too good hiding it."

Alisa nodded and stirred her drink with a swizzle stick. "I know how hard marriage can be, especially the first year. When we first married, Grant was gone constantly. Always working. Even evenings and weekends. It put a real strain on our relationship."

"What did you do?"

"I sat him down and had a talk with him. I told him that our marriage was more important than any single job and that at the end of his days, he would be asking for more time with his family and not with a client. I told him that if he really valued me and the children, he would make us the priority. No one's resume is listed on a tombstone. It's their relationships."

Beth nodded. "How did that go over?"

"It took some time, but gradually he changed. His father was such a go-getter. I think Grant believed he needed to best his dad at everything. But then he realized that inside, he wasn't happy. All the promotions he was getting at work weren't near enough to offset what he was losing at home. So, he changed." She took a long drink from her glass, then set it down. "The rest, as they say, is history."

Beth looked toward the water's edge. A blue heron walked gingerly across the shore, picking one long leg up and sitting it back down as if concerned the ground beneath it would give way. "I'm not sure how that speech would go over with Mark," she said, as she pushed her sunglasses on top of her head. "There's so much more I want out of life than," she extended her arms outward, "this. But he's totally happy."

Her eyes traveled to the dock. A family stepped off a small ferry that made round trips from Ft. Myers. Two children scampered around their parents and ran along the boardwalk. The man reached for the woman's hand. She smiled up at him. *Why can't it be that way with me and Mark?* she wondered. Not just reaching for one another's hands, but for one another's hearts? Were they so different that their marriage was no stronger than— she searched for a comparison and looked down at her glass— the rum in this drink?

She set her glass aside with disgust. Alisa drew her close. "You're in a hard place, sweetie. But I want you to know that Grant and I are here for you. That's why we jumped at the invitation – to make sure you knew that anything you need from us, we stand ready to do."

Beth squeezed her hand. "I may take you up on that."

"You got it, Rocky Top. We're your family. Don't forget it."

***

Later, when the two women returned to the bar, it took a moment for Beth's eyes to adjust from the brightness out-doors. But then she saw Mark. As she watched, he drew on his beer and leaned against the bar. His tanned face looked rugged against his white T-shirt. His long limbs were roped with muscle. For a moment, he looked as he had the night they met. Handsome. Desirable. Only now, instead of Beth in the seat beside him, he was glaring at a television mounted behind the bar. Grant sat next to him, pointing at the numer-ous dollar bills affixed to the walls and ceilings, probably wondering about the story behind them. The men looked to be on their second beer, but from their postures, Beth could see that the alcohol had done nothing to make them buddies. Mark practically had his back turned.

Grant saw Beth coming and nudged him. She took the bar stool Grant pulled out for her.

"Hey, you," she said when Mark turned around. "What's going on?"

He took another long drag on his beer. "I was just telling your friend how great it is to live down here." He gestured to the windows that framed the blue waters and green foliage of the island. "I told him I'd be on that water every day, if I could." He turned to Grant. "Tell me, man to man," he said, placing his empty bottle on the bar. "Wouldn't you rather be here than stuck up in Atlanta?" He wiped his mouth with the back of his hand. "Beth's an idiot for not realizing how great this place is." He turned to her. "Sorry, babe. But you are."

She felt the sweat cool on her arms. *You're an idiot. You're an idiot.* How many times had she said that to herself, espe-cially in college, when her world changed? From that day on, she had second-guessed every decision she made, like a run-ner stuck between second and third base. She drew a breath and looked first at Grant's shocked face and then Alisa's, who moved to hug her. With only a moment's hesitation, Beth slipped off her stool and walked out the door. Grant and Alisa followed, leaving Mark standing alone.

CHAPTER TWENTY-EIGHT

The Kentucky Derby was running when Beth heard Mark's convertible round the corner. She tensed and flipped off the television. Back to reality. No need fantasizing about being in Louisville with a two-dollar bet and a big hat. Even a block away, she could hear Dave Matthews blaring from the car's stereo. Beth watched as Mark pulled into the driveway. His daughter, Heather, was in the passenger seat – a black ball cap pulled low on her face, her bare feet up on the console. Beth snorted. The first time she and Mark had driven to Chattanooga, he chided her for doing the same thing. Now she wondered how he kept his mouth shut in the hour drive from the Ft. Myers airport.

After Alisa and Grant drove away three weeks earlier, Beth standing in the driveway and waving until their car was out of sight, she had struggled with her annoyance toward Mark. "You were rude to them," she had told him. "And that remark about me being an idiot was hurtful."

"Sorry," he had said, in a tone that meant the opposite. Plus, he now was becoming critical of little things about her, like the books she read and the care she took with her appearance. "Who are you trying to impress?" he asked one morning as he headed out.

Now a part of her – an ugly part, she had to admit – wanted him to experience a visit going sideways. Heather was the obvious person to invite.

But underneath her annoyance at Mark was another motivation for inviting Heather. She felt sorry for her, even at times identified with her. She had reasons for acting out, Beth believed – shuffled between two parents who apparently never forgave one another for whatever wrongs had occurred. Mark always blamed the ex for Heather's problems, but in Beth's thinking, Mark had a big part in it too. If Beth could help improve the relationship, she would do it. *Who knows?* Beth wondered. Perhaps she and Heather had more in common than she realized.

Fingers crossed, she thought as the car came to a stop. *Fingers crossed.*

Heather was out of the car first, slamming the door behind her. She wore a pair of frayed blue-jean shorts and black gladiator sandals that extended past her calves. *Keep your laws off my body,* her sweatshirt proclaimed. Beth wondered what her conservative father thought about that. She suppressed a smile. She didn't plan to ask him.

Beth gave Heather a slight hug before grabbing her quilted duffle bag from the back seat. Heather pulled back, ready to maintain her space.

"Come on in," Beth said. "I've got lunch ready unless you'd like to take a shower or relax first."

"Cool," Heather answered, following Beth into the house. She dropped her purse on the floor before walking to the lanai. "Is there a pool nearby?" Her voice sounded brittle.

"Just down the street. We can walk or bike to it."

Heather didn't respond. Beth looked at her back. From the tightness of her shoulders, she could tell she was nervous but trying to hide her discomfort behind a nonchalant attitude. Beth glanced at Mark. He was doing the same.

With a quick shake of her head, she put a pitcher of lemonade on the counter and tossed a salad. While they ate, she waited for Mark to speak, occasionally nudging his foot with hers. Finally, she couldn't stand the awkward silence anymore.

"Here's an idea," she announced, her voice higher than her normal pitch. "Why don't I pack a cooler with drinks, and we can all go to the pool?" She turned to Heather. "We have some floats in the garage, and I've got an assortment of magazines perfect for poolside reading. Afterward, I'll run by the grocery, if you'll tell me what you like to eat. That will give you and your dad a chance to catch up. Sound good?"

Beth looked from Heather to her father, their faces similar.

"Whatever," Heather responded, her voice disinterested.

Beth stared at Mark, eyebrows raised to her hairline. "Are you in?"

He shifted in his chair before standing. "You know what? Why don't I get the groceries, and you two hit the pool? I've got some other stuff I need to take care of today."

***

As Heather floated in the pool, Beth fumed. Once again, Mark was all about himself. *It's your daughter, for God's sake,* she fumed. What success did she have drawing them closer together if he didn't put forth an effort? She watched Heather flip onto her stomach and untie her top, exposing a snake tattoo that extended from her neck to her butt.

Bet her daddy would have something harsh to say about that, Beth thought. She flicked away a mosquito. Something was wrong in the Berger family portrait. But what to do about it? She picked up a float and walked into the shallow end. If you can't beat them, she reasoned, you work on a tan. What was that Scarlett O'Hara quote about thinking about it tomorrow? She stretched her arms above her head. Good advice.

***

"So?" she asked Mark that night when they were in bed. They could hear the television in Heather's room tuned to *The Bachelor.* "What are your plans for the week?"

He turned a page in his *Sailing* magazine. "Plans? You mean with Heather?"

"Yes, with your daughter. We've already talked about this. How do you want to entertain her?"

"Hadn't given it much thought. I figured you would take her shopping one day, and I'll take her out on the boat. You can come if you want," he added as an afterthought.

Beth felt tightness begin in her chest. This was not going well. "Alright. That's two days. What else?"

"What do you mean, what else?" He sounded puzzled. "She's not a child. She can entertain herself. I've already got a busy week planned. Hanging out at the pool seemed to work today. Can't she just do that for the week?"

"Don't you want to spend time with her and let her know you're glad she's here? I mean, the point of the visit was for us to make her feel part of our family."

"*I* thought the point of the visit was for her to catch some sun. What's the need for an itinerary?" He returned his attention to his article.

Beth struggled not to snatch the magazine out of his hands. "Okay, fine," she said at last. "We'll play it by ear," realizing that somewhere along the way she had become passive-aggressive. She waited, trying to control her aggravation, but then couldn't help herself. "Can you at least make some spa appointments for her at the club? Every girl likes that. I'd do it, but it would be nice coming from you."

He flipped to another article and didn't answer.

"Come on, Mark," she said. "That's not a hard thing to do for your daughter."

"Fine, Beth, fine," he muttered. "I'll call the club."

"And another thing – I could bring her to your tennis tournament. Let her see her old man in action." This was her trump card. If an activity focused on him, he was in.

He looked up from his magazine. "You think she would enjoy that?"

"Of course she would," she said. "She's here to build a relationship."

He sat silently in thought. Beth felt a glimmer of excitement. She was getting through to him. *Hallelujah*, she thought. "And with the television so loud," she added, "maybe I can see her old man in action right now."

Mark tossed aside the magazine and pulled her to his chest.

***

"Here's some water and aspirin," Beth said. "That should help take some of the pain away. You're running a low-grade fever too. I'll come back later and rub more aloe cream on your shoulders."

"It's just a sunburn," Heather answered, as she settled into bed. "No big deal."

"I know, but I feel responsible. I had no idea Mark's match would last that long. I should have noticed your shoulders getting burned. It happened to me when we first moved here. The sun is brutal. Maybe tomorrow, after I'm off work, we could drive to Ft. Myers and catch a movie. Keep you out of the sun for the day."

Beth turned off the light beside the bed. "Yell if you need anything, okay?"

"Can I ask you something?" Heather said as Beth was closing the door. "Tell me to mind my own business if you want, but who's this Wendi person? I mean, is she a good friend of yours?"

Beth turned. "You mean Wendi down at the club? That Wendi?"

"Yeah." Heather rolled onto her side and propped herself on an elbow. "She did my massage yesterday morning, and the entire time, she kept talking about Dad like they were best buddies – like she knew everything about him. She was at the tennis tournament too. I figured she must be a friend of yours."

Beth grew still. "I suppose she's a friend," she said at last. "We chat when I'm at the club. And I know she sails and crews for races. I saw her at a dock party."

"Okay," said Heather, as she lay back down on her stomach. "Just curious. She was talkative and kept asking questions about you and Dad."

Beth felt a cold sweat break on her forehead. She wiped it away as she pushed aside her bangs. "It's a small town," she said at last. "Everybody seems to know everything about everybody. You know...."

Beth closed the door and went into the living room. She collapsed on the sofa and drew a pillow to her lap. When Lizzie jumped up to join her, Beth pulled the cat close, hoping to draw warmth and comfort from her small body. It didn't work. Heather's words had exposed a raw nerve – a worrisome feeling she had had for the past month and hadn't been able to put into words. Now she had the words: Mark might be cheating on her.

She pictured Wendi at the dock party: tall, athletic, loud voice, sun-bleached hair. Always wore low-cut workout tops that showed off her muscular back and ample breasts. Without wanting to, Beth's mind shifted to the days when Mark lived on the boat. How long ago was that? Two months, maybe?

No, she kept telling herself. *No way.* She absently stroked Lizzie, as her mind formulated pictures. Mark throwing a casual arm around Wendi when they greeted one another at the club. His low chuckle on the phone when he arranged for her to crew with him for Sunday races. The times he would leave the house on the pretext of forgetting something in his school office and come home hours later.

Tears welled in her eyes and crawled down her cheeks. *No*, her heart cried. Mark wasn't that type of guy. No way would he be unfaithful. She squeezed her eyes tight to stop the tears. This wasn't happening. She would know. Mark loved her. He was committed to their marriage. *He isn't a cheater*, she told herself. *He isn't.*

But still, as she fought back the tears and listened to Lizzie's gentle purr, feeling the light, steady heartbeat under her palm, she wondered . . . and worried.

CHAPTER TWENTY-NINE

" Hurry. We're late," Beth called, as she removed the peach cobbler from the oven. She placed it on a cooling rack and then covered it with a kitchen towel. The recipe was her grandmother's and had been a Gardiner family staple. Beth had tweaked it some over time— adding more cinnamon to the topping and cutting back on the amount of sugar used to sweeten the peaches— but it was, essentially, the same dessert she had eaten after most Sunday dinners. In the summer, her mother had topped it with homemade vanilla ice cream – the custard kind – but in winter they used store-bought. It was one of the few pleasant memories she had of her mother – cooking the custard on the stovetop, allowing Beth to lick the spoon.

Beth checked the time. "Mark!" she called again.

Since Heather had left, she had replayed their conversation many times. *No*, she kept telling herself. Heather was wrong. Beth would have felt it in her bones. Seen it on his face. Tasted it in a kiss. Plus, they were back to getting along, even talking about taking a second honeymoon. It was just a phase they were going through. Hadn't the past two weeks been perfect? She looked at the roses on the dining room table. Those didn't come from a cheater.

"Stop nagging," he said, as he walked down the hall and into the bedroom. "I just got home five minutes ago. Had to meet with the principal. Some bullshit about a kid."

"But you knew what time the party started." She went no further. No need to risk an argument. Not now. She had hoped, if they had a good time tonight, Mark would drive to Clearwater for a dance weekend. All her Atlanta dance friends were coming. Perhaps Mark would agree to some private lessons. Maybe then they would have an activity in common.

They weren't into the same things at home. That was evident. Even if they drove to the club together, he was into spin class and weights, and Beth liked aerobics and yoga – one to get her moving and one to get her stretched. Plus, Mark didn't like to play tennis with her. She wasn't good enough, he told her. That left only biking and running. She hated running, especially in Florida. Anything but running.

Mark's phone rang as he was getting out of the shower. From the way he sounded, she knew it was Heather. He came into the living room with a towel draped around him and signaled for Beth to bring him something to drink. "I know, Heather, I know," he said. "You're right, but you can't chew out the restaurant manager in front of other staff and expect not to get fired."

Beth could hear Heather's voice rising on the other end of the line. She grabbed a beer from the refrigerator and took it to him. He nodded his thanks.

"He's a jerk. I'm sure you're right. But listen, Beth's signaling for me to hang up. We've got some party to go to." He listened more. "We'll talk tomorrow." He put down the phone.

"I wasn't trying to get you to hang up," Beth said.

"Drop it. I'm irritated enough as it is." He walked back into the bedroom.

She took the cobbler from the counter. "We'll go in my car," she called to him but got no answer. Ten minutes later, he joined her.

They were at the end of their street when his phone rang again. "Don't answer it," Beth suggested, but he took the call.

"Yeah," he said and then listened. "No, you can't quit your lease. That will go on your credit rating." He listened more. "No, Heather. Don't do that." More listening. "I'll call you tomorrow. Or call your mother. You two can figure it out." He ended the call.

Beth could tell from the color of his face he was crossing over from irritated to angry. "What's happening?" she asked. "Is she in trouble?" He didn't answer. "What's happening, Mark? Talk to me."

"Stop the car," he yelled.

"What?"

"Stop the damn car. I'm in no mood for a party."

She braked, but before the car stopped, he flung open the door and stumbled to the ground.

"Mark!" she yelled and jerked open her door. "What the hell are you doing?"

He looked around, then, seeing a length of rebar, picked it up. He looked at her.

"Oh, my God." Beth jumped back into the car. Just as she got it into gear, she glanced at the rearview mirror and saw Mark take a swing. The car jolted with the impact to the rear bumper and a shock wave reverberated in her heart.

For a moment, she froze – her eyes locked to his. He was breathing hard, the bar still in his hands, the sound of metal on metal still ringing in her ears. When he took a step toward the car, she hit the gas and drove – down unfamiliar streets, turning onto back roads, before pulling over beneath an underpass to the interstate. She sat there with her head on the steering wheel and her hands pressed to her face.

She took long, deep breaths, and when her heart rate slowed, she reclined the seat. The sunroof was open, and she stared at the overpass. The concrete beams were covered with grime from engine exhaust, and the air smelled of gasoline and rotted vegetation. Without realizing it, she counted cars as they rumbled across the overpass. When she got to fifty, she raised the seat. *Don't tell anyone your business*, she heard her mother caution. That had been the Gardiner family motto. Not *love thy neighbor as thyself.* That would have been too easy.

Of course, she had driven straight to her mother that day in college. Of course, she had believed that was the right thing to do. *And look what happened*, she now thought, as she stared at her face in the rearview mirror. *And look what has happened now.* Not knowing what else to do, she put the car into gear and made a U-turn.

Ten minutes later, she eased onto the shoulder of a familiar street only four blocks from her house. Parked cars lined both sides of the road. Leaning her head once more against the steering wheel, she drew deep breaths. Her heart was still racing, and her whole body shook. When a couple walked by and noticed her, she faked looking for something on the floor of the car. With one hand, she felt in her purse, hoping to find a prescription bottle before remembering that those pills had been flushed down the toilet a year ago. But she located eye drops, and with a straightening of her back, doctored her eyes. Once the redness cleared, she fluffed her hair and opened the car door. *Showtime*, she thought.

Forcing herself to walk, she followed another couple into the house. "Shit," she murmured as soon as she saw the buffet table. She had forgotten the peach cobbler in the back seat. She turned toward the door just as Clare, the hostess, waved to her. "I forgot my dish," she mouthed. But Clare waved her over, holding a bottle of white wine and two glasses above her head.

Beth willed her body to relax and followed her to the patio.

The two women knew one another from the club. They had the type of friendship where they chatted before yoga or played tennis from time to time. Not close friends, but Beth had hoped she and Mark would get to know Clare and her husband better at the party. That wasn't happening now, and Beth didn't want to think about what awaited her at home.

She looked around. The house was on a deep-water canal that opened into the harbor with a view worthy of a tourist brochure. Beth could see the couple's sailboat a short walk from the pool deck. Lounge chairs, potted palm trees, and umbrellas were placed so guests could lounge and watch the sunset. *This is how the other half lives*, she thought.

"Love your place," she told Clare, not knowing what else to say. Across the pool, she saw Wendi draped onto a lounge chair, talking to a guy Beth didn't recognize. Beth gave her a weak wave hello. Wendi seemed not to notice.

"Thanks," Clare said. "I handled the remodeling. It was a lot of work but worth every penny. The tiles were imported from Italy and the wood from Brazil." She greeted another couple as they walked by, and then turned back to Beth. "Where's Mark?"

Beth had rehearsed a response walking from the car. "He got back late from teaching sailing and was bushed ...." She shrugged her shoulders and took a drink of wine.

Clare gave her a questioning look but didn't pursue it further. Beth rolled her shoulders to release tension and finished her glass. When Clare offered a refill, she nodded.

It was like that for the rest of the evening. Meeting couples. Answering questions. Explaining why Mark wasn't with her. *Why move to Porto Verde?* they all seemed to wonder. *Damned if I know,* Beth wanted to answer. Most of the guests had retired here or were winter snowbirds. Few were like her and Mark – fulltime residents, still in their thirties, and far from retirement. She waited until Clare was busy with other guests before making her exit.

She prolonged the drive home as much as possible before easing her car into the garage beside Mark's. Drinking wine had given her false courage at the party. Now she had none.

She stared at the door leading into the house. Her parents had never argued the way she and Mark did, she realized, and her father would never have raised a hand against her mother. Never. Their form of disagreement was more the cold stare, the overly polite remark, the stillness that would settle on the house and not melt for days. Beth knew when the frost came she needed to be on her best behavior and do nothing to upset her mother. Often, she would walk to her grandparents' house with a book tucked under her arm. Her papaw would take one look at her and pat a seat beside him. Her grandma would join them, bringing her quilting. Later, Papaw would walk her home, holding her hand the whole way.

Those days seemed a lifetime ago.

Mark was sitting in the living room and stood when she walked in and sat the uneaten cobbler on the counter. He held a bouquet.

"Look, I'm sorry," he said and moved to hug her.

Beth backed away, behind a chair. She picked up a pillow and held it to her chest. Lizzie jumped onto the seat, and she scratched her head in an abstracted way.

She stared at him. "You came after me," she said at last. "You swung a metal pipe at me and hit my car."

He bit his lip. "I wasn't coming after you. I was frustrated. Work. Heather..." his voice trailed off. "I've got things on my mind. I just needed to punch a wall." He swallowed. "I'll take care of the car."

"But you came at me," Beth said again. "I was scared. Do you have any idea how that affected me? I mean, if you only knew..." Beth stopped herself. Now was not the time to go into something from long ago.

"I know, I know," Mark was saying. "I was in the wrong."

Beth drew a breath, bringing her thoughts back to the present. "Well, keep that in mind the next time you lose your temper or want to take it out on me when something isn't going right."

"Got it. Enough. I've apologized. Okay?" He extended the flowers toward her. "It won't happen again."

She regarded him and then accepted the bouquet. "Remember, Mark. No one touches me or threatens me. Especially you."

He nodded. "How can I make things up to you?"

Beth sat the flowers aside. "I don't know. But I'll think of something and let you know. Right now, I'm going to bed. This might be a good time for you to give me some space."

She turned away, leaving the flowers lying on the table.

CHAPTER THIRTY

*B*eth caught up with Mark at the top of the St. Augustine Lighthouse, bending over to catch her breath, with her hands on her knees. She had to stop three times before completing the 219 spiraled steps but was determined to take in the view overlooking Mantanza Bay and the Atlantic Ocean. Just like she was determined to save her marriage. That's what she and Mark had agreed to when they sat down and talked.

"I married you for better or worse," Beth told him. "Now's a good time for the better to begin."

The trip was supposed to be a fresh start. "Our second honeymoon," she had told Mark. She said the same thing to Helen. She, like Dr. Em in Atlanta, still urged Beth to include Mark in their sessions, but Beth had all but put her hands to her ears about suggesting this to him. Plus, she had downplayed what happened to her car, saying Mark was stressed by work.

Now, as she took in the cloudless sky, she thought again about the night of the party. It had been a month, and Mark had not yet fixed her car. Each time she went into the garage, she stared at the dent in the bumper and relived her fright. She could still see the swinging of the metal bar, feel the shock, taste the fear that worked up her throat. Never again would she think of peach cobbler without remembering the smell in the car as she pressed the gas pedal.

Now, as she stood at the top of the lighthouse, she tried to order her thoughts and take great cleansing breaths, the way she did in yoga. But her worries interfered with her serenity. Either something had changed in Mark since their marriage, or she had missed something fundamental when they were dating. He had everything he wanted. The water, the job, the boat. Had she been that blind to his core nature when they were dating? Was his temper more than his standard expletive at a bad line call in a tennis match? Was something other than work bothering him? She took off her dark glasses and turned her face to the sun, hoping its rays could beam insight.

Mark already had his binoculars to his eyes when she joined him on the lookout and was scanning the horizon as if watching for passing ships. Without speaking, he passed the glasses to her. She adjusted them and mimicked his stance, zooming in on pelicans that were dive-bombing for fish, before turning her gaze to the coastline. She blurred the glasses, so the scene looked like swashes of blue, white, and green fabric.

A new perspective, she thought. That's what she needed. She had visited lighthouses in the past on the North Carolina Outer Banks, but as she turned in a circle, she agreed with the hotel desk clerk who recommended they visit this structure on Anastasia Island. Striped black and white, with a cherry red lantern room, surrounded by a garden and outbuildings, overlooking a picturesque town and bay— it appeared the perfect seaside village, just as she and Mark seemed the perfect couple to an outsider.

She handed the glasses back to him. Appearances were deceiving.

They had arrived late the night before and spent most of the day wandering the historic area of the city. While the town had elements of Old Florida, including the wooden schoolhouse and the old jail, like most tourist towns, it boasted far too many tacky souvenir shops and over-priced clothing stores, Beth decided. She loved to shop but was disappointed and settled on a sea glass charm as a souvenir. Or, at least, the sales-clerk said it was sea glass. It could have been plastic for all Beth knew.

The second honeymoon was not going as planned, she admitted, as she clambered down the iron stairs.

***

By late afternoon, Mark lagged Beth as they entered the main structure of Flagler College – a gilded, turn-of-the-

century former hotel that now served as offices and class-
rooms for the school. "You're on your own," he told her,
passing on the guided tour.

Now, as she stood in front of the Tiffany windows and chan-
deliers, she was glad she could admire the handiwork by
herself. Mark wouldn't have appreciated the construction the
way Beth did. The spacious rotunda supported by solid oak
pillars. The light that filtered through the stained-glass windows. She sat on a bench in front of a mural, envisioning
herself pausing between dances at one of the elegant balls that
once took place there. She drank from her water bottle, its
warm taste a far cry from the crisp champagne she'd imagined.

"Ready to go?"

She turned and saw Mark's dark shape framed in the doorway by the brilliant sun. He had his hands in his pockets and
the bill of his hat pulled so low it seemed to rest on the top of
his dark glasses. He motioned to her and then walked back
out the door. Beth stood and took one more look around before following him.

That night, after wandering the town looking at menus,
they settled on the Kingfish Grill, a seafood place near the
harbor. Mark had muttered at each place about the "jacked-
up" prices before Beth said, "Let's just split something." *Honestly*, she thought, as she ordered the house white wine, *could
he not at least try to enjoy himself?* She felt her chest tightening and again tried her yoga breathing. It still wasn't working.

As they waited for their food, Beth watched the locals gathered at the bar and felt a pang of loneliness for the dancing
friends she once had at Flamingo Joe's in suburban Atlanta.
They would gather there on Thursday and Saturday evenings
– talking, laughing, dancing until all hours— and then call
one another to say they had arrived home. Just like a family.
She looked at Mark, who was staring out the window toward
the harbor, and wondered what scene from his past he might
be envisioning.

It was still early in the evening when they walked back to
their inn – not speaking, not holding hands, just walking. On

the drive to St. Augustine, Beth had convinced herself that this trip would change the stalemate between them, but now the effort and failure weighed on her.

"Why are you working so hard to preserve this marriage?" Helen had asked at their last session.

"Because I want someone to be my partner in life," Beth had answered. "Because I'm tired of being the only single woman in a room full of married people. Because Mark needs me."

That's what he had said, as she turned away from the flowers he thrust toward her. "Baby, I need you," he said.

"You're in a marriage because you're needed?" Helen had asked.

Beth took her time answering. "I'm accustomed to being needed," she answered. "I'm experienced at it." When Helen remained silent, she continued. "I guess I learned early in life that if I busied myself taking care of others, I could keep my head below the drama that swirled above me."

"What you're experienced in," Helen had answered, "is absorbing and hiding the pain. What do you think would happen to Mark if you weren't in his life? More importantly," Helen pressed, "What do you need? Just a husband? Any husband? Or just Mark?" Beth didn't have an answer for that, not yet anyway.

"Give it thought," Helen had said at the end of their session. "A lot of thought."

Her words were inside Beth as they opened the door of their hotel room. Mark flipped on the television to the tennis channel and piled up pillows for his back on the bed. Beth looked at him and then at the screen. Andy Roddick was making a comeback, according to the announcer, and was up one set against Rafael Nadal. She thought of snuggling up to Mark but sat in a side chair and reached for Thomas Hardy's *Far From the Madding Crowd*. She and Mark had recently watched the old movie starring Julie Christie. While Mark had dozed off, she had found herself captivated by the dark, impenetrable eyes of Alan Bates, the co-star, and now was reading the book in search of insight into his character.

She was nearing the end of the story when Mark reached for the remote and turned off the tennis. "Let's drive back tomorrow."

She looked up, startled. Her attention had been so deep into the novel that at first, she wasn't sure she had heard him correctly. "Let's do what?" she asked.

"Drive back. I've got things I need to check on." He pulled off his jeans and T-shirt and then crawled under the covers in his boxers. "And remember, you said if we did this trip, you would join me for a lobster dive next month." He gestured around the room. "We've done it. And this place is costing an arm and a leg."

"But I thought we would take advantage of the room tomorrow," she began, her mind on images of a leisurely breakfast of scones and jam and plates piled high with fluffy scrambled eggs and Applewood bacon. Afterward, they would find a private beach and spend the afternoon there before returning to their spa tub and back into bed with a bottle of chilled champagne. Then, after making love, they might talk, *really* talk. She remembered times like that when they were first dating – how they would spend hours in bed, losing track of time. That was the Mark she married – a charming, romantic man. The person whose back was turned to her was someone she didn't know.

Putting aside her book, she watched him. Within five minutes, he was asleep. She shook her head in disgust at her romantic notions and thought back over the past month. When was the last time they had really good sex? She couldn't remember. Somehow, they had progressed from ardent lovers to a married couple who had sex once or twice a week, to living apart. What had caused that? And could it be fixed? Not just the sex, but the relationship? Helen's questions returned to haunt her.

And Wendi. God, how she hated that name. On occasions, she had nearly gathered her courage to ask Mark, "What is it with you two?" But she would lose her courage, or maybe it had nothing to do with courage. Maybe she was doing what

Lizzie always did – hiding at the first sign of danger. Avoiding conflict.

Beth laid aside her book and got her nightgown. It was made of soft blue cotton with a rounded neck, cap sleeves, and lace trim. She held it up.

When had she become someone who slept in a cotton nightgown? And when had Mark become the man who snored in his boxers?

“ It's a tradition," Mark told her, as they drove back from St. Augustine. Every year, at the start of lobster season, divers plunged into the waters off Key West in search of spiny lobsters. "It's a Florida thing," he kept saying.

"At midnight?" Beth questioned. "Does it have to be a night dive? Can't we just dive during the day?"

He looked at her as if one of his freshmen had challenged the need for pre-season training. "Are you kidding me? The whole point is to be the first in the water. That's the fun of it."

"I can name twenty things that sound like more fun in the Keys."

Even as she spoke, Mark shook his head like a bull. "We made a deal. Remember? I went to St. Augustine with you, and now you're lobster diving with me. The season starts at one-minute past midnight, and I plan for us to be in the water. We can each bag six that night and six the next day. That's the limit. Just think, baby," he said, reaching for her hand. "In two shallow dives, we can bag twenty-four lobsters. And the boat operator will clean them for us and pack 'em on ice."

"Why not," she answered, recognizing a brick wall when she saw one.

His plan was to drive to Islamorada after work the following Friday, check into a motel close to the dive center, grab some dinner, change into their gear, and then board the boat around eleven. The plunge into the ocean would be at midnight.

"But here's what we'll do if it makes you feel better," he offered. "We'll take one quick daylight dive at the site with the dive master as soon as we arrive. That way, you'll know the terrain. But it will cost more," he added.

"Great idea," she said, but still, she didn't feel safe about a night dive. Just the day before, she'd read an online article about a college football player who had died on a night lobster dive the previous season. "No bug is worth your life," the article had said, quoting the Florida Fish and Wildlife director. She had printed the article and handed it to Mark. A few minutes later, he wadded it into a ball and tossed it into a wastebasket.

"That guy was an idiot," he said. "He went in the water without a buddy like a dumb jock. You need to relax, Beth. I'll be right beside you. Nothing can go wrong."

***

That weekend, Beth followed him through a sporting goods store, pushing a shopping cart. As he headed toward the lobster nets on the opposite side of the store, he pulled a list from his pocket, jostling around shoppers who were in his way. The cart was already piled with tickle sticks, snares, measuring sticks, rubber gloves, scuba flags with reeled lines, and a mesh lobster hotel for storing their catches. In Beth's calculations, they had pulled well over two hundred dollars' worth of gear from the shelves, and that didn't even factor in the cost of fishing licenses, two nights in a motel, and the dive boat.

She thought again of the cost of one extra night in St. Augustine. It paled in comparison.

This is an awful big deposit into the love bank, she concluded. She had learned the concept from a relationship book, having spent an afternoon at a bookstore in Ft. Myers, perusing the self-help aisle. Now she was reading it for a second time, hiding it behind a fashion magazine like a teenage boy looking at porn. She wasn't ready to discuss the content with Mark. It wasn't that she was worried about 'saving' her marriage, as the author stated it. She was now convinced that nothing was going on with Wendi. But the book gave a clue for what might be wrong between them.

The author explained that sometimes couples lose their instinct to make each other happy. Their love bank balances get overdrawn, and they no longer meet their partner's emotional needs. When this happens, they need to make deposits into one another's love bank – do and say things to build back up the negative balances, before things take a turn for the worse.

Their love bank account was low, Beth had decided. She was determined to rectify it. Mark had made a deposit into hers by going to St. Augustine, even if the trip wasn't ideal. Now she would make her deposit by catching a lobster.

Give and take. That's what the book stressed.

As she followed him through the checkout line, she reminded herself of her resolve. The only problem, however, was that her survival instincts were fighting back hard. She thought again of the 'dumb jock.' Maybe the poor guy was diving to make a deposit into his girlfriend's love bank.

As Beth watched the clerk place their purchases in a large bag, she felt her stomach lurch, remembering the night dive on their honeymoon. She had protested that dive too, knowing as soon as she jumped into the black waters she was in trouble. Divers had been told to keep their torches pointed downward, but like a group of kids piling off a school bus for a field trip, lights were shining in all directions, causing the sea to feel like an underwater light show. She became blinded, disoriented, and couldn't tell up from down. In a state of panic, she even imagined she was under the boat and about to hit her head on the hull. Plus, that dive was in the same waters as the shark feed, and she could sense their sleek bodies and razor teeth coming closer with each foot they descended. She had jerked Mark's arm several times, adamantly pointing upward, before he had reluctantly joined her in ascending.

As they left the store, Mark smiled at her, and she looked at him like a celebrity assessing a new bodyguard. Hopeful, yet cautious. "It's not out in the middle of the ocean," he said, reading her mind. "It's shallow and close to shore. You'll be fine."

She straightened her back and reached for his hand. He squeezed it.

Maybe the relationship book was right, she decided. Maybe she just needed to build back up their love account balance. She had said as much when she last talked with Lori.

"Really, Beth?" her friend had replied. "You think you haven't deposited enough into his love account?"

***

It was five minutes until midnight, and Beth struggled to stand. Her scuba tank weighed close to fifty pounds, and her balance was further compromised by the amount of extra gear Mark had clipped to her dive vest. He planned to carry the lobster bag, but Beth still needed her own snare, tickle stick, measuring rod, dive flag, net, and light. The items clanged against her tank like a peddler's cart rolling down a cobbled road. Just a few hours earlier, when they made their exploration dive, none of these items were on her.

She pulled a massive rubber glove, which would protect her from the prickly backs of the lobsters, onto her right hand and then adjusted her mask and snorkel. Mark reached behind her and turned on her air. She inhaled and gave him a shaky okay sign. He grinned and handed her a dive torch with the light turned on.

The dive boat captain had paired Mark and Beth with two veteran divers. This was their tenth-year diving, and Mark was excited to learn from them. All the way to the dive site, he pelted the men with questions, not just about hunting lobsters but questions on their favorite deep dives and wrecks, the type dives Beth had little or no interest in doing. A part of her wished he would find another dive buddy to take these trips with, but she felt disloyal allowing this thought to cross her mind. Her mind flicked to Wendi and her athletic body. Maybe disloyalty wasn't the only reason she had made the trip. But now, as she stood at the rear of the boat and the captain signaled it was her turn to jump, she wished she were anywhere but here.

As the four descended, Beth reeled out the line that led back up to her dive flag. Because they would drift during the night and be unable to sight the boat above, the dive crew would scan the water, keeping an eye on everyone's flag.

As she touched down, she glanced at her gauge and saw they were at forty feet – ten feet deeper than Mark had indicated. He was already swimming ahead of her, fanning out from the other dive pair so as not to explore the same coral beds. Beth followed him, feeling her gear drag on the ocean floor. She watched Mark as he peeped under coral shelves and poked with his tickle stick. It wasn't long before he netted a lobster, but when he turned it over, it revealed the orange eggs of a female, and he let it go.

Beth released her snare from its clip and fired it a few times, just to get the feel of it. The salesman in the sporting goods store had convinced them this was the one piece of equipment guaranteed to catch lobster. The trick was to slip the noose around the neck and then fire the pen to tighten the loop. It seemed cruel. Maybe her yoga instructor had a point about being a vegetarian.

Her light cut through the dark and played across the coral reef, revealing its ridges and valleys. An outcropping, the color of a sunset, caught her attention. She inched a gloved hand forward, expecting it to give like a soft bath sponge. It was rock hard. On the ocean floor below, startled creatures scurried for hiding, their movements raising small clouds of sand from the lunar surface. In the distance, a murky shape swished. *Not a shark*, she told herself. That's what the dive master had said. *Not in these waters*. But still, in a night dive, anything was possible. She shivered despite her dive vest.

Turning away from the reef, she looked for a light, but all she saw was black water. No light beam. No blue fins. At forty feet below the surface, nothing was visible, she realized. Not even herself, in this all-black gear.

She wrapped her arms around herself, fighting off panic, but still it came, closing around her like a coffin. Only a few hours earlier, she had explored these same waters with the dive master. He had pointed out schools of turquoise fish and a seahorse hidden in a bed of orange fans. She had smiled at him, grateful for his presence. But tonight, as she peered through a fogged mask, all she saw was this inky black.

Nausea crawled up her throat, and she bent over, expecting to heave into her mask. "Oh, God," she whimpered, her heart beating rapidly like a triggerfish ready to attack. "Oh, God. Help me."

She turned again in a slow circle. A beam of light caught her eye. Swimming hard, she caught up to Mark, who appeared unaware he had left her behind. He held up two fingers to indicate his catch. Grabbing his arm, she gestured upward. He adamantly shook his head *no*, before swimming to the next coral outcropping. She did another three-sixty degree turn to look for the other dive pair but saw no one.

What seemed like an hour later, she checked her gauge to see how much air she had left, hoping Mark would realize it was time to surface. But she still had half a tank. The dive could last forever.

At that moment, a large lobster swam into view. She felt her pulse race and readied her snare. The lobster was swimming in a zigzag pattern, and she slowly closed the distance. She reached with her left hand and encircled it with the noose. Then she fired the trigger. The lobster lurched with more power than she had expected. It fought the snare and carried her bouncing along behind it. She looked over her shoulder, hoping to see Mark, but he was nowhere in sight. She felt another lurch from the lobster. It wasn't giving up the fight. She called Mark's name, but all that did was emit a cloud of bubbles. She looked at the lobster on the end of her snare and released it. It darted beneath a ledge.

She turned in another slow circle, shining her light in all directions. Nothing. She tried to orient herself back to where she had last seen Mark, but now, each coral boulder looked the same. "Oh, God," she began praying. "Oh, God. Oh, God. Oh, God."

She remembered the dive master. "Stay with your partner," he had stressed. "Surface when you're down to a quarter tank, and we'll bring the boat to you."

Beth began to cry big gulping tears. Her dive vest compressed her body, and her panic grew. Her mind flooded with all the training she had received about the proper speed to ascend and the risk of contracting the bends, but all that left her. She had to get to the surface.

With a crouch, she pushed her feet against the ocean floor and scissor-kicked to the surface. When her head popped up, she circled her light. "Mark," she yelled. "Help! Anybody!" She again turned in a circle, her voice sounding thin and weak in the night air. On her third turn, she saw boat lights some forty feet away and heard the revving of its motor. She grabbed the whistle from her vest and blew it, still waving the flashlight in the air. She kept blowing and waving her light until she felt the strong arms of a crewman pulling her onboard.

***

The silent ride back to Porto Verde allowed Beth time to think. She pictured again when Mark surfaced from the dark sea, looking like a creature from the deep – all bluster and vibrato. "What happened to you?" he yelled, as soon as he removed his mask. "Why didn't you keep up with us?"

But Beth turned away and refused to say a word to him – a vow she kept on the boat ride back to shore, through what little time they spent in their motel room, and during the next day's dive, where she sat on board without her gear, answering only with grunts or head nods.

She waited until they were inside their house before she looked at him and said, "You asshole."

"What?" he countered. "You're the one who got lost."

"No, Mark. You were my dive buddy, and you didn't look out for me. You were so concerned about catching your limit and impressing your new friends that you forgot your own wife on the bottom of the ocean."

His face turned red, his anger causing a vein in his neck to pulse. "Oh, please, Beth. Don't get all dramatic. We were only thirty feet deep. You knew what to do and everything worked out fine, except you went into a pouting fit afterward and refused to dive the next day."

"Of course, I refused. What was I supposed to do? Put myself right back into harm's way? Even the dive master knew you did the wrong thing."

"Bullshit." He pushed past her and walked down the hallway to the guest bedroom, yanking back the covers on the bed.

Beth followed. "You have no consideration for anyone but yourself," she yelled, slamming her palm against the door frame. "You're a lousy partner, and I don't mean just in diving. You stink at being a husband, and right now, I can't stand the sight of you."

She was standing at the foot of the bed when she said those last words. In one fluid move, Mark stepped toward her and pinned her against the wall.

"Don't touch me!" she screamed, bringing a knee up toward his groin.

He dodged it and tightened his hold. "Do you want to fight me? Is that what you want to do?"

"Let me go!" she screamed, struggling against his grip. She brought a heel down hard on his instep, and he winced. Adrenaline shot through her veins, and she brought her head up to knock against his chin.

He let go and shoved her toward the door. "Go cry to one of your girlfriends, Beth." He pushed past her and stepped toward the front door. "You little slut," he said.

Only it wasn't Mark's voice she heard. It was another dark-headed man with Mark's build and Mark's voice. There was a door, and a bedroom, and a wall. *You coeds are all alike,* the voice said. *All tease.*

Beth shook her head, trying to stop the voice. It was close. It was familiar. She could feel her head pressed against the wall once again, the voice burning into her brain like a tattoo. Now, like then, she was scared for her life.

She fought the memory away and ran down the hallway to the door. Mark was already backing out of the driveway. "Don't come back," she yelled to his taillights. "And don't you dare ever touch me again!"

CHAPTER THIRTY-TWO

" Did you call the police?" Helen asked. "I picked up your message this morning. That's what I would have told you to do."

Beth shook her head. "No, I didn't do that. I locked myself in the bedroom after he left, then finally went to bed. I barely slept. Around three, I packed a bag with his things and put it outside on the porch. I must have fallen asleep after that because when I woke, the bag was gone."

Helen leaned forward, forcing Beth to look at her. "I've got to ask you some questions. You know I'm obligated to report all incidents of abuse to authorities. Do you feel endangered? Do you think you should take out a restraining order? Request court-ordered anger management classes for him?"

Beth shook her head. "No, I don't think that's needed. It was an argument. A bad one, and it escalated. I think he was as shocked by his actions as I was. I shouldn't have followed him into the room. That was my mistake. I should have waited until we were both calm to talk." She crossed her arms and stared out the window, shaking slightly. "But do you think I did the right thing? Throwing him out of the house? I mean, it's his home too."

"Does it feel like the right thing?"

"Yes and no," Beth answered, her heart still pounding from the memory. *Two wrongs don't make a right,* she heard her mother saying.

She looked back at Helen and turned her head from side to side to release tension.

Helen nodded. "Let me tell you a story. A few years ago, I took horseback riding lessons. I've always admired horses but was afraid of them. Their power and all. My instructor was trying to teach me to use my legs to control the horse, rather than my hands, which felt wrong. I mean, you drive a car with your hands, right? But she wanted me to steer with my legs by applying firm but gentle pressure to the horse's flanks. Here's what she said: 'If it feels wrong, it's right.' Get it? Whenever we're learning a new skill, it requires turning loose of an old habit. At first, the new skill will feel wrong when actually it's right."

Beth unwrapped her arms. "You think the reason I'm feeling I did the wrong thing by throwing Mark out is because I've never done anything like that before? If it feels wrong, it may be right?"

Helen leaned back and smiled. "Bingo! I always knew you were a quick learner." She allowed Beth to process her thoughts before speaking again. "Of course, that's not the final answer to the problem, but it's a start. Now, I know you. You will go home and convince yourself this is your fault. You'll put together a care package to take to his boat. Right? And what little I know about Mark, I imagine he's already ordered a truckload of flowers. Great. You both feel regretful for your part in the fight. But nothing will change if you sweep the problem under the rug and go back to the way things were before. Peace will only last until another problem pops up, and another, and another." She sat back. "That, my dear, is why you are here. Things have happened in your life and keep happening. Things won't change until you change."

"This is probably the end of our marriage."

Helen fixed her with a look. "Let me ask you a question," she said at last. "What is the first word that comes to your mind when I say divorce?"

"Failure," Beth responded.

Helen nodded. "Okay. What else?"

"Loneliness. Heartache. Old age." She clasped and unclasped her hands, then stretched them out. "Doomed for the rest of my life."

Helen gave her a soft smile. "A little dramatic, don't you think?"

"But it's how I feel. It's not something I want to think about right now."

Helen leaned forward so she could look into Beth's eyes. "But that's what you need to do. Sometimes it helps to visualize the worst that could happen. Once you've faced it in your mind, you can then work past it. When you call fear by its name, you can gain control over it, take away its power. Right now, you're allowing Mark and your fear that your marriage is over to take control of you. What I want you to think about before our next session is who *you* are. What goals can you set for yourself? What resources of strength do you have? Your life isn't just about Mark and making this marriage work. It sounds like you've been trying that, and it isn't working. Your life is about you – what makes you whole, what makes you happy." She sat back. "You're stronger than you think, Beth. All of us are."

Beth nodded as tears welled in her eyes. "I wanted this marriage to work so much, you know? I was convinced that all I needed was someone big and strong by my side." She wiped at her eyes. "How stupid is that?" She turned and gazed out the window, visualizing another room, another window, another time. "There's other stuff I've never told anyone," she said. "I thought I was over it long ago, but...."

Helen waited until Beth made eye contact.

"I'm not ready to go there," she said.

"We'll get there. If you're willing, we'll explore all that old stuff. It's not called baggage for nothing." She patted Beth's knee as she saw her tears return. "I'm here for you, Beth. This is a safe place." They sat together until Beth wiped away the tears and nodded. Helen smiled. "Remember, if it feels wrong..."

"It may be right."

CHAPTER THIRTY-THREE

*E*lbowing aside her calculator, Beth stared at the spreadsheet. One-hundred fifty dollars and change. That's what she would have in her bank account after the mortgage and utilities were paid. One-hundred fifty dollars for food, gas, and any other expenses that came her way. Maybe she could ask Mark for his share of the mortgage, but, if they were on a path to a divorce, she would need to pay her own bills. Things would have to be cut, like the fitness club membership and maybe Helen too. She couldn't afford the copay. And until the house was sold, she wouldn't have money to live on. Returning to Atlanta wasn't an option. Not yet.

She pushed her chair back and walked to the window. Outside, it was the same old same old. Blazing hot sun, dull green foliage, and a paved road leading to nowhere. What was the expression Janet used when she had been upset with her husband? *I hate my life and everyone in it.* She turned her back to the window. No. She would remain positive. She wouldn't let anger or fear rule her life. She would get into problem-solving mode and stay there.

Should I stay or should I go now? The lyrics from an old song played in her head. *If I go, there will be trouble. If I stay, there will be double.*

Without thinking, she tapped the rhythm on her desk. "Better the devil you know,' my Mama used to say," she told Lizzie, who was curled at her feet. The cat opened one eye and then yawned before rearranging herself and going back to sleep.

Beth exhaled in frustration. She now understood the temptation behind the saying. It was easy to feel strong and powerful in Helen's office. Now all she felt was helpless, no matter how many positive affirmations she said. So here she was: Helen on one shoulder, her mother on the other, Mark pulling her heart apart, and The Clash still singing that annoying song.

"Shit," she said in disgust. It would only take one phone call. Plus, an apology. And taking all the blame. And resigning herself to more of the same.

She pushed away from her desk and walked to the window where her blue bowl sat. She picked it up and turned it in her hands. She pictured a smile as the bowl was placed in her hands. So long ago. Its blue color almost the same shade as those eyes.

She put the bowl down and paced, questions cramming in her head. How did she miss so much about Mark when they were first dating? He'd had a temper, no doubt about it. Like the time he yelled at the valet who squealed the tires of his Mustang. He nearly chased after the kid. Or the time he cursed an opponent who made a bad line call in a tennis match. After the match, Beth had tried to calm him down, and he pushed her away. Or the way he talked on the phone to his ex, like she was a "stupid bitch." His words. Add that to what Anna had told her, before her marriage. What had she said? *Get answers before the I do's.* But no, Beth had been so in love she was blind to what stared her in the face. A man with serious anger issues.

She turned again from the window and went back to her desk. She knew why she had ignored warning signs. Dr. Em had all but written it in bold letters on his whiteboard. She was programmed to be passive around angry people. She had been so convinced that Mark was 'the one' – she grimaced, recalling how she had used that phrase with Lori – that she didn't see he was not the man for her. *Stupid Beth*, she chided herself. The man who first called her that was right. She was an idiot with tits. Didn't know the first thing about men. Perhaps her mother was right too. None of them could be trusted.

She remembered when her mother drilled that lesson into her. Beth was in sixth grade and had just turned twelve. She had begged her mother for a training bra. Not that she needed one, but she had wanted to be like her friends. Cheerleading practice had ended, and she was waiting for her mother to pick her up, when Tommy, the quarterback of the football team, came over to talk with her. They had been in class together since first grade, and he had passed a note to Beth saying he 'liked' her. Beth was looking up at him with her arms folded across her chest, nervous about how she looked in the training bra and trying to keep her lips together to conceal her new braces. He had one arm slung across her shoulder and was holding his helmet in the other hand. She had no memory of what they were talking about, only that it was a beautiful fall day – the kind that made you want to make big piles of leaves and jump in them.

The next thing she knew, her mother was grabbing her by the arm and pulling her to the car. "Don't let that boy touch you," she yelled, slapping Beth hard across the face. "All he wants to do is get in your pants."

Shame and her mother's handprint lit her face. Shame for letting a boy touch her. Shame that her friends had seen how her mother treated her. The next day at school, she had avoided Tommy. She had been a junior in high school before she went on her first date with a dull boy from church, from a family whom her mother said was 'good stock.' What would her mother have said about Mark? Probably, *if you lie down with dogs, you get fleas.*

Beth went to the front door and flung it open. She needed to work out her aggravation. A storm had blown through during the night, leaving palm fronds and sticks strewn across the yard. With a surge of energy, she picked them up, tossing them into a pile outside the garage. Thirty minutes later, she had worked her way around the house, avoiding the fire ant mounds scattered across the yard. With hands on her hips, she assessed the shrubs close to the house. They needed pruning, she decided. She went into the garage, hoping to find clippers, when her eyes landed on Mark's stuff. His golf clubs, his scuba gear, his spare lines for the boat, his tennis racquets. She picked one up and removed its cover. It was a Head Extreme, Mark's favorite racquet. He must have had it restrung and the grips replaced because a receipt was still attached to the handle for seventy-five dollars.

Beth hit the strings with the palm of her hand, and again, harder and harder. She remembered the first time he had used this racquet. It was at a tournament in Orlando. He had won the first set easily, but his opponent figured out his difficulty handling backspin drop shots. The third time Mark lunged and missed the ball, he came up cursing and hitting the net with his racquet. She remembered sitting dead still with embarrassment as spectators seated around her jeered him. He lost the set 2-6. Beth had to trail after him as he stormed to the car, throwing his gear into the trunk and kicking it shut.

She looked at the grid pattern on her hand and then spun around and walked outside. She attacked the bushes below the front windows first, whacking them with the racquet back and forth, back and forth, again and again, until small branches littered the ground below. Her left arm grew tired, and she switched to her right hand, hitting and hitting until satisfied.

In the back of the house, she continued her work. Over and over, she struck the foliage, ignoring the sweat, the heat, and the sting of mosquitoes. An hour later, she wiped her face with the bottom of her shirt and regarded her handiwork. The bushes were stumps now, nearly level with the ground. She hit her palm against the racquet face to knock away some of the debris. Two strings had broken loose. She laughed once, then spun around and returned to the garage. She tossed the racquet toward the golf clubs and slammed the door.

Lizzie was curled asleep in Beth's office chair when she returned to her computer. She placed her on another chair. "Mama will find a good job," she told Lizzie, but all she got in return was a yawn. Beth laughed. "You're right. As long as you have your Fancy Feast, you're happy."

When the computer booted, she typed in her search terms, leaning close to the screen. Again, no results for marketing, and only a handful for sales. But scrolling down, she saw one at a camera shop. The store needed someone with experience in desktop publishing. She reached for her calculator and plugged in what she estimated would be her salary. It wouldn't solve all her problems, but at least it was in her field. Leaning back, she gripped the arms of her chair. If only she could think. If only she didn't feel blood pounding in her temples like an incessant steel drum band. If only, if only, if only. She clicked on a file marked *Resume* and proofed it one more time before typing a cover letter, attaching both documents to an email.

She got her first job in Atlanta by answering a blind ad. Maybe luck would visit her again. She hit *Send*.

***

Beth arrived at the club early on Saturday. It was the last week she could afford the membership, so she wanted to soak in the whirlpool before her massage. She had cleaned the house to stay busy the night before and then settled in with *Somewhere in Time.* She remembered watching it with Lori one Sunday while they cooked together. Both had wept at the end, hugging and swearing it was the best movie ever. She dialed Lori's number while the credits were running. "Sounds like you're at a party," she said with forced gaiety.

"I'm at a concert at Chastain Park," Lori answered. "Here. Let me hold the phone up, and you can hear. It's Coldplay!"

Beth had put the phone against her forehead, unable to listen and keep tears out of her voice. When she heard Lori's voice again, she returned the phone to her ear.

"I'll let you go," she said. "Call you next week. Have fun!" she added, before snapping the phone shut. She had cradled it in her hand, feeling a flush of longing for her old life.

That night, she hardly slept, still hearing Lori's easy laughter and her own shrill voice. Now, as she soaked in the club's whirlpool, she tried reciting a mantra she had found online. "My life is special. I live my truth. I nurture my spirit." *What a load of crap*, she thought, as she climbed out of the tub and checked the time. Too late to cancel the appointment. What she wanted was to get back home and dig into some research that might lead to a job.

"We had to change your masseuse," said Rebecca at the front desk, as Beth signed in, her mind still on her job search. "You asked for Wendi when you called. I know Mark uses her a lot, but she's out of town, so Jennifer will take you. Hope that's okay." She smiled.

"That's fine," Beth answered, not caring. She turned before realizing that Rebecca was still talking.

"Wendi always goes to Miami for the boat show. She sets up shop in the lobby where the sailing association members stay and does back massages. It's easy money, she says. Gives her the chance to hang out at South Beach." She hesitated. "I thought you might want to know why she's not here."

"Oh," Beth replied and resumed walking toward the locker room. But then she stopped and looked back. Rebecca met her gaze and then looked away.

Beth stood still. If there was a boat show, would Mark have gone? And would he have stayed at the same hotel? Cold sweat spread across her face. Funny, how Wendi's name kept being linked to his. For a moment, she couldn't breathe. The room seemed to sway around her.

When Jennifer came to get her, she followed.

"Relax," Jennifer ordered, as she dug into Beth's back muscles. "You've got way too much tension. What's going on with you?"

Beth's head was pounding. She tried slowing her breath. In and out. Deep breaths. It didn't work. Nothing worked – not movies or her favorite foods or talking to Lori or Helen or meditation or even the possibility of a new job. Nothing. And now she was blowing one hundred dollars she didn't have.

CHAPTER THIRTY-FOUR

"Sweetie, are you okay?" Alisa asked.

"I'm fine," Beth replied in a small voice. She could hear Grant in the background.

"No, you aren't. You can't be. And I'm mad you waited this long to call us."

Beth had put off calling the couple, indecisive about what to say and what to do. At last, like a trip to confession, she called Alisa the Sunday after the massage and told the whole story of the lobster dive and Mark attacking her. She didn't say it that way, but that's how it loomed in her mind. And she didn't mention Mark's possible trip to Miami and the way Wendi's name kept being linked to his. It was shameful enough.

Beth pulled her mind back and realized Alisa was talking to Grant. "Mark hit Beth," she heard her say.

"He didn't hit me so much as—"

"I'll rip him to shreds," Grant said, having taken the phone from Alisa.

"Please. That's not needed. He's living on the boat now, and he didn't hit me. We had an argument, and he pushed me against a wall. I'm fine!"

"Goddammit, Beth. We're getting in the car right now and coming there."

"Don't do that. I'm fine. Plus, I've got Lizzie for company."

"We know that pet is like your child, so put her in a carrier and come here. Now."

"Yes," she heard Alisa agree. "Take a few days off from that minimum wage job."

Three days later, as she sat on their screened porch, she felt the tension leave her body. A late summer breeze gently moved the curtains while the afternoon sun played across a row of hydrangeas, highlighting their purple and blue petals. She had left a voice mail for Mark, saying she was driving to Atlanta. It was the polite thing to do, she had decided, masking her desire he call her with an apology.

She smiled weakly as Alisa joined her on the porch, bringing with her a tray of antipasto and a bottle of white wine. When Beth's phone rang, both women's eyes locked.

"It's Mark," Beth mouthed to Alisa. After the third ring, she answered and listened for a moment.

"Oh, God," she said, standing. "When?"

"What's happened?" Alisa asked. Beth waved her away.

"What hospital?" she asked and listened more.

"What is it?" Alisa said, but Beth shushed her.

"I'm leaving right now. I can be there in fifteen minutes. What time will you arrive?" More listening. "What do you mean you're not coming? She's your daughter!" Another pause. "That's ridiculous. Get the next flight to Atlanta. My God, Mark. Screw your sailing class. It's your daughter!" Beth closed her cell phone and stared at it before looking at Alisa.

"What's happened?" Alisa cried.

Beth looked at her with an open mouth and wide eyes. "You won't believe this. Heather's been in a car wreck. The police just called Mark, and, wait for it." She held up a hand. "He needs me to handle it for him. He's not coming."

"Of all the selfish things he's done," Alisa began, but Beth interrupted her.

"I gotta go." She turned in a circle before locating her purse. "According to Mark, she isn't seriously injured. A broken wrist and ankle. Lots of cuts and bruises. A mild concussion. My guess is more scared and in shock than anything. Her airbag saved her, plus she had her seatbelt on. The car's totaled. Not sure what his definition of serious is, but there you have it."

"Mark needs to be here," Grant finished for her, having walked in the room while Beth was on the phone.

Alisa nodded in agreement. "If something happened to one of our children, we would be there in a heartbeat."

"Let's just go," Beth said. "He wants me to handle things."

"How did it happen?" Grant asked.

"She was drinking. At least, that's what the police implied. They're waiting on a tox screen. But knowing Heather...."

"All the more reason he should come," Alisa interrupted. "My God, Beth. It's his daughter."

Grant put a hand out to quiet Alisa. "Let's just get to the hospital and assess how she is."

***

When Beth walked into Heather's room, a nurse was checking her pulse rate. She stood beside the open door, until the nurse was gone, before approaching the bed. Heather had her head turned away and her eyes closed. Her long blond hair was matted to her head, and her broken right arm was extended by her side, on a pillow. Her foot was elevated, and the side of her face was bruised. She looked twelve rather than twenty. A sheet was pulled over her chest and folded, the way a mother might tuck a child into bed. Beth waited a moment before saying her name.

Heather turned her head and looked at Beth. "Where's Dad?" Her voice was small and weak.

Beth released a long breath before answering. "He's—"

But Heather cut her off. "He's not coming." Tears welled in her eyes. "I've been in a car wreck, and my father is not coming."

"He wants to be here," Beth said. "But he was already booked for a sailing class—"

"And it's his weekend, and he doesn't want to be bothered." Turning away from Beth, she wiped her eyes. "You know, he's done this before." She reached with her left hand for her water, and Beth handed the cup to her, guiding the straw into her mouth. She took a gulp and handed it back. "I know. I was in the wrong that time. I was out with some kids drinking, and we got picked up for being underage and taken to jail. I called my dad, and do you know what he did? He hung up on me. I was fifteen and scared and in trouble, and he let me sit in the Fulton County jail overnight." She locked eyes with Beth. "What kind of father does that?"

Beth stroked her arm. "I don't know, sweetie. But you need to rest now. Things always look better in the morning." Beth turned and saw an armchair. "I can settle in here and keep you company. I'm sure your dad will call soon, and who knows, he may already have a flight booked."

Heather looked old and tired. "Don't count on it. I know Dad." She looked up at the ceiling and then back at Beth. "When the going gets tough, Dad gets going." She turned her face away and closed her eyes.

You may know him better than I do, thought Beth.

***

It was after two that night, long after a whispered exchange in the hallway with Alisa and Grant, before Beth slipped out of the room and drove the deserted streets back to their home. Heather's question kept repeating in her head. What kind of father was Mark? What kind of man?

By ten in the morning, she was back at the hospital in time to meet Megan, Heather's mother. Beth always pictured Mark's ex the way he described her – a shrill blonde with big boobs and a bigger attitude, but the woman who walked down the corridor toward her seemed like someone who would fit right in with the Core Four. She had brownish blonde hair pulled back with a headband and wore running tights and a well-worn pair of sneakers. Her face was clean of makeup. She was taller than Beth, but not by much. Pleasant looking, like someone's best friend.

She walked straight to Beth and enveloped her in a hug. "Thank you," she said. "Thank you, thank you, thank you."

"It was nothing," Beth answered. "I know Mark would have been here with me, but—"

Megan held up a hand to stop her in a gesture like Heather's. "It's okay, Beth. You don't need to make excuses for him. You were here for my daughter, and I appreciate it." She turned and pushed open Heather's door before turning back. "Can you wait?"

"Sure." Beth gestured toward a couch in the waiting area. "I'll be there."

An hour later, Megan dropped beside her. "She's asleep," she said, stifling her own yawn.

"Did you drive?"

Megan nodded. "Left around five this morning. Tried to get a flight from Raleigh, but...." She yawned again.

Beth went to a vending machine and brought back coffee.

Megan nodded her thanks and took a gulp before setting the cup down. "Thank you again." She waved toward Heather's room. "She likes you."

"Heather? Really?"

Megan nodded. "She said you made her feel welcome in Florida." She reached for Beth's hand. "That means a lot."

A comfortable silence surrounded them. "What was she like as a little girl?" Beth asked, nodding her head toward the closed door.

Megan smiled. "She was a delight. Full of energy. Always laughing and smiling. Had a way of taking over a room, as if everyone was there for her to entertain." She smiled. "I was even stopped in the mall one day by a modeling agent who represented children. Wanted to know if I was interested."

"And were you?" Beth asked.

"No. I didn't think that was the right influence for her. Plus, when I mentioned it to Mark, he worried that it would cost more than it made." She released Beth's hand, lost in thought. "And then she grew up," she said at last.

Beth sat silent as Megan looked away. Finally, she turned back to Beth. "I had hoped things would get better between Mark and her, but...." She paused again. "Now I don't think they will ever bond." She stopped herself and drank her coffee. "I'm talking too much. Too much time on the road to think."

"That's fine," Beth said. "I want to help as much as I can." She laughed. "I had a difficult time growing up with my mother. So, I know what Heather's going through." She patted Megan's arm. "Talk if you need to. I'm a good listener."

Megan shook her head, clearing her thoughts. "When we were married," she began, "I felt he blamed her existence for keeping him from achieving some great goal in his life." She grimaced. "It was an unplanned pregnancy." She looked down the hallway, lost in thought. "I remember when I met his dad at the wedding. A big hunk of a guy. Booming voice. Pushing people out of his way to stand front and center for family pictures. His wife trailing behind him saying, 'What do you need, Crush? What can I bring you, Crush?' That was how she addressed him. Not Matt or Mathew but Crush, like his nickname, 'The Crusher.'" Megan made air quotes around the name. "I remember looking at that woman and thinking, I don't want to be you."

Beth tensed. "That's not the picture Mark painted of his dad."

"I'm sure it isn't."

Again, the two women sat silent as other visitors took the remaining chairs in the waiting area. Beth was about to pick up her purse and leave when Megan turned toward her. "I'm sorry. I'm talking about your husband's family. That's rude of me. I'm sure Mark has changed a lot. When I knew him, he was all about the chase." She shrugged. "I was a cheerleader, and he chased and got me and then left. End of story."

Beth interrupted. "It's okay. I'm learning some things about him I didn't know before."

Megan patted her hand. "Underneath, he's a decent guy, but when we were married, he had a way of hiding it. I always blamed his father for being a bad role model – like an overgrown bully, and when he died, Mark seemed to lose his way." She stopped herself. "I'm tired and saying too much. I'm sure he's a different husband for you than he was for me."

Beth allowed Megan's words to settle in her head, feeling the stillness of the room. Megan glanced at Heather's door. Beth took it as a sign and reached for her purse.

"You need to get back in there." She pulled out a business card. "Here," she said, handing it to Megan. "Call me and keep me posted about Heather." She turned to walk away and then stopped. "Also, maybe it's time we got to know one another better."

Megan looked surprised and then smiled. "That we do," she answered. She put the card in her purse and pushed open the hospital room door before turning back to Beth. "You're not what I expected," she said.

Beth laughed. "You aren't either. Frankly," she added. "Nothing is."

CHAPTER THIRTY-FIVE

"   That's great, Megan. Thanks for calling."

Returning her phone to her purse, Beth checked her watch. Two hours until closing time and not a customer in sight. At least Megan's call had interrupted the monotony of the day. She had called to let Beth know that Heather was settling into life in Raleigh. "Her driver's license is suspended for a year," she had said, "but she's working at Ann Taylor and not drinking. I think she will begin classes in January, maybe study marketing. She says you got her interested in that as a career."

Beth thought about this and smiled. Only a month since the wreck, and Heather was making progress. "Baby steps," she had told Megan. She knew about those. Wasn't that what she was doing too?

She gazed out at the frame shop parking lot and thought about the past month and the steps she was taking. She couldn't claim she and Megan were friends, but it seemed they both realized that morning in the hospital that each had a faulty impression of the other. Her job research was progressing, and the part-time job at the camera store was providing the bump in income she needed. Plus, to her surprise, Mark dropped off a check for half the mortgage the Monday after she returned from Atlanta. From the look of the house, he seemed to drop by when she was at work to use the laundry.

But beyond that, nothing. Like a low-pressure system hovering in the distance with the promise of rain, the air around their marriage was filled with crashing ions. Beth knew this feeling. It had engulfed the home where she grew up. Burning, crashing ions, and not a drop of relief in sight.

"But not tonight," she had told Lizzie as she left the house. Tonight, was for dancing. Alisa had told her about a new

186 · Sarah Jones

dance spot in Sarasota with an instructor looking for a new partner. "Why not audition?" she had challenged Beth.

***

Anthony took Beth's hand and led her onto the dance floor. He held her in a closed position, their hip bones almost touching as he moved her into a four-count starter step. But instead of following the lead-in with a traditional slingshot throw out and back to a sugar push, he executed a smooth underarm turn that drew her back into his arms. Then with a wink, he placed her into the slot using a double-spin followed by a whip with an outside turn. When they hit the first break in the song, they paused. Beth's eyes sparkled, and Anthony released a low whistle. "You move well, girl," he said. Her only response was to smile even more.

He was the best West Coast Swing partner she had ever danced with. He had solid footwork and a rolling count style that displayed his Latin roots. Beth had no expectations he would select her as his partner and didn't even know if it was something she wanted to do. *But wow*, she thought, the dance was worth the drive.

She was proud of herself for making this decision. Dancing was freedom, and by God, today she was declaring her independence. No more repeating under her breath 'walk-walk-triple-step, tri-ple-step' to keep Mark on beat, as she had done when they first met. No more being jerked and shoved around the floor. She could dance with a partner who knew how to lead and how to make his partner feel attractive. Whoever said dancing was a vertical form of love–making knew what they were talking about. Nothing made Beth feel sexier than dancing.

As the number ended, Anthony kept her hand in his and led her off the floor, ignoring the brunette who approached him with a hand extended to grab him for the next dance. They walked to the water station, where he filled a glass for her, and then leaned against the table to watch the other dancers. His eyes traveled the room, and his head nodded with satisfaction. The DJ was excellent, the floor smooth, the lights and temperature just right. She knew he had started the studio after leaving Houston with the hopes of building a community of dancers in southwest Florida. Sarasota was a natural place to put down his dancing shoes. The city had a cool vibe, with an emphasis on arts and entertainment. Had Mark listened before they moved, she could have lived happily in Sarasota. But no need to dwell on what could have been. She was here not to think but to dance.

They turned to one another when they heard the opening bars of Patti Austin's *Ability to Swing*. "I love this one," Beth said. "It's the first song I learned to dance to."

"Come on," Anthony said, pulling her from the table. "Show me what you got."

It was midnight before Beth got in her car to head back to Porto Verde. She and Anthony had taken a break from dancing around ten to talk in his office. He wanted to show her videos of some of the competitions from around the country. She knew the names of many of the couples, having attended the Grand National Dance Championships held every Memorial Day weekend in Atlanta. But committing the time it would take to bring her skills to that level was more than she wanted, she explained, avoiding mentioning that she was separated from her husband. She wanted to dance as often as possible with someone like Anthony and enjoy herself. It was time to put some fun back into her life.

"At least do one pro-am event with me," he said, as he walked her to her car, and to her own surprise as much as his, she agreed.

As she headed south on I-75, she plugged a CD into the player and tapped the beat on the steering wheel. The last dance with Anthony had been to Johnny Lang's "Lie to Me." As the song now blared from the speaker, she sang along. *It doesn't matter anymore. It could never be the way it was before. If I can't hold on to you. Leave me with something I can hold onto. For just a little while, won't you let me....*

She opened the sunroof. The warm night wind whipped her hair. This was what she used to do every weekend in Atlanta – dance until late at night with friends and then go home to soak her tired feet so she could come back the next night and do it again.

"Why me?" she had asked Anthony toward the end of the evening. "Why enter a pro-am competition with me?"

"Because you're real," he answered. "There's nothing fake about you. And when you dance, you only have eyes for your partner. Do you have any idea how sexy it is for a woman to have eyes only for her man? Sure, lots of other dancers are above you in technique, but that isn't what I want to showcase. Other women dance for the judges. You glow for your partner. That's the person I want at my studio. Not those who can do splits and lifts, but people like you, who get the joy of dancing. And you, Beth, get it. You're the real thing."

His words followed her to bed that night and brought with them a question: *If I was my true self tonight,* she wondered, *who the heck have I been for the past year?*

CHAPTER THIRTY-SIX

*F*or the following week, Beth reveled in her night of dancing. She was happy, she realized. Not jump-up-in-the-air happy. Not pop-a-bottle-of-champagne-and-throw-a-party happy, but feeling-good happy. No-stress happy. Normal happy. Like she had a future. *Who knows*, she speculated. Maybe things might turn around with her and Mark. Since she had returned from Atlanta with greetings from Heather – granted, she had fabricated the greetings – they were talking more often. Not about things between them but more "How's your day been" and "Did you hear about" kinds of conversations. Topics that allowed them both to pretend that their love bank balances weren't in the red. She had noticed he still wore his wedding band. That was a plus.

She hit her brakes as soon as she pulled into the driveway. Here she was, thinking of Mark, and there was his car. She stepped out just as he walked out of their house. His face looked haggard, and she felt the urge to hug him. "What's going on?" she asked.

"Hurricane Edward. It's headed out of the Caribbean and moving up the coast. I need to get the boat secured and, well, thought I would help you with the house and maybe stay here tomorrow, just in case. There's supposed to be a big storm surge."

Her mouth went slack as she tried to absorb the news. Mark paid her no further attention and instead walked past her, taking long strides toward a nearby construction area. She watched his blue cap disappear around the bend. By the time she caught up, he had on work gloves and was stacking cinder blocks. He looked over his shoulder.

"Go back and get your car," he ordered. "We'll put the furniture up on these in case of flooding. The house is above the flood plain, but better safe than sorry."

For the next hour, they worked in silence – loading blocks into Beth's trunk and then carrying them into the house. It took three trips to get enough for the living room and bedroom furniture. With hands on hips, they stared at the dining room table. It was too heavy to lift.

"Put a blanket over it and we'll stack smaller pieces on top," Mark said. He walked over and picked up the coffee table. "It's just furniture."

Beth automatically nodded in agreement.

Back outside, she looked at the sky. It felt odd to prepare for a potential flood on such a clear day. The weather was sunny with a honeycomb of high white cirrus clouds that looked like paint strokes against the Wedgewood blue sky. It seemed more a day for walking on the beach or reading a book in a hammock.

When Mark left to secure the boat, Beth made ham sandwiches and joined him. Working together to prepare the house had brought an ease that had been missing for some time. It felt good. Like a team. Like a marriage.

After he tied the last line, she passed him a sandwich and a beer and then surveyed his work. The boat looked like a giant bug caught in a spider's web with lines back and forth to nearby pilings. She nodded her head in approval. "It looks secure."

"She should ride out the surge. I left enough play in the lines that she can ride the tide. Plus, we're inland."

For a moment, it seemed peaceful sitting with him on the dock – just like it had been back in Atlanta when she would join him after his sailing students left. He would drape an arm around her shoulders and pull her close. She had liked the feel of him. His day growth of beard was just rough enough to make him seem even more handsome and masculine.

As she watched him now, she moved to sit closer. But just as their hips touched, he jumped up. "Gotta go. A friend needs my help."

"Oh. Who is it? I can come too."

"No. Just go on back home. I'll call later."

His car was out of sight before Beth realized he hadn't said whom he was helping. But the knot in her stomach told her she knew.

***

The next morning, she awoke early from a restless night. Turning on the television, she flipped through channels. All stations were broadcasting the weather. She settled in to listen to meteorologist Jim Farrell's predictions. Edward was closer, he said, pointing at the map behind him. She leaned toward the set to better see the satellite image and didn't notice when Mark walked in and sat down beside her. Unsure whether to start a conversation – about the weather, about Wendi, about them – she regarded his profile before turning back to the television. Conversation could wait until the storm passed. Together, yet apart, they watched as Jim switched from a satellite shot to a radar image of green, blue, and red, looking more like a child's drawing than a force of nature with wind speeds of 150 miles per hour.

"Edward's wobbling," Mark commented. "It's changing its path. It was headed toward Tampa but now may reach land further south."

Beth stood, feeling her first jolt of fear. "What does that mean for us?"

"Don't know. But I think I'll grab more lines for the boat."

"Shouldn't we do more here? Tape the windows or something?"

Mark ignored her and headed down the hallway. She looked at his back, remembering the closeness she felt while sitting on the dock. Now his physique looked hard and unwelcoming. Her eyes traveled back to the television. Jim was still pointing at the storm, and Beth's stomach clenched. She noticed the date across the bottom of the screen – Friday the thirteenth.

***

With Mark gone, she spent the morning bringing plants and outdoor furniture inside, picking up anything that might become a missile if hurled by a strong wind. With this task done, she lay on her stomach and dragged Lizzie from under the bed. "You'll be safe," she told the cat, as she placed her in a pet carrier and placed it on the floor of a storage closet.

With her phone close by, she settled again in front of the television and waited – for what, she wasn't sure. By one o'clock, Jim announced that Edward had 'wobbled' more. Beth walked outside to look for Mark. Gone were the blue skies and gentle clouds of the day before. In their place were towering gray masses, heavy with water. Up and down the street, she could hear hammering, as neighbors readied their houses for the worst.

By three, Jim said that Edward had made its last wobble and would touch land on Cayo Costa Island in forty-five minutes, before crossing Charlotte Harbour and slamming straight into Porto Verde.

A coldness descended on Beth as she realized what was about to happen. She dialed Mark's number. It went straight to voice mail.

Time seemed to slow as Beth walked room to room, straightening a picture here, fluffing a pillow there, as if Edward were a houseguest who would soon be ringing the doorbell. She listened as the wind raised its voice to a crackling, searing howl. Returning to the television, she leaned forward, feeling like Jim was talking only to her. When at last the storm brought its fury ashore, her eyes were still glued to the screen – watching it like a movie about a storm and hearing the sound effects. When the electricity went out, silencing Jim's authoritative voice in mid-sentence, she jumped and dialed Mark's number. *I'm scared*, she wanted to tell him. *Please hurry*. But there was no dial tone.

Her hands pressed her chest to hold down her panic. By now, the wind had changed from a rumbling growl into an eerie cry. What felt like boulders slammed again the side of the house, and without warning, the lanai roof collapsed, bringing down with its hunks of insulation, screen, and bent metal. Beth screamed. Pulling a sofa cushion to her head for protection, she ran into the hallway – the only interior area of the house.

With knees drawn to her chest, she heard the pounding increase. A crashing sound like crushed metal made her jump. Her car. The garage must have collapsed. "Oh, God," she cried out and punched the wall with a fist. "Damn it, Mark. Where are you?" But all she heard in answer was the steady roar of the wind. A nearby window shattered and soon water soaked her clothes. She got up, and with strength she didn't realize she had, dragged the sofa from the living room into the hall and flipped it over. As more windows broke, and more water puddled around her, she crawled under the sofa as the house took hit after hit.

For what felt like hours, she listened to the brutality of the storm as it crawled its way out of the Gulf and onto land. Each time something crashed to the floor, she jerked as if she were being whipped. At one point, Edward seemed to ease, and she realized its eye was passing. But after that brief break, the winds picked back up, finding even more items to hurl against the house.

When the storm had passed, Beth remained under the sofa – too numb to move, too scared to assess the damage. At last, she crawled out and walked into the living room. A scream escaped as she looked about. The room was trashed. Pictures had fallen from the walls, their shattered frames in splinters. Window shades were twisted in grotesque shapes, and curtains hung in tatters. Water and broken glass covered the floor. "Oh my God," she kept repeating. Glancing toward the master bedroom, she cried out again. A tree protruded through a smashed window, its limbs tangled in shredded drapes.

Shock. Bewilderment. Disbelief. Fright. A range of emotions as wide as Edward's path surged through her. She dropped to the floor and squeezed her knees to her chest to control her shaking. She stayed in that position for some time until her senses returned. Sounds from outside pulled her from the floor. When she opened the front door, she could smell the storm still in the air – like a mixture of chlorine interlaced with damp grass, wet sand, and garbage.

Chaos greeted her when she stepped outside. The lawn was littered with roof tiles, shutters, street signs, screens, and gutters. Looking up and down the road, she watched neighbors doing the same thing she was – staring at the damage and standing in wonderment at what had just occurred. Overhead, she heard helicopters, and in the distance, sirens.

She bent over, fearful she might throw up.

"Are you okay?" a voice asked. It was her next-door neighbor – a man in his seventies from Wisconsin.

Without looking up, she nodded.

"This is terrible," he said as he walked away. "Terrible."

Lizzie, she thought and returned inside, needing the cat's comforting purr now more than ever. But what greeted her was horror, not comfort. An overturned metal cabinet had crushed the pet carrier. Frantically, she pulled away the debris. "No!" she cried out when at last she reached Lizzie.

The cat made no sound as Beth lifted her into her arms. With shaking hands, she examined her and located a bloody gash across Lizzie's side where the storage cabinet had landed. She rested a shaky hand on the cat's stomach. Her breathing was labored, but she was still alive. With one hand, Beth ripped off her shirt and wrapped it around Lizzie's middle to stop the bleeding. Then she leaned against the wall and rocked the cat in her arms. She turned the small face toward hers. Lizzie's green eyes were barely open.

"Please stay alive," Beth cried. "Don't leave me." But as she sat and rocked, she realized that Lizzie had breathed her last breath.

Tears soaked her face as she voiced her sorrow. Telling Lizzie how much she loved her. How much she needed her. How sorry she was for endangering her. Still holding the cat, she rummaged in the closet and found a beach towel. Clearing an area on the floor, she placed Lizzie on the towel and folded the cloth around her, making a small bundle. Then she carried her into the guest bedroom, the only place that had escaped damage, and placed her in her favorite chair. Beth dropped to

the floor beside the chair, oblivious to heat, sound, and time
– feeling only deep sorrow.

When the front door opened much later, she sat up and
listened to Mark's heavy footsteps as he walked down the hallway. He stopped in the doorway. His face was drawn and gray,
his shirt soaked with sweat.

"I'm sorry," he began. "I didn't—"

"Lizzie's dead," she interrupted, her voice void of emotion.
She nodded toward the bundle in the chair.

His face said it all – pain, confusion, regret. "I'm sorry,
Beth. I am. I meant to be here, but it took longer than I
thought to secure the boat and, well, help a friend."

She looked away and gave no indication she had even heard
his apology. "I don't think you ever realized how much she
meant to me," she said at last. "What comfort she gave me."

He exhaled. "Probably not."

"I don't know how to manage without her. It's my fault."

"It was an accident, Beth. No one's fault."

Now she looked at him. "She would still be alive if I hadn't
brought her here."

He exhaled. "Don't go there. Not now."

A silence as uncomfortable as the afternoon heat hung in
the air between them. "I'm thinking of burying her in the yard
under this window," she said, as Mark continued to lean
against the door frame. "It's where she liked to sit."

He nodded. "I'll do that for you. I need to check on the boat,
but I'll be right back."

"You need to check on your boat right now? Not bury Lizzie? Not comfort your wife? Not even ask if I'm okay? Your boat
is all you care about?"

"That's not true," he said. "I came straight here when the
storm let up. I didn't even stop by the boat. But now I need to
assess the damage and see if it even survived the storm." He
walked out of the room and headed down the hall. She followed him and grabbed for his arm.

"No, Mark. You're needed here. We just had our house
blown apart. Lizzie was killed. I was scared, Mark," she
screamed. "I was scared and afraid that at any moment the

196 · Sarah Jones

house would collapse on me. And where was my husband? Helping a friend. And where is he going now? To his boat." She spat out the last word.

Mark shook her loose and started down the driveway at a jog.

She ran a few steps after him. "Look at me, Mark!" she called out.

But he kept walking as if he didn't hear a thing except, perhaps, the helicopters still circling above.

When he disappeared around the corner of the road, Beth went inside, dropped to the floor, and wept.

CHAPTER THIRTY-SEVEN

*T*he smell of rotted food greeted her. "Shit," she said, leaving the door open behind her. Mark must have forgotten to throw everything out of the refrigerator. That was supposed to be his part of the cleanup – emptying the kitchen of all perishable food items and stacking trash beside the road for pickup. It appeared he had done the second, as evidenced by the pile of debris beside the mailbox, but not the first.

She backed onto the porch and took deep breaths. *Forget it,* she thought. *It doesn't matter. Nothing matters anymore.*

September 9, 2004, AE. Three weeks after Edward. That's how everyone in Porto Verde now tracked time. "AE," they would say to one another, as they bought more lumber to cover broken windows, or a generator to provide some power, or gallons of water to store in bathtubs. After Edward. From news broadcasts, she had learned that as the hurricane continued its path across central Florida, it flattened thousands of homes, plundered miles of power lines, uprooted countless trees, splintered boats into matchsticks, ripped mobile homes to smithereens, and destroyed churches, schools, businesses, hospitals and fire stations – damage that would later be calculated as exceeding fourteen billion dollars. But to Beth, all she could think about was one shattered house. That was enough to process. That, and one shattered marriage.

According to Mark's last message, repairs to their property would begin soon. Her job was to pack anything she wanted to salvage. Then she would be finished with Porto Verde. She didn't know her next steps, but she did know they would take her away from here.

Eager to get on with the task, she walked into the house and played her flashlight around the room. Boarded windows

198 · Sarah Jones

kept out sunlight and stifled what little breeze there was on a hot afternoon. Furniture remained stacked on concrete blocks, and the sofa was still in the hallway, its pillows scattered on the floor. Her chest tightened, and she dropped the packing boxes she carried under her arm, too overwhelmed by memories to be bothered by the odor of mold.

When Mark had returned that night after Edward passed, she heard him ransack through the garage in search of a shovel. When the spade cut into the earth below the window, she lifted Lizzie, still wrapped in a towel, and placed her in a plastic storage box. Willing herself not to think about what was inside it, she had sealed the box with packing tape.

Mark was waiting for her beside the turned earth. She'd knelt, lowered the box, and then sat back on her heels. Sweat streamed down her face, but when she touched her cheek to wipe it away, her skin felt cold as if she, too, were no longer alive. Looking down at the grave, she had wanted to say something profound – about life, about love, about the joy of having a pet. But all that came to her mind were two words – "I'm sorry." Her throat had constricted with the urge to cry, but no tears fell.

Looking about, she found some broken ceiling tiles. "So the box doesn't accidentally get dug up," she said, her voice breaking as she placed them on top of the container. Then she stood and signaled for Mark to close the grave. She shut her eyes and felt in her heart each shovel of sandy soil as it hit the plastic box. When she heard Mark patting down the earth, she opened her eyes and looked at the small mound. After a few moments, she had walked back inside and returned to the guest room, the only room left untouched by the storm, and closed the door.

Up and down their street that night, neighbors lit outdoor grills. Mark did the same, but when he knocked on her door, she had turned down the steaks he offered. Sometime around midnight, as the heat of the day, at last, gave way to a gentle wind, she must have fallen asleep. She woke the next morning without any memory of dreaming and found a note from Mark saying he had gone to find a place where he might get cell service to call their insurance agent. She looked at the handwriting, envisioning the hand that held the pen and seeing instead the hand that held her to a wall not so long ago. The same hand that had signed their marriage license. The same hand that, at this moment, was probably comforting another woman.

The following day, when rescue workers knocked on their door, Beth had crossed the street with them to go inside a neighbor's home. When they pushed open the battered front door, the house stank of rotten food and the floor was littered with water, glass, and debris. In a back room, they found an elderly woman huddled in a wet bed. A thin cover was pulled over her frail body, and the window behind her was smashed. She was bruised, addled, and dehydrated.

Beth held the woman's hand as the workers checked her vitals and bandaged her cuts. They left her with water and food, and a promise of returning. Beth stayed with her for some time, patting her hand until she could persuade the woman to allow her to change the bed sheets. "Clean clothes always make me feel better," she said. "And clean sheets are like a breath of fresh air."

The woman didn't answer – still in too much shock to respond to her surroundings. "I'll be back later," Beth had told her, as she closed the front door.

For the next two days, Beth had visited twice a day until the woman's son arrived from Birmingham and moved her out of the house. "Thank you," he said as he squeezed Beth's hand. "Mom's independent, but it's time she moved in with us."

She watched him drive away, wishing she were in the backseat. By now, she had cleaned away the broken glass and water and had done her best to restore some order to their house. She no longer kept up with Mark's comings and goings. When their insurance adjuster arrived five days later, he gave them a check to cover the apartment rental where Beth now lived in Ft. Myers. After he had left, they had each packed suitcases.

"I'm staying around," Mark had said, his back turned to Beth. "I'll keep an eye on the house."

On that note, they had parted. Since then, they had spoken only about house repairs. Where Mark spent his time, she didn't know. His boat had survived the storm, so perhaps he was there. She assumed he was preparing to go back to school. As for Beth's job, well, it was gone with the wind, as she told Lori and Alisa when she called them. The Porto Verde Frame Shop was now a pile of rubble, like most structures in the town. So, too, was the camera shop.

Freeing her mind from those memories, she picked up her boxes and got to work. Turning to the dining room hutch, she looked at a crystal vase – a wedding gift from Mark's tennis team. She examined it, finding one small crack. She set it back down. Mark could decide whether to save it or toss it.

She opened the hutch and drew out two large champagne flutes. They were a gift from Alisa and Dean. She and Mark had toasted one another at their wedding reception with them. No idea how they survived the storm, but they were going with her. She found two dish towels and wrapped them.

In her bedroom, she held her blue bowl. Rubbing its surface. Admiring its color. Feeling the hands of the potter in its shape. She placed it in her purse. It would go onto her window ledge at the apartment, with rosemary in it, just as it had sat in college. She smiled in memory of looking up from her studies and being distracted by the fragrance and the warmth of the boy snuggled beside her on the bed.

Sweating from the heat, she continued her packing – taking items that were personal and leaving everything else for Mark. The adjuster had given them until the weekend to clear the house. It was Mark's life now.

An hour later, Beth shoved the last box into her trunk and leaned against the car, holding a tray of pink flowers. Looking up and down the street, she saw every roof covered with blue tarps, including theirs. Cars in various stages of disrepair sat in driveways, and mounds of debris waited to be hauled away. There was only one last item on her to-do list for the day. She walked to the back of the house and squatted down under the kitchen window, beside the small earthen mound that was Lizzie's grave. Using a spade, she planted primroses across the mound, a colorful quilt to cover Lizzie. When she finished, she ran her hand back and forth over the pink flowers, stirring their delicate scent. Opening her purse, she drew out a plaque with Lizzie's name on it. Using her spade like a hammer, she secured the plaque at the head.

She stared at her work for a long time and then sat back against the house wall, allowing her thoughts to return to a time when the name *Lizzie* was not just a cat's but her own. A name she had taken in high school, not wanting to be Elizabeth anymore. A name that had stood for a hopeful girl in love with a sweet boy. She closed her eyes and, for the first time in a decade, opened the vault that held her memories of the day Lizzie died, and Beth was born.

***

Professor Matthews had touched her on the shoulder as she passed him. "You ask intelligent questions," he said. "Can you wait a minute? I want to invite you to something."

Her eyes lit up. Chase Matthews was the leading authority on Henry James and had written the introduction to the textbook she now clutched to her chest. It was an honor to be the only undergraduate invited to attend the visiting professor's seminar, and now to be complimented and perhaps invited to another discussion was more than thrilling. She watched as the other students filed out, trying to look nonchalant but feeling her body tremble with excitement. Her ambition was to become a college professor of English, just like him. To be an expert on some writer. Perhaps Flannery O'Connor or Edith Wharton. Maybe he would mentor her in her studies.

He closed the classroom door and walked over to her. "I'm staying at the downtown Hilton and have asked a handful of grad students to drop by for an impromptu discussion and cocktail hour. Why don't you join us? Say around seven?"

She had nodded. "That's great. Thanks. And, well, if it's no trouble, would you sign my book?" She thrust the text toward him. "Here's a pen," she added.

A slight smile crossed his face as he took the pen and opened to the last page of the introduction. He scribbled something and signed his name with a flourish. "See you at seven," he said, as he gave her back the book.

She waited until she was back in her dorm room to read the inscription. *To Elizabeth – who has a lovely mind and a lovely smile. Chase.*

At seven sharp, she knocked on the hotel door and adjusted her backpack. She had changed out of jeans and into a bright blue skirt, a floral blouse, and high-heeled sandals. This was the first cocktail party she had ever attended, and for a moment, she wondered if she should have brought flowers or a gift. She could hear jazz playing inside the room and was about to knock a second time when the door opened.

"You made it," he said. He had changed into a black cashmere sweater and had pushed the sleeves above his elbows. His thick brown hair was falling across his forehead in a way that set off his deep brown eyes. She hadn't noticed how handsome he was in the classroom because she was so busy taking notes. He held a drink in his hand.

"Thanks again for inviting me, Professor."

"Call me Chase."

"Okay. And I go by Lizzie." She released a nervous laugh and looked around the room. "Am I the first?"

He turned and searched the room in a playful manner before looking back at her. "Looks that way," he had said and then nodded toward the bar. "I'm having a gin and tonic. Can I make you one?"

Without waiting for an answer, he went to the bar and mixed her drink, while she stood in the middle of the room, her ankles crossed. It was a mini suite with a small sitting area. She could see into the bedroom, where the maid had already turned down the bed. She took her backpack off and selected a chair by the sofa, adjusting her skirt and crossing her ankles.

He came and sat on the sofa near her chair and handed her the drink, his fingers touching hers. He lifted his drink toward her. "Cheers," he said.

She clicked his glass and took a sip, her eyes opening wide. "How is it?" he asked.

"Strong," she had answered. "I'm not much of a drinker. The occasional Miller Lite or perhaps a glass of white wine."

He chuckled. "Wine's fine, but liquor's quicker. At least, that's what we used to say when I was an undergrad." He leaned back into the cushion and fixed her with a look. "Tell me, Lizzie Gardiner. What got you interested in Henry James?"

She sipped her drink. "I read *The Turn of the Screw* in high school. I liked the way James created mystery and suspense around his characters. Most of the kids in my class didn't get the story, but I liked the way it forced readers to draw their own conclusion." She took another sip before placing the glass on the coffee table.

"And from there, let me guess, you read *Daisy Miller*."

She nodded. The drink was giving her a nice warm glow. "I'm not sure I understood it when I read it, I mean, the life-style was so different for women back then, but after I finished it, I read Edith Wharton's *House of Mirth* and realized how contemporary these turn-of-the-century novels are. I mean, society is different, but the conflicts that young women face are the same."

She took another drink and felt foolish. Had she slurred her words? Did she sound like a stupid girl? That's how she felt. And when would the others arrive?

She glanced at Chase. His brown eyes looked even darker, and again a smile played across his face. He patted the cushion beside him. "Why don't you sit by me?"

"I'm fine." She scanned the room for a clock but didn't see one.

He patted the cushion again. "Your professor has assigned your seat, young lady."

She laughed and changed seats, taking her drink with her.

"Looks like you need a refill."

"I'm fine, thanks. I'll wait until the others arrive."

But he was already at the bar. When he turned around, he winked. "Two's company. Right, Lizzie? I think we can have our own seminar on Henry James or any other writer you like."

A hot flush had crossed her face, and when she stood up, her head had spun. He reached out a hand and grabbed her wrist, causing her to drop her drink. It hit the table edge and crashed to the floor. Beth gasped.

"Forget about it," he murmured. "How about we get more comfortable?" He reached behind his head with his free hand and pulled off his sweater. "Come on, Lizzie. Henry James is a sexy writer." Again, the smile, but this time more leering.

"I'm not feeling well," she stammered. "I think I ought to go."

But he was still holding her wrist, and she felt his grip tightening.

"Come on, Lizzie," he'd murmured into her ear. "I saw the way you looked at me this afternoon. This is why you're here." He half walked, half dragged her toward the bedroom.

"No," she said, grabbing the door frame with her free hand. "Please don't."

But her words were shoved back into her throat by his mouth, his tongue thrusting into hers, his chest pushing her against the wall. He still held her by the wrist and was now yanking down her skirt. She heard a small rip as it passed over her hips.

"No," she said again. "No."

But now his pants were undone, and she felt her panties ripped away. He thrust his hand between her legs.

"Ah," he murmured into her ear. "I think this little coed is ready for me."

He spun her around, slamming her face against the wall and pinning her with both arms.

"Great ass, Lizzie. Has anyone ever told you that? I bet your boyfriend has never fucked you the way I'm going to." He turned loose of her arms and pulled her hips before him.

She cried out when she had felt him enter her. "Please, no," she cried over and over.

He came with a deep growl, then withdrew and turned her toward him, the smile still on his face. Only now, the face was sweaty, and she could see the red veins in his eyes.

"This time, I want to see your face when you come."

Vomit worked its way up her throat. She put a hand to her mouth to hold it back. He was pounding her harder, her head knocking against the wall in a rhythmic pattern.

"No!" she cried when he came again, but her voice was a whisper.

Then it was over. He backed away from her as she sank to the floor on top of her discarded clothes. She picked up her skirt and held it to her mouth. "I'm sick," she muttered.

"The bathroom's there," she heard him say, as he walked back to the bar.

She got to her knees and, with the help of the door handle, stood, and ran to the bathroom, slamming and locking the door behind her. She held her head over the sink and tried to vomit, but nothing came out. She turned on the cold water and splashed one handful after another on her face. When she looked at herself in the mirror, she gasped and grabbed a towel to wipe away the smeared lipstick and ruined eye makeup. She sat down on the toilet and buried her face in her hands.

A knock at the door. "Hello," he said. "Everything all right in there? I've got a drink waiting for you."

She stood and pulled on her skirt, leaving the blouse untucked to cover the rip in the side seam. She took one last look in the mirror and ran a shaky hand through her hair.

When she had opened the door, he once again sat on the sofa, a newspaper unfolded in his lap, a drink by his side. He put the paper aside when he saw her.

"Where did we leave off? We were talking about the similarity between Daisy Miller and Lily Bart, weren't we? And this fantastic sophomoric observation you made about how, what was the word you used, contemporary? That was it, right? How 'contemporary' these books are and what women your age can learn from these fictional characters."

He took a long drink from his glass.

"Well, Lizzie. I think you got a bigger education tonight. Wouldn't you say so?" He laughed. "Or maybe you need to run on back to your dorm and cry yourself to sleep on your pillow or tell your roommate you had sex with a real man." He drained his drink and slammed it onto the coffee table. "You coeds are alike. All tits and no brains. Just a tease in high heels. You can find your way out the door, can't you?" He picked the newspaper back up and reached for the TV remote.

She stood, frozen.

He glanced up. "Go on, now. Class dismissed. Oh, and remember. You're the one who came here. It was your choice."

She had nodded her head once and then scanned the room, looking for her backpack. On legs that were about to buckle, she had walked over and picked it up, hanging it over one shoulder. Without looking back, she had opened the door and walked out, closing it behind her.

She had scrubbed herself hard until her skin all but bled. Then, before she could lose her courage, she had gotten in her car and drove south to home, comfort, safety, love. She needed these things so much. A cool washcloth pressed to her forehead. A bowl of chicken and dumplings. Sleep between crisp white sheets. A mother who understood what it's like to be a young girl in a man's world. This most of all.

But that wasn't what she got when she had sobbed out her story – wiping her face with the arm of her sweatshirt, her mother looking grim and judgmental.

"That's not how I raised you," her mother had said. "Don't you know better than to go to some man's apartment?"

Then later, as Beth was packing to leave, she heard a whispered exchange outside her room.

"She's an embarrassment to this family," her mother had murmured to her father. Then adding with a sigh, "Soiled girls often find themselves alone for life."

The next morning, dressed all in black, Beth had gone straight to Drew's apartment and given him back his engagement ring.

"Done," she had told herself as she drove away, refusing to look in the rearview mirror, hardening herself even as his words followed her.

"What's happened?" he had cried out. "What's going on? Talk, Lizzie. Talk to me."

***

Tears ran unchecked down Beth's face. She lay on the grass beside the grave, running her hand again, back and forth, across the flowers. After some time, she realized what she was feeling. She was mourning her own death. The young woman who thought if she worked harder, ran faster, changed her name, and dyed her hair, created a protective castle guarded by loyal friends, that she would never again be hurt as she had been that night. Mark was supposed to be the guardian of her heart – the knight who risked his life to protect his lady and his love.

But now, everything was gone. Everything was a failure. Beth saw herself for what she was: a sham. A pathetic lovelorn girl, like in the fairy tales she had once consumed. And Mark was another version of that first man who had ripped rose-tinted glasses off her face.

She stood, brushed the dirt off her shorts, and walked to her car. It was now clear what she had to do.

CHAPTER THIRTY-EIGHT

*D*riving through town, she forced herself to look at the damage. Piles of debris stood along curbs, and twisted metal signs watched over boarded storefronts. Wires to traffic lights still dangled above intersections, and volunteer policemen directed cars. Some side streets were still blocked by fallen trees. One flipped car leaned against a fallen telephone pole, its roof cut in half from the impact. Signs regarding the hurricane lined the street: *Good Riddance, Ed,* read one. *God, we need to talk,* spoke another. Signs offering free water, promising to shoot looters, promoting hurricane liquidation sales – many hand-painted on pressed wood panels and propped against dilapidated structures. *Thanks for nothing, Edward.* This one was giving a middle finger to the heavens.

She stopped beside the collapsed entrance to Windmill Village and rolled down her window. Bulldozers were pushing the remains of mobile homes into piles that reached fifteen feet high. A young woman in white shorts and sandals watched from nearby, her hands to her mouth in shock and dismay. Beth's eyes traveled across the trailer park to a VW van that lay on its side against a splintered mobile home. Nearby, a green lounge chair sat amidst shattered furniture, as if someone had witnessed the destruction of his home from the comfort of a La-Z-Boy recliner. She felt the earth tremble as a bulldozer lifted and then dropped a metal roof onto a mound of garbage. She had wanted to see if these sights and sounds affected her, but as she listened to the sputtering of the engines, her brain felt as numb as a shot of Novocain. Beyond Lizzie and the task ahead, she felt nothing.

She put her car back into gear and took the entrance ramp to I-75 north. Twisted metal highway signs lay scattered along the pavement. On the radio, newscasters still reported on the damage left by its category 5 winds, but like most Porto Verde residents, Beth no longer cared about the statistics in their reports. She turned off the radio.

Exiting the highway at Venice, she drove straight to the beach where she and Mark had spent their first morning in Florida a year earlier. It was deserted in the hot noonday sun. Following a footpath, she walked straight to the water's edge, dropped her purse and car keys to the sand, and felt the gritty earth beneath her feet, allowing the ebb and flow of the water to pool around her. She gazed at the horizon, listening to the waves and the distant cry of birds. Then, with eyes closed, she walked into the surf, feeling its push and pull against her legs. The tide was going out. It sucked the sand from beneath her feet, causing her to lose her balance. She raised her arms to steady herself and walked deeper into the water. Its gentle slope encouraged her to walk further and further from shore. As she crossed a submerged sand bar, she saw the ocean floor drop deeper, changing from cerulean to indigo. Stepping from the ledge, she drew a deep breath and collapsed, cross-legged, under the water. With both hands, she grabbed the sand to keep herself submerged, fighting the buoyancy of her body. Pressure built in her chest, and her lungs cried for air, but she maintained her grip, allowing only a small trail of bubbles to escape her mouth.

She leaned back her head, feeling her hair flowing behind her, and opened her eyes. Salt stung her eyes, but she kept them open. The light was glistening. Particles of plant life floated past, and deeper in the water, she saw a school of small fish. Across the ocean floor, the sunlight created a pattern among the soft mound of shell and sand. She looked at the sun's white orb, its rays causing the water to pixilate. Straining to keep her breath held, she released her grip and allowed the current to pull her deeper. It was an easy motion, much more freeing than swimming with fifty pounds of Scuba gear on her back.

Her chest now pounded, demanding air. She looked once more at the sun and its flickering light. It would be so easy to allow the current to drag her deeper, but the light called. She pulled her feet under her in a crouch. With one fluid motion, she pushed herself up from the ocean floor. Her shoulders cleared the water, and she coughed, clearing her lungs of water and mucus. With her head dropped back, she floated on the surface, her arms and legs extended outward. When she heard a bird cry, she opened her eyes and watched the acrobatics of a gull as it swooped down and plucked a fish from the water.

"Hush, you silly," she told the gull, using an expression she always did when Lizzie cried for more food. She laughed and flipped over, turning until her body faced the shore. With strong breaststrokes, she swam to land.

When she reached the shore, she removed her phone from her purse and dialed the number from memory. It went to Helen's voicemail. "It's Beth," she said. "I need to talk with you. It's about something that happened a long time ago."

She closed the phone. The sounds of the waves were now joined by the laughter of children climbing out of a minivan. She looked again at her phone and saw she had missed a call from Anna. It sounded important. She walked back to the car and grabbed a towel from the back seat. As she dried herself, she dialed her friend's number.

CHAPTER THIRTY-NINE

*B*eth sat on the porch steps in the shade. The fronds of a lone palm tree rustled with the wind, making a dry, cracking sound. From a distance, she heard hammering, as another neighbor's roof was replaced. She and Mark were fortunate, she concluded. Three months after Edward and their house looked brand new. That's why they had a quick offer. A family whose home was destroyed wanted to buy it as soon as possible. She straightened the papers in the packet from the realtor and checked her watch. Mark should have already arrived. She stretched her neck from side to side to relieve tension. Nothing could bother her today.

Before driving to the house, she had dropped off a gift basket to Helen. Beth's last appointment was the week after her drive to Venice. Helen had held her hands as Beth told her story and cried the tears she never allowed herself back in college. Their session lasted for hours, as Helen unraveled Beth's pain piece by piece.

"You were raped," Helen told her. "You were attacked by a predator who should be behind bars. You can still put him there, if you wish. You did nothing wrong."

And, as dusk had settled, casting long shadows among the fallen trees, Beth saw the path she needed to take.

Now Helen and her children were moving to Virginia, where she would join a new practice. Her house had been one of the many leveled, and like many Charlotte County residents, the trauma of Edward, followed by Frances, Ivan and Jeanne – three hurricanes that visited Florida within weeks of Edward – was more than Helen wanted to experience again. She had hugged Beth, enveloping her in an embrace.

As Mark's car rounded the corner, Beth stood. How many times had she awaited him since their first meeting – peeping out a window, staring down a street, listening for the sound of his footsteps down a hallway? Too many. He unfolded his body from the Mustang. The car looked brand new, its red color polished to a high gleam. He must have had it detailed. She remembered the first time he had arrived at her condo for a date in that car. It seemed a lifetime ago.

He hooked his dark glasses to the front of his shirt and walked toward her. It had been two months since she had last seen him, when they both signed the final insurance payment. His fit body and tanned limbs still caused her to feel a rush of attraction. He moved to hug her but then, seeing her arms crossed, drew back, unsure.

She turned to unlock the door, and he followed her in. The house was empty, and, as they walked through each room, their footsteps echoed.

"Looks like they did a good job," Mark said.

Beth only nodded.

After a look in each room, they stood in the kitchen – their backs against counters opposite one another. Mark shifted from one foot to the other, and just as he stepped toward her, she moved away and walked out the door.

A moment later, he followed. He found her seated on the porch steps with the realtor's packet on her lap. She held it up to him.

"Here's the offer. I think we should take it." She pressed her lips together as if to remind herself not to say more.

Mark sat beside her and flipped through the pages, grunting only once. Beth waited and watched a truck of roofers stop at the house across the street and unload red ceramic tiles.

"You're happy with this?" he asked, gesturing toward the packet.

She nodded, her eyes still on the activity across the street.

He looked away and then back to her. "If we wait a little longer, we might make a lot more money."

She turned toward him. "No, Mark. I want this over now. I never want to live here again."

A car passed down the road, and they both watched as it turned a corner. Mark removed his visor and wiped sweat from his brow.

"Okay," he said. He tapped the papers. "Let's do it." He leaned his forearms on his knees and turned his head toward her.

"Things didn't work out as I had planned," he began. "The job, this house, the boat. You." With a nervous laugh, he paused. "Damnit, I had a speech all rehearsed."

He removed his visor and wiped his brow and then shifted his body. Beth did nothing except to continue staring across the street.

"You were right," he said at last and released another short laugh. "This place wasn't good for us." When she didn't make a sound, he turned toward her. "Dammit, Beth. You can say 'I told you so' if you wish."

Beth shook her head and didn't reply.

He twisted toward her and then stood and faced her, arms hanging by his side. "Here's the good news. A week ago, I drove to Naples to talk with some of the sailing school instructors. Edward didn't do any damage down there. You would love it. Anyway, last week, I went back down for an interview and was offered a job as director of a sailing and boat rental program. Get this. It's a full-time position with lots of benefits. I won't have to teach or coach, which should make you happy. I told them I couldn't decide until talking with you." He laughed. "I've learned my lesson."

When she didn't speak, he squatted in front of her and placed his hands on her shoulders. She recoiled.

"We can move there, Beth. You'll love it." He grinned. "And here's the best part. There's dancing every Sunday night at the Ritz. I know you'll like that. And one more thing. I bet you could get a job in sales or marketing, maybe for the Ritz. That is, if you want to work. Or you could just play tennis. Get another cat. Whatever you want."

He watched her face, trying to read her response, and moved his hands down to her left hand.

"What do you think?" he said at last. He shifted to kneel in front of her, still holding her hand. "I'm sorry for all that went wrong. I want to start again with you. Don't make me beg you, Beth. Say yes."

Beth stared at him for a moment but then pulled her hand away and stood. She walked into the yard before turning around.

"Thank you for the apology. It means a lot." She shrugged her shoulders. "It means a lot, but it doesn't change my mind."

He stood and tried to speak, but Beth held up a hand to stop him.

"I know about Wendi. I've known for some time. That's something else you'll try to explain away, but don't insult me."

He again tried to speak, but she kept her hand raised.

"After your trip to Miami, I put two and two together. And then with the hurricane...." She shook her head.

"Beth, I—" Mark began, but she interrupted.

"And that's not all I know. I know what happened back in Atlanta too. Not just the private school thing before we met. You already explained that one away. But the incident last August, right before you announced we were moving here."

"Wait a minute," Mark said. "That charge was bogus. I was teaching a kid a wrestling move. That's all. I never hit him." He stood up, huffing, ready for a fight.

Beth watched as he paced in front of her, like a caged animal. "No wonder you wanted to get out of town," she continued. "You lost your temper and manhandled the kid, just like you did the time before. Just like you did to me." She clenched her hands and glanced away, before looking again at him. "But guess what? That kid's family goes to Anna's church. What are the chances of that? But there you have it. And the kid had bruises on his arms. His mom mentioned it one Sunday to Anna. You have a pattern, it seems. It makes sense you'd want to skip town."

Mark stepped toward her. "Hold it right there," he said. "Let me explain."

But Beth waved him back. "No. I already know what you will say. It was the kid's fault, or you lost your temper, or it got blown out of proportion. Blah, blah, blah. Just like you can explain away Wendi. We were fighting, and you got angry and wanted to do something to get back at me, and Wendi came on to you, and it didn't mean a thing." She fixed him with a look. "But Mark, it meant something. It meant that whenever we have a disagreement or you get annoyed or you think someone has disrespected you, then you have the right to become angry and lash out or," she shrugged, "have an out-of-town hookup. Whatever." Now she was the one nodding her head in agreement. "I lived in fear down here. In fact, I've lived in fear for a long time. I've worked hard at being the good girl and the good student and the good employee and the good wife, and you know where that's gotten me? It's gotten me, time after time, in a situation where the other person is the dominant one and I'm...." Beth stopped to take a long breath. "I'm the one left feeling hurt and unworthy of love."

Beth looked away as tears filled her eyes. Mark took a step toward her, and she backed away again before speaking.

"Mark, something happened a long time ago, and guess what? I thought it was my fault, just like I've blamed myself for everything that has gone wrong down here. But I see things differently now."

She again turned from him and forced herself to take deep breaths, wanting to continue what she had started. She sensed Mark stepping closer and spun back around. He stopped, startled by her reaction.

"Here's the thing, Mark. In some ways, I still love you. Not enough to stay with you. Certainly not enough to be your wife. But some love remains. It may be there for a long time. I don't know. But this storm...." She turned in a circle, with her arms stretched wide. "You know what this storm did? It knocked some sense into me. Woke me up. Made me think. Made me realize that boats and houses and cars aren't important. Friends are. Lizzie was." She leaned toward him, looking into his eyes as she pointed to her heart. "I am. I'm important, Mark. You may not think so. Others may not think so. I don't care. *I* think so."

She reached to her left hand and pulled off the wedding ring.

"No," Mark said, but she shook her head and held the ring toward him. He placed his hands on his hips. "Shit, Beth," he said.

She continued holding the ring out to him. "You told me this ring was your mother's. If so, she wasn't honored by our marriage. Lock it away. Sell it. Maybe give it to Heather when she gets married. It would mean a lot to her."

At last, he took it and rolled it in his hand for a moment before putting it in his pocket.

Beth walked to her car. Opening the door, she turned one last time toward him. "I'll file the papers, and we can split the profits from the house. It will be over in a month." She stared at him for a long time. "You'll be fine, Mark."

She closed the car door and pulled out of the driveway. She didn't look back.

eth sat as Grayson, her former boss, examined her packet of materials. A smile flickered across his face.

"There's a PowerPoint presentation on a disc in the back," she said, leaning across the desk to point to it. "It covers the same information but with graphics to give you a visual of the research I did."

He closed the packet and patted it. "You always were thorough, Beth. That's one thing I liked about you." He tapped his fingers on his desk and looked out his window at the January skies. "You think they're looking for new show management?"

Beth leaned forward. "I'm confident they are. I talked to people in marketing, the crew who set up the venues, their finance director, anyone I could to verify they are seeking new management." She leaned back, not wanting to oversell her proposal.

"Your strategy is that we could take over the St. Pete boat show and use that one as a stepping-stone to shows in San Diego and Annapolis."

"Not immediately. But we could build to it. There are smaller shows all along the Gulf Coast we could approach first – Mobile, Biloxi, to name a few. It's a lucrative market." She laughed. "Boaters are an avid bunch. Take my word for it. Even when other industries are in a downturn, boaters are out buying their next piece of paradise. They live for blue skies and open water."

Grayson leaned back in his chair and looked at her. "I suppose you see yourself as the marketing director for this new boating division of our company?"

Beth shook her head. "No."

He leaned forward and opened his eyes wide. "No?"

Beth nodded. "No. I see myself as show director." She sat up straighter in her chair. "I know the industry. I wasn't just living in a boating community for the past year; I used every opportunity to research it. I know what power boaters are looking for and what sets them apart from sailors. I know the do's and don'ts of show layout. I know which manufacturers to approach for each show and what crafts they make that appeal to the waters in each area. I know the advantages of a wide beam versus a deep hull. I even know what brand of rum and beer they prefer." She sat back and smiled. "And what I don't know, I'll learn. As you said, I'm thorough."

Grayson placed his hands on his desktop and stood up. Beth did the same.

"All right, then. Let's get us a boat show." He held his hand out for Beth to shake. "But one last question on something that wasn't covered in your packet."

Beth's eyes opened wide in surprise.

"Can you still bring in those scones you make?"

Beth smiled. "Every Monday. Except when I'm on the road at a show."

***

Grant and Alisa were waiting for her when she arrived at Chops. Grant let out a whoop when he saw her face. "You got it, didn't you?" he asked, as he enveloped her in a hug. "I knew you would."

Alisa signaled the waiter, who stepped forward with a bottle of champagne. "To Beth," she proclaimed, as the cork popped. "I've got some other good news for you," she continued, as Beth drained her glass. "You know the condo you liked best?"

Beth nodded. "The one with the big balcony overlooking Piedmont Park?"

Alisa grinned. "They're ready to accept your offer."

"How can you know that? I haven't heard anything from my realtor."

Alisa laughed. "Let's just say I know someone who knows the owners."

Beth's phone rang.

Alisa nodded toward it. "I won't be surprised if that isn't the call."

That night, as Beth sat in her car in front of Lori's townhouse, she smiled as a flurry of snowflakes covered her windshield. She knew what this meant. Schools and businesses would close the next day. The snow would be gone by the afternoon, but no one in Atlanta took a chance driving on icy roads. It was one of the many things she loved about the city. It was busy and vibrant, but when snow arrived, everyone took a holiday. She assumed that Lori had already made a trip to the grocery store. They would make French toast in the morning, with thick slices of Benton smoked bacon on the side.

When she had driven back to Atlanta from Porto Verde a month earlier, all she could think about was surrounding herself with her friends. She had planned to live in an extended stay hotel and work as a picture framer while she job searched, if Grayson didn't go for her proposal. But Lori had insisted she stay with her. It was cramped, but that didn't matter. They were close enough friends to make it work. Meanwhile, Beth hired a moving company to bring her belongings from Florida to a nearby storage unit.

She stepped out of the car and looked up at the sky. Snow was falling. She thought back to the last time she had felt snow on her face. It was the night she met Mark. They had been crazy for one another back then. Like a couple inside a snow globe, they were caught up in the magic of love. Helen and Dr. Em had helped her realize that. She found her courage to see Dr. Em two weeks after moving in with Lori. He helped her get past her sense of failure and realize what was missing in their marriage was partnership, respect, empathy – and love. And he continued to guide her in healing from the rape.

Mark's last email said he was considering moving to the Virgin Islands to be a captain for hire. He had met a guy in Naples who owned a company that moved boats up and down the Atlantic coast to the Caribbean. He had told Mark there was a ton of money to make doing it. Beth hadn't responded to his email. There was no need. They had used a mediator to set the terms of the divorce, and she had received notice a month afterward. She was Beth Gardiner again, perhaps forever. And that was okay.

The porch light went on as Lori appeared at the door. "Get in here," she yelled to Beth. "I've got popcorn and a movie already lined up. In the morning, we can make snow angels."

Beth waved and quickened her steps. She hoped the movie was *Dirty Dancing*. Like Baby, no one was putting her in a corner again.

CHAPTER FORTY-ONE

*A*s she turned left on Highway 64, Beth opened the sunroof. Spring had come early to the Tennessee mountains, and Beth couldn't get enough of it. She had thought about this trip for over a year since returning from Florida. Now she was making it.

She settled into the familiar curves of the road, as it snaked its way between the granite walls of the Chilhowie Mountain and the fast-flowing Ocoee River. The locals still called the highway 'the River Road,' and as Beth rounded its curves, she was transported to her past. Many weekends, her brother and father had fished along the tributaries that fed the Ocoee, bringing home baskets full of trout and bream.

As she crested Boyd's Gap, she recalled the school bus rides she had taken as a cheerleader between her hometown of Benton, below the mountain, and their Copper Basin rivals upstream. Some students would become so car sick from the curves that the bus driver had to pull off the road, but Beth always glued her face to the window, taking in the swirling white water and the steep banks of Big Frog Mountain. Her father had taught her to drive on the River Road, coaching her on how to bank the curves and when to accelerate. Those Sunday drives were the most time she ever spent with him. She remembered how proud she had felt when she drove the whole length of the road without once touching her breaks. Her father had given her back a firm pat, his only form of affection.

Before reaching Benton, she turned onto a narrow road and followed the signs to Blue Springs Pottery. She knew the road well. It was her high school's unofficial make-out place, and Beth smiled as she saw the well-worn parking spots that dotted the sides of the road. When she reached the pottery, she kept the car idling as she viewed the building. It was made from hand-hued logs, with a deep porch that wrapped around three sides of the building. A cheery red metal roof complemented the hanging ferns that swayed in the breeze from the porch roof.

Beth twisted the rearview mirror and applied lip gloss, then cut the engine and stepped out of the car. Cobalt delphiniums standing two feet high surrounded the parking area like sentries, while massive pink hydrangeas framed the porch steps. A calico cat crawled out from under the steps and joined Beth as she climbed them. It darted through the showroom door as if it belonged there.

When she closed the door, she turned in a slow circle. Shelves arranged with glazed platters, vases, and bowls of various sizes stood against each wall. The colors mirrored the outdoors, including the cobalt blue of the flowers. Beth walked slowly along them, picking up an item here and there and rubbing her hand over its surface.

"Can I help you?" a voice behind her asked. Beth turned. A young woman in jeans, an orange shirt, and an apron splattered with clay stood beside her.

"Not right now," Beth answered, returning the vase she held to the shelf.

"Take your time," the woman said.

Beth crossed the room to another display and then turned back to the woman. "Is this the work of just one person?" she asked.

The young woman nodded. "It is. He's rather famous. And the best part is he allows art students to mentor under him. I'm doing a month program focusing on glazing techniques."

"Good for you," Beth said. She regarded her for a moment, trying to decide about something. Then she opened her purse and took out the blue bowl.

"How beautiful," the woman remarked. "The way the potter contrasted the moss green interior with the brilliant blue exterior.

"I was wondering. Could you ask the potter if he could make me one just like this?"

The woman took the bowl from Beth. "I'll go ask him. He does lots of commissions. In fact, he's working on some large pieces for an exhibit in the New York Museum of Modern Art. Who knows?"

Beth watched as the woman exited the showroom through double doors at the back. She walked to a window. Looking back at her was a pale face with perhaps too much lip gloss. Beth took a tissue out of her purse and blotted her lips. When she heard heavy footsteps behind her, she turned.

The potter was her age and had light brown hair that curled against his shirt collar. He wore dark-rimmed glasses that framed intense blue eyes and a red checkered shirt with the cuffs rolled up. He carried Beth's bowl in one hand. When she turned, he stopped walking. He ran a hand against a day's growth on his face, glanced away and then back to her.

"Lizzie," he said, his voice low and soft.

"Hi, Drew," Beth responded.

He released a deep breath and tossed the bowl back and forth between his hands. He shook his head, considering and rejecting some thought, before looking again at her.

"When Jen brought this bowl back, I had this strange out of body experience." He ran a callused thumb around its lip. "It took me a while to remember making this."

"Freshman year. Art class," Beth said. "I came over and admired it...."

"And I gave it to you," Drew said.

Beth nodded and took a step forward. "It's always been on my bureau. It's traveled everywhere I've been."

A smile played across his face. "Is that right?" he asked.

Beth nodded.

They stood in an awkward silence until he spoke again. "I heard your mom passed a couple of years ago. I thought about sending flowers but decided against it. Heard the house sold, too."

Beth smiled. "Sounds like you're keeping up with the Gardiners."

Drew laughed. "Not hardly. It's a small town." He looked across the parking lot and laughed. "I remember all the times

I stood on the porch steps waiting for you. Your dad always drilled me on driving safely and getting you home on time."

"Lots of memories," Beth said and then gestured to the surroundings. "But look at this place. It's fabulous."

"Thanks. I'm proud of it."

"I remember you talking about it, back in college. You even had the name already picked. I saw your sign by the road. Blue Springs, the color of your favorite glaze."

"Like on this bowl," he said. "I remember it sitting on the ledge of your dorm window with rosemary stuck in it." He tossed the bowl into the air and caught it. He did this a second time before removing his glasses and looking at her.

She shifted her stance and reached one hand toward the other, about to twist a ring she no longer wore.

He regarded her for some time, his face shifting with his emotions.

She met his gaze.

"Ten years," he said at last. "Ten years and not a word from you."

"I know," she answered.

"And now you're here."

She nodded.

He looked at the sky and released a harsh laugh. "You broke my heart that day, Lizzie. Do you know that? You knocked on my door and...."

"I gave you back your ring."

"You said it had nothing to do with me."

"It didn't. It still doesn't. It was all me. It's still all me. You did nothing wrong."

Drew walked to the window and leaned back against the sill.

Beth turned to face him, her arms at her side.

"I don't know how many times I've replayed that moment," he said. "I stood there, looking at the ring I'd worked all summer to buy. No explanation. You just gave it back and walked out of my life. Not answering phone calls, anything." Again, he released a bitter laugh and glanced at the ceiling before looking again at her. "Dammit, Lizzie. Are you finally going to tell me why?"

***

An hour later, they were seated on the porch steps. Drew still held the bowl, and Beth was stroking the calico. She reached up and wiped the remaining tears from her face, then picked up the cat and put it in her lap.

"I would have understood, Lizzie," Drew said at last. "I would have first killed the sonofabitch, but I would have understood. The trauma. Your mother's reaction. All of it. Why didn't you let me do that? Why did you shut me out?"

Beth turned toward him. "I'm still wrapping my head around that. The easiest way I can explain it is to say I had too much shame. I mean, I should have known better than to go to some man's hotel room. I shouldn't have been so stupid. Afterward, I had so much guilt. The only way I could process it was to close myself off from everyone – dig a hole and cover myself with the dirt. The only thought running through my head was an expression of my mother's: 'They that dance must pay the fiddler.' I danced, and I paid."

Drew shook his head. "Fuck your mother's aphorisms. She was way too critical of you." He sat silently before asking, "Do you still feel guilty, like it was your fault it happened?"

"No," Beth responded. "He was a sonofabitch like you said, and he committed a crime. I volunteer now at a rape crisis center one night a week. You'd be surprised how often this happens to young women, especially in college."

Drew nodded, accepting her answer before looking at her. "Why are you here?"

"To apologize. And to ask your forgiveness." She reached for his hand and then drew hers back. "You're the best person I've ever known, and I hurt you. I'll never forgive myself for that."

He looked down at the bowl and then up at her. "A lot's happened since then."

Beth nodded. "With me too. Some good, some bad. But now, I'm good." She looked around and then back to him. "And you. Well, look at this place. It's everything you talked about."

Drew smiled. "It is." He looked at his hands. "You know it's all I ever wanted to do. I mean, I took all those fine arts classes in college, but all I wanted to do was throw clay and make things."

They sat that way for some time, in comfortable silence – Beth stroking the cat and Drew leaning against the porch railing.

Finally, he looked down at her hand. "No wedding ring, I see."

"There was but not for long. It was a mistake. The second biggest I've ever made."

Drew nodded. A smile worked its way up to his eyes. "You think you can buy my forgiveness with a truckload order of little bowls?"

Beth smiled for the first time. "Maybe not forgiveness. Not yet. And not a truckload. But how about just one bowl? This one has been lonely for some time."

Drew nodded and then reached for her hand. "Dammit, Lizzie. I've missed you."

She rubbed a thumb across his knuckles. "I go by Beth now, and I've missed you, too."

He squeezed her hand. "Beth, it is," he said.

Later as she sat in her car, he leaned his elbows against her open window. "Are you sure you want to take that cat? It's just a stray."

Beth reached into the box, where the calico was curled on a towel and stroked her head. "I think she needs a proper home and a good mama. She can always come back and visit."

Drew smiled. "I'd like that."

She reached again for the cat and accidentally knocked over her purse. A paperback fell out.

Drew laughed. "I see you still carry a book everywhere you go. What are you reading now?"

Beth held it up. *A Doll's House*, she said. "The Ibsen play, remember? About the housewife who leaves her husband and children to start her own life?"

Drew's smile was broad. "You and your literature. That's one of the things I always liked about you."

***

As sunset approached, Beth parked her car in front of a white clapboard house on a side street in Benton. Two little girls were playing in the front yard, chasing one another around a bird feeder. The younger one squealed with delight when the older one allowed herself to be caught.

"Tag. You're it," the little girl yelled.

The door opened, and a woman in cutoffs came out, a pitcher of lemonade and three glasses balanced on her tray. A box of cookies was tucked under her arm. The girls ran to her, clambering to sit as close as possible. The woman glanced up and saw Beth.

"Can I help you?" she called out.

Beth took a step closer. "I used to live here. You bought the house from my family. My brother handled the closing, so we never met. I'm Beth Gardiner." She looked around. "I like what you've done with the house." She pointed to the blue shutters and the red front door. "I was just passing through town and wanted to stop by."

The girls reached for the cookies, and the woman turned her attention to them. Beth watched and then removed a small camera from her purse. "Would it be alright if I took a picture of the house, so I can show my brother and sister how good it looks?"

"Sure, why not?" called the woman. "Take your time," she added, as she and the girls went inside.

As Beth left Benton, she took Interstate 75 through Chattanooga. Several miles later, she pulled off for gas and checked her messages. There was one from Grayson confirming their meeting in St. Petersburg on Wednesday. She smiled and reached down to pet the cat, scratching it under its chin.

"How are you doing, Dorothy?" she cooed. "I think you will like your new home." The cat rubbed its head against her hand and meowed.

As she merged onto the highway, she again checked her rearview mirror. *Funny,* she thought. She never used to look back much while driving. But as she put more distance between herself and her past, she continued to glance into the mirror, smiling each time a special memory came to mind and admiring the sunset, as it settled behind the mountains.

THE END

Acknowledgements

This story went through many drafts, numerous cups of tea, two back surgeries, and the occasional bottle of wine. Encouraging me along the way was my dear friend, Rosalyn Waldron, who read those early drafts, shared the wine, and listened to my struggles (both in writing and in life). You are a true friend. For guidance in story craft, my gratitude goes to writers Sarah Lovett and Anne Corbitt. Both women were incredibly giving of their knowledge and experience, supporting me and encouraging me to become the best writer I can be. Their advice was spot on. A special acknowledgement goes to poet Will Wright who nudged me to take a small short story and turn it into a novel. I would never have had the courage to tackle writing my story without him. The clean-up job of my manuscript became the task of Chris Fenwick of Sunbury Press. Thank you for your patience and for guiding me along the path of publication. Gratitude also goes to the beta readers who gladly donated their time to read and respond to my drafts: Barb Newey, Trish Woody, Ellen Ward, Katya Svetova, and Alice Cekleov. Thank you, ladies. And for making all those cups of tea and for loving and believing in me, I thank my husband, Des Martin.

ABOUT THE AUTHOR

Sarah Jones is a graduate of the University of Tennessee and has worked as an English teacher and a business writer before retiring to a lake community north of Atlanta, Georgia. Her memoir, *Quicksand: A Cautionary Love Story*, was published in 2011 and turned into a screen play. *Summer Squall* is her second book. Her book reviews and wine pairings can be found on her website *www.sarahjonesauthor.com*.

Readers Guide

1. Beth's friends, the Core Four, serve as her sounding board and offer wise counsel. How do they individually and collectively influence her? Why did she go against their advice regarding Mark?

2. Beth and Mark are an example of the attraction between opposites. What is different about their approach to life? What is similar?

3. Why did Beth agree to move to Florida? By the end of the story, in what way did she benefit from the move?

4. Beth remains haunted by a traumatic event in college. In what ways has this trauma affected her life choices? What situations seem to trigger her trauma?

5. How is Beth finally able to vanquish her mother's critical voice? Or does she? Do her mother's saying sound familiar or different from those voiced by your parents?

6. Which moments do you think had the biggest impact on Beth's decision to leave Mark?

7. What do you think will happen to Beth in the future?

Made in the USA
Columbia, SC
03 September 2019